D0249594

Ali. He'd called her *Ali.*

Frank's deep, rich voice had wrapped itself intimately around her nickname, making it sound so right as he drew her even more deeply into the heart of his family.

Alison suddenly wanted to run and hide. But all she could do was stare at Frank, mesmerized by his brilliant blue eyes.

"Come on, Ali," five-year-old Joey urged. "Put the star on the Christmas tree!"

"Yeah!" twin Jake insisted, hopping from one foot to the other.

Giggling, Joey placed Alison's hand in his father's. "There you go."

Alison allowed Frank to help her onto the stool, then took the star from him, meeting his intense gaze. Oh, yes, she mused, there she went.

Straight down a road that could very well end in ruin.

Dear Reader,

Welcome to Silhouette **Special Edition**...welcome
to romance.

In this festive month of December, curl up by the fire
with romantic, heartwarming stories from some of
your favorite authors!

Our THAT SPECIAL WOMAN! title for December
is *For the Baby's Sake* by Christine Rimmer.
Andrea McCreary's unborn baby needed a father,
and her decision to marry friend Clay Barrett was
strictly for the baby's sake. But soon, their marriage
would mean much more to them both!

Lisa Jackson's LOVE LETTERS series continues this
month with *C Is for Cowboy*. Loner Sloan Redhawk
is hot on the trail of his prey—a headstrong, passionate
woman he won't soon forget! Also returning to
Special Edition in December is reader favorite
Sherryl Woods with *One Step Away*.

Rounding out this holiday month are *Jake Ryker's Back
in Town* by Jennifer Mikels, *Only St. Nick Knew* by
Nikki Benjamin and *Abigail and Mistletoe* by
Karen Rose Smith.

I hope this holiday season brings you happiness and joy,
and that you enjoy this book and the stories to come.
Happy holidays from all of us at Silhouette Books!

Sincerely,

Tara Gavin
Senior Editor

Please address questions and book requests to:
Silhouette Reader Service
U.S.: 3010 Walden Ave., P.O. Box 1325, Buffalo, NY 14269
Canadian: P.O. Box 609, Fort Erie, Ont. L2A 5X3

NIKKI BENJAMIN

ONLY ST. NICK KNEW

Silhouette®

SPECIAL EDITION®

Published by Silhouette Books

America's Publisher of Contemporary Romance

If you purchased this book without a cover you should be aware
that this book is stolen property. It was reported as "unsold and
destroyed" to the publisher, and neither the author nor the
publisher has received any payment for this "stripped book."

For my dear friend Shari Anderson,
with thanks for always making me smile

 SILHOUETTE BOOKS

ISBN 0-373-09928-2

ONLY ST. NICK KNEW

Copyright © 1994 by Barbara Vosbein

All rights reserved. Except for use in any review, the reproduction
or utilization of this work in whole or in part in any form by any
electronic, mechanical or other means, now known or hereafter
invented, including xerography, photocopying and recording, or in
any information storage or retrieval system, is forbidden without
the written permission of the editorial office, Silhouette Books,
300 East 42nd Street, New York, NY 10017 U.S.A.

All characters in this book have no existence outside the imagination of
the author and have no relation whatsoever to anyone bearing the same
name or names. They are not even distantly inspired by any individual
known or unknown to the author, and all incidents are pure invention.

This edition published by arrangement with Harlequin Enterprises B.V.

® and TM are trademarks of Harlequin Enterprises B.V., used under
license. Trademarks indicated with ® are registered in the United States
Patent and Trademark Office, the Canadian Trade Marks Office and in
other countries.

Printed in U.S.A.

Books by Nikki Benjamin

Silhouette Special Edition

Silhouette Intimate Moments

NIKKI BENJAMIN

was born and raised in the Midwest, but after years in the Houston area, she considers herself a true Texan. Nikki says she's always been an avid reader. (Her earliest literary heroines were Nancy Drew, Trixie Belden and Beany Malone.) Her writing experience was limited, however, until a friend started penning a novel and encouraged Nikki to do the same. One scene led to another, and soon she was hooked.

When not reading or writing, the author enjoys spending time with her husband and son, needlepoint, hiking, biking, horseback riding and sailing.

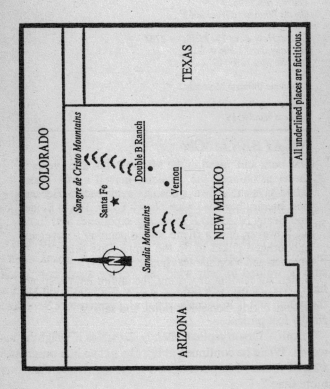

COLORADO

N

Sangre de Cristo Mountains

Santa Fe ★

Double B Ranch •

Sandia Mountains

• Vernon

NEW MEXICO

ARIZONA

TEXAS

All underlined places are fictitious.

Chapter One

"So, tell me, Orson . . . are you calling with good news or bad?" His grip on the telephone receiver tightening, Frank Bradford paced across the kitchen.

Though he'd stuck close to the house most of the morning waiting for Orson Hyde to return his call, Frank wasn't sure he wanted to hear what the literary agent had to tell him. Over the past few days he'd tried to prepare himself for the worst, but if Rebecca's editor at Overstreet & Sons had finally lost patience—

"Both," Orson replied, then hesitated as if weighing his words. When he continued at last, he did so in a pragmatic tone of voice. "Margaret agreed to extend the deadline one more time."

For just a moment, Frank leaned against the tile counter, his head bowed and his eyes closed, as a wave of relief washed over him. Then, aware that Margaret Locke's granting of another extension for a manuscript already almost a year overdue was the *good* news, he squared his shoulders and turned to retrace his steps.

"But?" he prodded as nonchalantly as he could. He'd gotten the reprieve he wanted. Still, he knew better than to think it was going to be anything but temporary.

"She wants the manuscript on her desk no later than January 15. If she doesn't have it by then, you'll have to repay the advance."

"I see...."

Pausing once again, Frank stared out the wide, arched window above the sink. As had been the case for over a week now, the sun shone brightly in the clear blue sky. But, typical of northern New Mexico in late November, the temperature probably hadn't risen much above freezing.

Which didn't seem to bother his five-year-old twin sons much at all. Not quite thirty minutes ago, they'd come home from kindergarten. Now, bundled into identical fleece-lined denim jackets, their strawberry-blond curls tucked under black knit stocking caps, Jake and Joey played a haphazard game of kickball on the scruffy patch of grass that served as a backyard. Their Australian shepherd, Molly, sat on the sidelines, keeping tabs on them, while over near the barn his father, Bert, tinkered under the hood of his ancient pickup truck.

At one time, the very normalcy of the scene outside his kitchen window would have been enough to assure Frank all was right with his world. But since his wife had died unexpectedly eighteen months ago, he'd had a hard time believing that would ever be the case again. And now, to make bad matters worse, he had less than two months to either complete the historical novel that had meant so much to her or allow her dream of making the bestseller list to die, too.

"I know seven weeks isn't a lot of time, especially with the holidays coming up, but Margaret had to beg her boss to agree to any extension at all," Orson advised, interrupting

Frank's reverie. "She had such high hopes for *Hunter's Edge.* She certainly doesn't want to give up on the project, but the powers that be at Overstreet are growing impatient."

"I can't say I blame them," Frank admitted as he turned away from the window.

When he'd offered to complete Rebecca's manuscript almost a year ago, Margaret had had some reservations. But he'd been so sure he could do it that he'd talked her into letting him give it a try.

He hadn't really thought he would have that much trouble picking up where Rebecca had left off just before she died. As he'd done in the past, he'd worked on the plot and characterization with her. He'd also done most of her research for her. And, having read everything she'd ever written, he was as well-acquainted with her writing style as anyone could be. Yet he'd finished less than fifty pages in the last eleven months. To think he could write at least a hundred more in a matter of weeks was downright crazy.

"How much more do you have to go?" Orson asked with obvious concern.

"Too much," Frank muttered, hoping he didn't sound quite as defeated as he'd begun to feel.

"Maybe you ought to call it quits, then. Under the circumstances, I don't think anyone would hold it against you."

"I can't do that."

"Well, you've spent almost a year trying to finish Rebecca's manuscript and you haven't been able to do *that,* either," Orson retorted, his exasperation evident.

"Gee, thanks for reminding me," Frank shot back sarcastically. Then, aware that he and the agent were supposed to be on the same side, he beat back his growing frustration and continued in a calmer tone of voice. "Look, Orson, I can't give up yet. As long as Margaret's willing to let me have a few more weeks, I've got to give it one last try.''

After all Rebecca had done for him, he owed her that much. Somehow he'd find a way to write the rest of her story. Because if he didn't, he'd spend the rest of his life feeling as if he'd let her down.

''If you're worried about repaying the advance—''

''I'm not,'' Frank cut in quietly.

With over twelve hundred acres of prime New Mexico ranchland and eight hundred head of fine-wooled merino and rambouillet sheep to his name, Frank had always been more than able to provide for his family. They'd never had to live off the money Rebecca made on her books. Instead, they'd set it aside for the twins' college tuition and the traveling Rebecca had dreamed of doing. So, if worse came to worst, and he had to pay back the advance, he could.

''So...'' Orson paused for several moments, as if carefully considering Frank's simple statement, then continued almost affably. ''Sounds to me like your mind's made up.''

''It is.''

''In that case...''

''What?'' Frank prodded, his patience beginning to wear thin again.

He'd already made it plain that he intended to do his damnedest to complete the manuscript. And if he couldn't, he'd pay back Overstreet & Sons. As far as he was concerned, they had nothing left to discuss.

''I was wondering if you'd be interested in having a little help.''

''What kind of help?'' Frank asked warily.

''Obviously you've had a hard time finishing *Hunter's Edge* on your own. But I know someone here in New York who might be willing to give you some help with it.''

"You want me to hire a ghostwriter?" Frank growled, none too thrilled with the turn their conversation seemed to be taking.

"Not exactly," Orson soothed. "Alison Kent is actually more of a ... book doctor."

A book doctor?

Moving away from the counter, Frank paced across the kitchen and paused in front of the refrigerator. As he eyed the hodgepodge of drawings attached to the door with magnets and masking tape, he considered Orson's suggestion as equably as he could.

If he understood correctly, the man wanted him to consider allowing someone named Alison Kent to finish writing Rebecca's book. His first inclination was to flatly refuse. More than anything, he wanted his wife's manuscript completed, but he wanted to be the one to do it. Yet, in all honesty, despite his protestations to the contrary, Frank knew there wasn't much of a chance that he actually could.

Even if he hadn't had the twins and his father and eight hundred head of sheep to worry about, writing more than a hundred pages in seven weeks would have been beyond him. To continue to insist otherwise would be silly.

Still, he couldn't say he was thrilled with the alternative Orson was offering him. He didn't like the idea of some *stranger* tampering with his wife's manuscript. He didn't like it at all. However, much as he hated to admit it, accepting Alison Kent's help might be the only way he could guarantee that Rebecca's book would make it to publication.

"So, tell me ... exactly what does your Ms. Kent do?" Frank asked, trying not to sound as grudging as he felt.

"Up until three years ago, she was a senior editor at Norville Press. Since then she's free-lanced occasionally for Norville and a couple of other publishing houses. She's also worked one-on-one with several writers who have had problems with a project. She can read through a manuscript once, pinpoint what's wrong with it, and suggest revisions. Thanks to her uncanny ability to take on a writer's individual tone and style and make it her own, she's also completed a couple of manuscripts for writers who haven't been able to do so themselves."

"She sounds like just the person I need," Frank admitted, then added only half-jokingly, "Does she make house calls?"

"I'm not really sure," Orson replied. "She's become something of a recluse over the past few years. I think she's met with a couple of her clients here in New York, but to my knowledge, she usually confers with the writer via telephone, then works on the manuscript on her own."

Frowning, Frank leaned against the counter once again. He found it hard enough to accept the fact that he was going to have to have help in order to finish Rebecca's manuscript. And even then, he'd assumed he would work *with* Alison Kent. Entrusting her to complete the manuscript on her own was something else altogether.

Apparently Orson held the woman in high regard. Yet Frank had no intention of allowing her to do whatever she wanted with *Hunter's Edge*. Albeit inadvertently, she could end up destroying the integrity of the story Rebecca had wanted to tell, and he wouldn't know it until it was too late to call a halt. So, either he had a say in Ms. Kent's day-to-day "contributions," or he made a last-ditch effort to complete the manuscript himself.

"Do you think she'd consider coming out here to work on it?" he asked.

He wasn't exactly thrilled with the prospect of having a strange woman underfoot. But if that was the only way he could make sure Ms. Kent finished Rebecca's book the way he wanted, he imagined he could put up with her for a few weeks. Otherwise, he'd have to go to New York, and he couldn't afford to do that. Not when he also had a ranch to run. While his father was a big help, Frank couldn't expect the older man to keep up with the twins and eight hundred head of sheep on his own for more than a day or two at a time.

"I can't say for sure, but under the circumstances, she might. Of course, you'd have to pay her expenses along with her usual fee."

"Which is?"

Orson named a sum that seemed quite reasonable. Frank could pay it, as well as her airfare and car rental, out of Rebecca's advance. He could also put her up in a hotel in Santa Fe if that's what she wanted. But commuting from there on a daily basis would be foolish when he could easily accommodate her at the house.

He said as much to Orson and the agent seemed to agree. Ms. Kent probably wouldn't mind staying at the ranch. That way she could spend the majority of her time working on the manuscript, and with luck, she'd more than likely be able to head back to New York before the Christmas holidays.

"You don't think she'd have any objection to being away from home so close to Christmas?" Frank asked, trying not to get his hopes up.

In the past few minutes he'd resigned himself to the fact that he'd have to have help if he wanted to complete Rebecca's book, the kind of help Alison Kent seemed quite capable of providing. But time was of the essence, and most people liked to be with their families during the holiday season.

"Her husband and son died a few years ago, and to my knowledge she doesn't have any other close relatives here," Orson replied. "As long as she isn't working on anything else at the moment, I can't see that she'd mind spending the next few weeks in New Mexico." He paused, then continued thoughtfully. "In fact, I'd say she might even welcome the opportunity to get away for a while."

Frank knew he couldn't ask for much more, especially if the woman turned out to be as ready, willing and able as Orson seemed to think she would. But he still had some qualms about her. From the little Orson had said, he gathered she was an older woman used to living alone. As long as she understood he'd be calling the shots, her age didn't matter to him one way or another. But unfortunately, although he could offer her *some* privacy while she was at the ranch, he couldn't guarantee that he'd be able to keep his sons from driving her crazy on a daily basis.

"What about the twins?" he ventured, determined to cover all the bases as best he could. "Do you think they'd get on her nerves?"

"As far as I know, she's always been fond of children, so I doubt that will be a problem," Orson assured him without hesitation.

"You sound like you know her pretty well," Frank said, then added as casually as he could, "Is your relationship with her based on anything other than . . . business?"

He'd heard both admiration and affection in Orson's voice each time the agent had spoken of the woman, and he couldn't help but wonder if they associated with each other on a personal as well as professional basis. Not that it made any difference to him. Orson obviously held her in high regard, and that meant a lot to Frank. Still, he'd never been especially fond of surprises. So he saw no reason why he shouldn't try to find out as much as he could about her.

"Her husband taught me all I know about the publishing business, and he was also one of my best friends," Orson stated simply. He paused for several moments, then continued quietly. "However, I'd never have recommended her if I didn't think she could do the work."

"I wasn't suggesting you would," Frank hastened to reassure him. He hadn't intended to insult the agent, but apparently he'd come close to doing just that. "I was just . . . curious."

"I can't say I blame you," Orson admitted in a more amicable tone. "But believe me, I've got nothing to gain by selling you a pig in a poke."

"Yeah, right." Aware that the time had come to make a decision about Alison Kent, Frank paced across the kitchen yet again. "So, where do we go from here? Do you want me to call her or what?"

Though he still had his doubts about working with the woman, he had to admit that he really didn't have much choice. What could it hurt to give Ms. Kent a crack at Rebecca's manuscript? If they didn't get along together or her work didn't measure up to his expectations, he'd pay her for her time and trouble and send her back to New York City without any hard feelings on his part.

"I think it would be best if I talked to her."

"All right," Frank agreed. Despite the impression he'd given earlier, he trusted the agent's judgment. And he figured Ms. Kent would be more amenable to the idea of spending a month or so in New Mexico if Orson was the one suggesting it rather than some stranger.

"If she's interested, when would you like her to be there?"

"The sooner the better." Frank eyed the calendar hanging on the pantry door. Tomorrow was Thanksgiving, and aside from roasting a turkey, they weren't doing anything special over the holiday weekend. But that didn't mean Ms. Kent hadn't made any plans for herself. And anyway, he'd need the next few days to get the house in order. "How about Monday or Tuesday?"

"Sounds good to me. I'll get back to you later this afternoon after I've talked to her, and if she's agreeable, we can work out the details then."

"Talk to you later." Frank cradled the receiver. Then, hoping he wouldn't regret the decision he'd made, he walked back to the window.

From his vantage point, he watched Jake and Joey climb onto the front seat of Bert's pickup truck as their grandfather slammed the hood shut. A few moments later, the old man joined them in the cab. The sound of the starter grinding drifted across the yard. Then, after a round of coughing and sputtering, the engine finally turned over.

With a sigh of relief, Frank turned and headed toward the open doorway on the far side of the kitchen. He hadn't planned on buying a new truck until the sheep had been sheared in the spring, and Bert liked having his own wheels almost as much as Frank did. They got along better than a lot of fathers and sons, but there were still times when one of them needed to get away from the other. And living out in the middle of nowhere the way they did, neither of them could risk being left alone without any means of transportation.

Standing on the threshold, he surveyed the combination bed-sitting room that had been Bert's since he'd moved back to the ranch five years ago, after Frank's mother had died. Under the circumstances, he didn't think his father would mind moving into one of the spare bedrooms on the far side of the house for the next few weeks. As for Ms. Kent, he could only hope she'd find the accommodations he had to offer acceptable.

The double bed sported a new mattress and box spring, and he'd recently refinished the old oak nightstand, dresser and chest of drawers. An easy chair and ottoman sat near the Franklin stove, and the little bookcase angled into one corner held a TV and stereo system. Granted, the furnishings were nothing fancy. But she'd have her own bathroom. And since the door in the outer wall opened into the backyard, she could come and go as she pleased without disturbing anyone. Of course, she'd have to venture into *their* part of the house to get to Rebecca's office, but otherwise everyone ought to have at least a little privacy.

Following his thoughts, Frank turned and crossed the kitchen, and headed down the hallway. He paused at the living room doorway, eyeing the piles of wooden blocks and assorted plastic action figures littering the floor, then moved on to the closed door across from the master bedroom. After hesitating a moment or two, he reached out, turned the knob and stepped across the threshold.

No matter how many times he walked into Rebecca's office and found it empty, somewhere deep in his heart he still expected to see her sitting at the old rolltop desk, immersed in another time and place as her fingers flew over the computer keyboard. But he was all by himself in the little room that had been hers, and hers alone.

Although he'd worked there off and on over the past year, trying to complete her manuscript, everything was pretty much as she'd left it that night when she'd come to bed early, complaining of a headache. The papers on her desk were neatly stacked, the books on the bookshelves lining one wall were all in order, and her patchwork quilt was neatly folded over the arm of the small blue-and-white-striped love seat tucked under the row of tall, narrow windows overlooking the front drive.

As if she weren't really gone forever...

Maybe he should have done as Bert suggested six months ago. Maybe he should have accepted the fact that Rebecca's last manuscript wasn't meant to be finished, then packed up her books and papers as he'd finally done her clothes, and given everything away. But he'd never been one to walk away easily. Or to allow another's dream to die quietly.

As he stood in the doorway, staring at the dust motes that drifted in the sunbeams slanting through the windowpanes, he thought of all the hours his wife had spent in that room, weaving words into one captivating story after another. Most of the time she'd preferred to be alone, but occasionally, when she'd needed his help, she'd allowed him to join her. But never anyone else. Not even the twins.

Now he was going to have to share the office with a total stranger. It wasn't going to be easy, not by a long shot, but he'd manage somehow. Simply because he had no other choice.

The sound of a door slamming drew him from his reverie. Then, from the kitchen, he heard his father's rumbling voice punctuated by the twins' light, bright chatter. Sighing inwardly, he turned to leave the room. He didn't want them to catch him brooding yet again. But before he could close the door, the boys clamored down the hallway, then skidded to a halt as they saw him. Their smiles fading, they stared at him, their gazes all too knowing for their years.

"Are you going to be sad again today, Dad?" Jake asked. The older of the twins by fifteen minutes, he often took the lead. But Frank saw the same question in Joey's blue-gray eyes as well.

"Why do you say that?" he asked, though he already had a good idea of what the answer would be.

"You always are after you've been in there," Joey stated with such candor that Frank's heart ached.

From the mouths of children, he thought, running a hand through his hair. But after all the times they'd found him sitting at Rebecca's desk, staring into space, what could he expect?

Suddenly aware of just how unfair he'd been to his sons, he hunkered down in front of them and drew them close. For the past eighteen months he'd been so caught up in *his* loss that he'd often shut out his sons when they had needed him most.

But not anymore. He was done clinging to the past. For his sake as well as his sons', he had to move forward and look toward the future. And that was exactly what he intended to do—once he'd seen to it that Rebecca's manuscript was completed. Then he'd have done all he could to guarantee a part of her would live on, not only in his mind and heart, but in the minds and hearts of everyone who would eventually have an opportunity to read what he believed would be the best of all the books she'd written.

"Truth be told, I'm actually feeling pretty good today," he said with a smile.

"You are?" Joey returned his smile with obvious pleasure.

"Why?" Jake demanded, not quite so easily convinced.

"Mr. Hyde's found someone to help me finish your mom's book."

"And who might that be?" Bert asked as he joined them in the hallway.

Glancing up, Frank met his father's speculative gaze. His smile widened into a grin. "A retired editor from New York City. Her name is Alison Kent."

Orson hadn't *said* she was retired, but Frank assumed that must be the case, especially since she was a widow without any family. He could only hope she and Bert wouldn't end up dealing each other a fit. Of course, there was also a possibility that the crotchety old rancher and the sophisticated lady from the big city might hit it off. As far as Frank was concerned, that would be just fine. His father got to feeling lonely sometimes, too.

"How's she going to help you from New York City?" Bert asked, rubbing a hand over his whiskery chin.

"Actually, she's going to come here."

"Oh, yeah? When?"

"Probably not until Monday or Tuesday."

"Good." Bert nodded agreeably. "That'll give us time to get the place cleaned up."

"Like we did when Aunt Ellen and Aunt Elaine came to visit?" Jake asked, sounding none too pleased by the prospect.

"Yeah, just like that," Frank replied.

They'd given the house a good going-over in August before his younger-by-five-years twin sisters had come to see them, Ellen from San Diego, where she was currently stationed, and Elaine from Seattle, where she owned a small bookstore. But they'd let the place clutter up again over the past couple of months.

"We had to put *all* our toys away, and Molly had to stay in the barn at night," Joey said, sighing woefully.

"Hey, guys, it's not going to be that bad," Frank chided softly, giving them a hug. "And since tomorrow's Thanksgiving, we won't start until Friday." He stood up once again. "Now, what do you say we drive into town, have lunch at Ruby's Café, then head over to the grocery store? We've got a turkey but not much in the way of fixin's."

"Oka-a-ay," they chimed gleefully, then spun around and raced past their grandfather.

"So, you gonna tell me all about Ms. Alison Kent?" Bert asked as they followed the boys into the kitchen.

"Everything I know," Frank said, meeting his father's twinkling eyes.

"She's retired, huh?"

"That's the impression I got." He grabbed the denim jacket he'd left on the back of one of the kitchen chairs and shrugged into it.

"Sounds interesting. Think she'll be able to put up with the four of us?"

"I hope so," Frank replied as they all headed out the kitchen door. "I certainly hope so."

* * *

She should have known better than to let Orson con her into joining him for a late lunch. But then, Alison had thought all he'd have up his sleeve was another eligible bachelor he wanted her to meet. She'd have had no problem dealing with *that*. She'd certainly had enough practice over the past year or so, ever since he'd decided it was time for her to get back into circulation. Maintaining an aura of indifference had worked like a charm on the other unwanted suitors he'd lined up for her, and she'd simply counted on it working again today.

What she hadn't expected was a request that she work one-on-one with a client of his out in New Mexico, she thought, settling against the plushly upholstered back seat of his Mercedes and staring out the window at the falling rain as the driver guided the car through the preholiday, midtown Manhattan traffic. Nor had she expected to find the idea quite so appealing. He'd definitely taken her by surprise when he'd broached the subject over the Caesar salad, and then she'd surprised herself with her own sudden interest in what he was saying.

Thanks to the money from Len's life insurance policy, she didn't have to work, and for a while that had been just as well. After her husband and their young son, Nathan, had been killed, she hadn't been willing or able to do much of anything but cry. She'd resigned her position as senior editor of women's fiction at Norville Press and virtually gone to ground.

About two years ago, however, Orson had taken it upon himself to bring her back to the land of the living. He'd badgered her into working with one of his clients who was having trouble rewriting a manuscript to her editor's satisfaction. Though Alison hadn't been all that enthusiastic about working with the woman, she hadn't been able to say no to Orson, either. He and Len had been best friends as

well as business associates. And Orson had been one of only
a few who hadn't deserted her during the early months of
her mourning, when she'd done everything she could to
isolate herself from everyone who'd ever mattered to her in
any way. She owed him for that, and she'd always been one
to pay her debts.

As it turned out, Alison had enjoyed working on Reba
Watson's manuscript a lot more than she'd anticipated.
She'd said as much to Orson, and before she knew it, other
agents began calling to request her services. Several editors
she'd worked with in the past also began to ask her to free-
lance for them. Lately, she'd been able to keep as busy as she
wanted, and she'd been able do so on her own terms. Which
had yet to include flying halfway across the country to work
with a writer face-to-face.

As Orson knew only too well, though she conferred with
her clients extensively at the outset, Alison preferred to work
on a manuscript alone. Also, after trying, with limited suc-
cess, to work with several men, she made a point of taking
on projects from women writers only. She not only found it
easier to tap into a woman's distinctive tone and style, but
was more comfortable with the kind of stories they tended
to write, as well.

At least Rebecca Francis fit *that* particular criteria.
However, much as she seemed to need the kind of help Alison had to offer, the woman didn't want to work with her
long distance. According to Orson, she wanted to keep a
close eye on her manuscript, and she was willing to pay Alison's travel expenses so that she could.

If anyone else had offered her the job, Alison wouldn't
have even considered it. Since Len and Nathan had been
killed on their way to pick her up at the airport three years
ago, she hadn't done any traveling at all, and she had no real
desire to do so now. Nor did she relish the idea of having
someone looking over her shoulder while she worked.

Yet, because she trusted Orson's judgment implicitly, she'd agreed to fly to New Mexico on Monday and spend the next few weeks completing Ms. Francis's manuscript.

Much to her surprise, she'd been intrigued not only by Orson's interest in the woman, but also by his enthusiasm for her work. Though he hadn't told her all that much about Rebecca Francis, what he *had* said had certainly roused her curiosity.

Ms. Francis obviously wasn't one of his top money-makers, not by any stretch of the imagination. Her sales had climbed steadily with each of the five books she'd had published over the past eight years, but she hadn't attained bestseller status...yet. However, from what Orson had told her, the book she'd been trying to finish for almost two years had been expected to put her on the *New York Times*'s list.

As to *why* she hadn't been able to complete the manuscript, Orson had been rather vague. When Alison had tried to pin him down, he'd mentioned something about personal problems. Then, instead of offering any details, he'd gone on to tell her how much Margaret Locke thought of the woman's work.

Alison had been impressed by the fact that one of the most respected editors at one of the most prestigious publishing houses in the country had taken Ms. Francis under her wing. And, as a result, she now realized that she'd allowed herself to be sidetracked before her questions had all been answered.

The next thing Alison knew, she was agreeing to work with Ms. Francis on the woman's terms, and Orson was sending her home in his car after promising to make the necessary arrangements.

"Here we are, Ms. Kent," Orson's driver announced as he pulled to a stop in front of her apartment building.

Grabbing an umbrella, he stepped outside and opened her door.

"Thank you, Randall."

She gathered her briefcase and the canvas bag full of Ms. Francis's books Orson had given her and climbed out of the car. Shivering as a gust of icy wind ruffled her short dark hair, she hurried up the flight of steps to the entryway of the elegant old brownstone where Carlson, the doorman, waited to greet her.

After thanking Randall once again, Alison wished Carlson a good evening, crossed the polished marble floor of the foyer and entered the waiting elevator.

Upstairs in her third-floor apartment, she dumped her briefcase and the canvas bag on the floor just inside the front door, hung her coat in the closet, then walked from one room to another, turning on lamps to dispel the gloom of early evening. Three years ago, when Len and Nathan had been alive, the place had often seemed too small. Now it always seemed much too big and, despite the lovely antique furniture filling the rooms, all too empty.

In the kitchen, she filled the kettle with water and set it on the stove to heat. Since she'd finished lunch less than an hour ago, she wasn't hungry, but a cup of tea would help chase away the chill she'd caught on her way into the building.

Sitting on a chair by the table, she pulled off her boots, then headed for the bedroom to check her answering machine. There was only one message. Orson's wife, Deborah, had called to remind her that she was welcome to join them for Thanksgiving dinner tomorrow at two o'clock. If she changed her mind, she should call, and they'd send Randall to pick her up.

Feeling like a thankless wretch, Alison stripped out of her gray wool skirt and ivory turtleneck sweater, then slipped into a long, quilted, green-and-blue plaid flannel robe and matching slippers. She really should take Orson and Deborah up on their offer and spend Thanksgiving with them. But even after almost three years, she still found the holiday season hard to bear. Getting through Thanksgiving, Christmas and New Year's alone was a lot easier than making an effort to join in the festivities organized by others, even her closest friends.

Which led her to the major reason why she wasn't going to call Orson and tell him she'd changed her mind about working with Rebecca Francis, despite the second thoughts she'd been having. While she still wasn't thrilled about traveling to New Mexico, getting out of the city for the next month or so had suddenly begun to seem like a good idea.

She didn't have any other projects lined up at the moment. Nor did she foresee anything coming her way until after the first of the year. Most everyone would be preoccupied with preparations for Christmas and New Year's, and any work that could be put off for a while would be. That meant she'd have way too much time on her hands. And, everywhere she turned, she'd be inundated with the kind of holiday cheer she simply couldn't share.

All things considered, Alison had to admit she'd probably be much better off out in New Mexico, working with Ms. Francis at her ranch south of Santa Fe. From the little Orson had said about her, Alison gathered she was somewhat reclusive. And, with more than a hundred manuscript pages to write by January 15, surely the woman wouldn't have time to bother about making a big deal of the holidays.

Gazing at the photograph of Len and Nathan on the nightstand, Alison recalled how she and her husband had planned to make their son's first Christmas as magical as they could. They'd splurged on all sorts of decorations, but they'd still needed a tree when she'd gone out of town on business that first week in December. They'd planned to stop and buy one on their way home from the airport when she returned.

As she'd waited for them to pick her up, she'd been happier than she'd ever been in her life. She'd lost her parents, then her beloved older brother, but she had a husband and a son, and she'd begun to believe that all would finally be well.

And it would have been, if only she'd taken the shuttle instead of so eagerly agreeing to let them make the drive to the airport that snowy Sunday afternoon—

The piercing whistle of the teakettle brought her back to the present with an unpleasant jolt. Unfortunately, *if only* had yet to change anything, she thought as she turned and walked back to the kitchen.

She dropped a tea bag in her little teapot and added hot water. Then, leaving it to steep, she returned to the entryway and retrieved the bag of books Orson had given her. She might as well start familiarizing herself with Ms. Francis's style. She certainly had the time, not to mention the desire. She'd just as soon not dwell on her hapless past any longer. Nor did she want to think beyond the very near future.

Over the past three years she'd finally resigned herself to the fact that she was going to have to spend the rest of her life alone. At the ripe old age of thirty, she'd lost everyone she'd ever loved. So obviously, she was meant to get by on her own.

She wished it could be otherwise. But she knew better than to tempt fate. If she allowed herself to love anyone, she'd only end up losing them as she had her parents, her brother, her husband and her son. She knew she wouldn't be able to bear the heartache, so she simply made up her mind that she'd never have to. No matter how many eligible men Orson Hyde dangled in front of her.

Which gave her another good reason for going to New Mexico. At least she wouldn't have to put up with his matchmaking out there, she thought, smiling as she poured herself a cup of tea. And that would definitely suit her just fine.

Chapter Two

"Still no sign of our Ms. Kent, I take it."

Frowning, Frank glanced over his shoulder at his father. "No sign at all," he growled, making no attempt to hide his annoyance with the woman. She should have arrived at the ranch almost three hours ago, but he had yet to see hide or hair of her.

Shoving his hands in the back pockets of his jeans, Frank turned away from his father and once again stared out the front window, which faced the narrow drive that led down to the ranch road more than half a mile away. Thanks to the snow that drifted and swirled on the shifting wind, he could see very little in the pale glow of the outside lights. Still, he stayed where he was, watching and waiting as a vague uneasiness began to edge under his irritation.

Damn it to hell, where was she?

"Maybe she decided to spend the night in Santa Fe," Bert said.

"Yeah, maybe she did," Frank agreed, though he had his doubts. Surely she would have had the courtesy to contact him if she'd changed her mind about making the drive down to the ranch that night. Wouldn't she?

According to Orson, Alison Kent's flight had been scheduled to land in Santa Fe around four-thirty that afternoon. Upon arrival, she was supposed to pick up the rental car she'd requested. Then, following the detailed directions Frank had given the agent over the phone, she was supposed to head for the Double B.

Under optimum conditions, the seventy-mile drive should have taken her no more than an hour and a half. When she hadn't arrived at the ranch by seven o'clock, Frank had called the airline to check on her flight. Due to bad weather on the east coast, the plane had been delayed almost two hours, but had finally touched down at six-thirty.

Thinking that she probably hadn't had time to pick up the car yet, he'd called the rental agency to leave a message for her suggesting she stay in Santa Fe until the following day. But by the time he'd gotten through to someone, she'd already picked up her car and gone.

He'd hoped that she'd have sense enough to check into a hotel rather than head for the ranch as planned, especially when the rental agent advised him that it had begun to snow in Santa Fe around the time her plane had landed. But it was almost nine-thirty, and he had yet to hear from her.

She had to know that he was expecting her and that he'd be concerned about her if she didn't show up as scheduled. Taking a moment to call and tell him where she was couldn't present that much of a problem, could it?

Unless she was out in the middle of the first major snowstorm of the season, somewhere between Santa Fe and the Double B....

Swearing softly, Frank grabbed the cord and gave it a yank, closing the wide, old-fashioned, wood-slatted blinds.

He had enough problems already. Having to worry about Alison Kent, as well, irritated the hell out of him. He'd hired her because he needed her help. But over the past couple of hours he'd begun to wonder if she was going to be more trouble than she was worth. Orson had led him to believe the old girl was smart and savvy, but only an addlebrained idiot would set out on a seventy-mile drive along unfamiliar roads in the midst of bad weather.

"Don't you think she'd have called if she decided to stay in Santa Fe?" Bert asked quietly, as if he'd read his son's mind.

Turning, Frank met his father's gaze and realized the older man was just as concerned as he was. "Yeah, I think she would have," he admitted.

"Which means she's probably out on the road somewhere."

"Probably," Frank agreed as he crossed to the old sofa, sat down and reached for the boots he'd kicked off a couple of hours ago when he'd come in for what he'd hoped would be the last time that night.

"So, what are you going to do?"

"First, I'm going to call the highway patrol and the sheriff's office and find out if anyone's run across her."

"And if they haven't?"

"Then I'm going to see if I can find her myself," he muttered.

He couldn't think of anything he'd rather do less than spend the next couple of hours driving around in the blowing snow and cold, especially when there was a good chance the woman was tucked away in a cozy hotel room up in Santa Fe. More than likely, he'd be wasting his time, not to mention risking his own well-being, going on what would probably turn out to be nothing more than a wild-goose chase.

Still, try as he might, he couldn't completely discount the possibility that Alison Kent was stuck out on the road somewhere. And, if that proved to be the case, then he was partially responsible for her being there.

Though Orson had indicated that she was satisfied with the arrangements they'd made, and though the weather hadn't really been bad earlier, Frank knew he should have gone to meet her plane. Then she could have followed him back to the ranch in her rental car. That would have been the gentlemanly thing to do. And, under any other circumstances, he wouldn't have thought twice about it. He'd have hopped into his truck, driven to Santa Fe, and been waiting for her when she finally arrived.

Unfortunately, by that afternoon he still hadn't come to terms with the fact that he'd begun to want the woman's help as much as he needed it. When he'd first agreed to hire her, he'd done so for Rebecca's sake rather than his own. He'd wanted nothing more than to guarantee that she'd always be remembered. But over the past few days he'd come to realize that he was also looking forward to finally being done with her manuscript once and for all.

As a result, his honorable intentions had been tempered by a hearty dose of self-reproach. And, before he knew it, he'd started thinking of Alison Kent as a kind of co-conspirator. Actually going out of his way to welcome her had suddenly seemed . . . traitorous. Thus, he'd chosen to postpone their first meeting as long as possible.

"How far do you plan to go?"

"Just up to the interstate."

Just was actually something of an understatement since the drive, one way, was more than fifty miles, but they both knew what he meant. If Ms. Kent had had problems on the outskirts of Santa Fe or along I-25, someone would have come along to give her a hand by now. But if she'd run into trouble on Highway 3 or the ranch road, there was a good chance no one would come upon her until tomorrow morning. No one there ventured out at night in the middle of a snowstorm unless absolutely necessary.

Of course, if she got stuck and stayed with the car, she'd be all right. She probably didn't have a sleeping bag or a wool blanket with her, but she would have a suitcase full of clothes. She could add layers to stay warm if necessary.

However, if she hadn't had sense enough to stay in Santa Fe, Frank knew better than to count on her having sense enough to stay in the car until morning. She'd probably assume that she could find help somewhere and go looking for it.

"Why don't I fill a thermos with coffee for you while you make your calls?" Bert offered.

"I'd appreciate that, Dad," Frank replied as he followed his father into the kitchen.

Fifteen minutes later, after being advised that neither the highway patrol nor the local sheriff had come across anyone by the name of Alison Kent, Frank shrugged into his fleece-lined denim jacket and clapped his battered cowboy hat on his head. Then, after promising to touch base with his father in an hour or so, he headed out to the shed where he'd parked his truck, thermos of coffee in one hand, mobile phone in the other, and a couple of wool blankets tucked under his arm for good measure.

Shivering as a blast of icy wind sent spatters of snowflakes down the back of his neck, he whistled for Molly. Heedless of the cold, the dog nosed open the barn door, raced across the yard and scrambled onto the passenger seat, her brown eyes bright with excitement. Not only would she be good company, if Ms. Kent had left her car and wandered off the road, Molly would be able to find her a lot faster than he. And, if worse came to worst, and *he* ended up in a ditch, the dog would gladly curl up with him and keep him warm until Bert could come to his rescue.

"So, girlie, you wanna go for a ride?" he asked as he turned the key in the ignition.

Wiggling close to him, the dog yipped once, then rested a paw on his thigh and nuzzled his ear with her cold nose.

"Yeah, that's what I thought, you old hussy. Anything to have some company for a while, huh?" Frank grumbled, smiling in spite of himself.

At least the dog was happy.

Swearing softly under her breath, Alison let up on the accelerator and switched off the engine. Despite the fact that she'd been driving at a snail's pace, somehow the car had gotten away from her, sliding and shimmying across the narrow road until it finally crunched to a halt, tail end slanted down in a ditch. And, no matter how she spun the back tires, she wasn't going to get the car back on the road again.

As she had off and on all evening, she wondered why on earth she'd been so intent on driving to the Double B that night. After numerous delays, her plane had finally arrived in Santa Fe two hours late. She'd been worn to a frazzle by then, yet she'd been determined to go on to the ranch rather than spend the night in the city. Now, as she stared at the snowflakes swirling in the glow of the headlights, she tried to recall exactly *what* had prompted her to act so irrationally. Granted, she'd been anxious to reach the end of her journey, but not anxious enough to endanger herself.

Of course, it hadn't been snowing much at all when she left the airport. And, after all the traveling she'd done that day, what was another seventy miles or so? She'd figured she might as well try to make it to the ranch, and if the weather worsened along the way, she could always find someplace to spend the night.

She hadn't realized that once she left the interstate, she'd be out in the middle of nowhere with nothing around for miles. Nor had she been prepared for how swiftly a few snow flurries could turn into a blinding storm. Still, she'd forged ahead slowly, watching the odometer ticking off mile after mile and checking at regular intervals the directions Orson had given her.

When she'd finally turned off Highway 3 onto the ranch road, she'd allowed herself to relax just a little. She had less than five miles to go to the Double B, and though the snow was much deeper than it had been on the highway, the rental car continued to slog along steadily. Or it had until about ten minutes ago when it spun around in a truly terrifying three-sixty that ended with the car stuck in a ditch.

Swearing yet again, Alison switched off the headlights, tipped her head against the headrest and closed her eyes. There was no way she was going to get the car back on the road on her own. So, now what? Should she stay with the car and hope that someone would come to her rescue?

Fat chance of that happening, she thought, recalling that she hadn't seen another car on the road since she'd left the interstate. She'd probably end up spending the night out there. At the very least. Who knew when somebody would venture onto the roads again, especially if the weather stayed bad.

Maybe she ought to try to walk the rest of the way to the ranch. Since she made a habit of walking almost everywhere she went in the city, she was in fairly good shape. And she'd had sense enough to dress warmly in tailored wool pants, a flannel shirt, wool sweater, boots and a calf-length wool coat.

According to the odometer, she couldn't be more than a mile or so from the Double B. In fact, if she wasn't mistaken, she'd seen a light up ahead on the right just before the car had started to skid.

Opening her eyes, she peered through the windshield thoughtfully. Yes, there it was, off in the distance . . . a pale glow that had to be coming from the Double B ranch.

"So, what'll it be—stay or go?" she muttered, drumming her fingers on the steering wheel as she watched the snow continue to drift downward.

Unless she started the engine and ran the heater, thus risking asphyxiation, the car windows would frost over all too soon. And just the thought of not being able to see outside the close confines of the car made her feel claustrophobic. Which was about all it took for her to make up her mind. Given her somewhat limited choices, she'd much rather spend an hour or so trudging through the snow and cold than stay in the car, courting a bad case of the screaming meemies.

Having come to a decision, she reached over, opened the glove box and took out the flashlight the rental company had so kindly provided. Then she pulled her woolen scarf over her head, wrapped it around her neck and tucked the ends inside the collar of her coat. She slipped on her wool-lined leather gloves and slung her purse strap over her shoulder. Moments later, aware that she was as ready as she'd ever be, she stepped out of the car, switched on the flashlight and started out along the edge of the road.

Thankfully, the wind had died down and the snow didn't seem to be falling quite as heavily as it had been earlier. Still, the air was icy cold, and the occasional knee-deep, powdery drifts made the going anything but easy. Yet she continued to trudge forward, the crunching of her footsteps the only sound disturbing the eerie, almost otherworldly, silence of the night.

After what seemed like a very long time, she turned to see how much distance she'd put between herself and the car. Not much more than a few hundred yards, she thought with dismay as the beam of the flashlight bounced off the vehicle's front bumper.

Okay, so maybe she'd underestimated just how long a walk she had ahead of her. But she'd already admitted she couldn't spend the night in the car and retain her sanity. And once she got to the ranch, she'd be able to take a nice hot bath and crawl into a warm, cozy bed.

Head down, she plodded onward, putting one foot in front of the other as she followed the pale glow provided by the flashlight. She wasn't really all that cold. But she found herself growing more and more weary with each step she took.

Maybe she ought to turn back after all, she reasoned after a while. At least she knew she could make it back to the car. The ranch was another story altogether. Though she'd been keeping an eye on the light up ahead, she didn't really seem to be getting any closer to it.

And what if she slipped and fell and hurt herself? She could very well die out there. Granted, she could remember a few times when she hadn't thought that she wanted to go on living, but tonight certainly wasn't one of them. Actually, now that she'd had some time to consider the possibly dire consequences of her decision to walk the rest of the way to the ranch, dealing with a little claustrophobia didn't seem all that bad.

She certainly didn't relish the thought of freezing to death out in the middle of nowhere. In fact, she had to admit that she didn't relish the thought of dying at all. She'd come a long way in the past three years, she realized, as she continued to tramp through the snow. Funny, she'd intended her trip to New Mexico to be nothing more than a temporary respite. And here she was, after less than a day away, discovering something unexpected about herself. Talk about a good omen. Now, if only she could make it to the Double B before she—

Pausing, Alison stared at the snow-covered ground, wondering if she'd heard what she thought she had over the swish of her footsteps. Yes, there it was, the sound of a motor running somewhere off in the distance. As she raised her head, she saw what had to be a pair of headlights angling toward the ranch road along what she assumed was the Double B's main drive.

"Oh, please," she murmured, picking up her pace as much as she could as she moved forward once again. "Head this way."

As if in answer to her plea, the vehicle turned onto the ranch road and rolled slowly toward her. Breathing hard, Alison stepped away from the verge, raised her arm and waved the flashlight. Within moments, the vehicle ground to a halt a couple of yards away from her.

After hesitating no more than an instant or two, Alison started across the road, hoping against hope that she wasn't about to throw herself on the mercy of a homicidal maniac. Considering the kind of day she'd had, she wouldn't be at all surprised if that turned out to be the case. But then, there was always a chance that her luck was about to change, she reminded herself with as much optimism as she could muster.

She was still a few feet away when the driver's door opened. She heard a deep, masculine voice mutter something that sounded a lot like "damn fool woman." Then, a tall, broad-shouldered, slim-hipped man wearing jeans, boots, a denim jacket and a cowboy hat strode toward her.

With the headlights behind him, Alison couldn't really see his face. However, considering the way he stomped through the snow, she had a feeling that his expression was probably rather grim.

"Are you—are you from the Double B ranch?" she stammered as he halted a foot or two away and eyed her up and down.

"Yes." He bit off the affirmation angrily.

Obviously, he wasn't thrilled to be out on a night like tonight. But then, Alison didn't imagine anyone would be. *She* certainly was none too pleased with her current situation. Yet she hadn't snapped at *him,* had she?

She was on the verge of pointing that out to him, then realized she'd probably only succeed in getting him more riled up than he already was. And *that* certainly wouldn't do her any good.

More than likely, Ms. Francis had begun to worry when she hadn't arrived as scheduled, so she'd sent him out to look for her. And for that, Alison was eternally thankful. Maybe if she made an effort to express her gratitude, he'd be somewhat mollified. What was that old saying about catching more flies with honey . . . ?

"I'm so glad to see you," she gushed.

Offering him the brightest smile she could muster, she took a step toward him and shifted the flashlight so that she could catch a glimpse of his face. Talk about a mistake. She hadn't really expected him to return her smile. But she hadn't thought his expression would be quite so severe, either.

"I'll just bet you are," he growled.

"Look, Mr. . . . .whoever you are," she began, her smile fading. The man was downright . . . insufferable.

"Bradford," he supplied with the barest hint of amusement. "Frank Bradford."

"Mr. Bradford." Her patience with the man wearing thin, Alison tipped her chin up and staunchly met his gaze. "I'm Alison Kent, and if I'm not mistaken, Ms. Francis is expecting me at the Double B. Unfortunately, my car went off the road—"

"*You're* Alison Kent?" he interrupted, eyeing her narrowly as his frown deepened.

"Yes."

"And you say *Ms. Francis* is expecting you?"

"Yes," she said again, making no effort to hide her exasperation. "I was scheduled to arrive earlier this evening, but my flight was delayed. Then I got caught in the snowstorm, and my car went off the road."

Not only was she dead on her feet, but in the short time she'd been standing still, she'd also begun to feel the cold. And just a few yards away sat a vehicle that could take her to the hot bath and warm bed she craved. Yet the vehicle's owner seemed much more intent on giving her the third degree than a ride to the Double B.

"*She* was expecting you?" he prodded, as if he wasn't sure he'd heard her right the first time.

"According to Orson Hyde, *she* was." Crossing her arms over her chest, Alison shivered violently. For the life of her, she couldn't understand why he seemed so disconcerted. Surely Ms. Francis had told him about her. Unless... "You—you did say you're from the Double B, didn't you?" she asked. Maybe she was the one who hadn't heard right, and Frank Bradford wasn't going to prove to be her savior, after all.

"Yeah, I'm from the Double B," he muttered. Closing the distance between them, he took her by the arm and steered her toward the passenger side of his truck.

"So, you work for Ms. Francis?" she continued, stumbling along beside him.

"You could say that." He opened the door, then turned to face her. "Take your scarf off."

"What?" Taking a step back, she eyed him uneasily.

"It's covered with snow," he explained. "If you take it off, I'll shake it out for you."

"Oh...okay."

As she fumbled with the ends she'd tucked into her coat collar, she shivered again, then swayed slightly as a wave of weariness washed over her.

"Here . . . let me," Bradford offered.

With surprising gentleness, he unwound her scarf, slipped it off her head, shook it out and handed it back to her. He brushed off the shoulders of her coat and, rather awkwardly, ran a gloved hand over her hair. Then, he caught her around the waist, hoisted her onto the seat, slammed the door and crossed to the driver's side.

If she hadn't been almost at the end of her rope, Alison would have bristled at his high-handed manner. In her current condition, however, she could do nothing but utter a small sigh of relief as she sat back, closed her eyes and basked in the blast of warm air emanating from the vents both atop and underneath the dash. She couldn't remember anything ever feeling quite so—

With a shriek of surprise, she sat up again, her eyes flying open as something cold and wet nuzzled her cheek. "What in the world—"

"Molly, let the lady be," Bradford admonished as he settled onto the driver's seat and pulled his door closed.

A woof sounded from the back seat of the double cab, then a medium-size, reddish-brown-and-white shaggy dog jumped onto the seat between them, curled as close as she could to Alison and rested her head in her lap.

"Oh...my," Alison murmured, staring at the animal. She liked dogs, but she'd never had an opportunity to own one, so she wasn't quite sure how to respond to the canine snuggling up against her.

"Why don't you give me that?" Reaching out, Bradford took the flashlight from her, switched it off and tossed it onto the back seat. Then he sat back and eyed her quietly for several seconds. "She won't hurt you, you know," he said at last.

"I know."

"You can pet her if you want. Take your gloves off and run your hands through her fur. It'll help to warm you up."

Alison did as he suggested, plunging her half-frozen fingers into the dog's silky coat. Almost immediately, the aching numbness was replaced by a warm, tingling sensation. Tipping her head back, she closed her eyes once again, and sighed in unison with the dog.

"Better?"

"Oh, yes," she murmured. "Much better."

"How about some coffee?"

"You have coffee?" Hoping he wasn't just teasing, she opened her eyes and turned to face him.

"Right here."

For just an instant, Alison thought she saw a smile tugging at the corners of his mouth. But then, he bent to retrieve the thermos he'd tucked under his seat. And, a few moments later, when he glanced at her as he handed her the metal cup of steaming coffee, he had that grim look on his face again.

"How far down the road did you leave your car?" he asked, capping the thermos, then setting it on the floor by her feet.

"Not too far." She cradled the cup in her hands and stared out the windshield. "Maybe half a mile, max."

"You shouldn't have tried to walk to the ranch, you know. You could have wandered off the road. Or worse, you could have fallen and hurt yourself," he grumbled.

"Mmm," she offered noncommittally, taking a sip of the strong, hot coffee.

She didn't really appreciate having her idiocy pointed out to her. But, since she'd already come to the conclusion that leaving her car had been a dumb idea, she resisted the urge to defend herself. Obviously, he didn't have a very high opinion of her, and Alison was fairly sure nothing she could say would change that. So, why waste her breath?

"I've got to make a call. Then, we'll go get your stuff," he advised, reaching under his seat again.

"A call?" She eyed him quizzically.

"Believe it or not, we have mobile telephones out here, too."

"How nice for you," she commented dryly. Annoyed by his sarcasm, she turned to gaze out the side window as she sipped her coffee and stroked the dog's furry head.

While he hadn't treated her badly, Frank Bradford certainly hadn't made any attempt to disguise the fact that he didn't have much use for her, either. And he seemed intent on taking exception to just about everything she had to say. Why that bothered her, Alison had no idea at all.

He was well built and, from what she'd seen of his face, reasonably attractive in a rugged kind of way. And she had to admit that he'd handled her gently, not only when he'd brushed the snow from her hair, but when he'd lifted her into the truck, as well.

However, she certainly didn't want or need his interest or his approval. She'd sworn off men in general, hadn't she? And she'd never had any fondness for macho men in particular. So why let him get under her skin?

After he dropped her off at the ranch house, she probably wouldn't see him again except at a distance. She'd be busy working with Ms. Francis, and though she didn't know a lot about sheep ranching, she doubted the hands spent much time at the house. And that suited her just fine.

"It's me."

Bradford's terse announcement interrupted Alison's reverie. Still staring out the window, she listened as he continued his conversation with the person on the other end of the telephone line. While she'd never been one to eavesdrop, under the circumstances, she didn't seem to have much choice. And since he was talking about her...

"Yeah, I found her," he stated rather trenchantly. "Her car went off the road about a mile from the ranch, and she decided to walk the rest of the way." He paused for several seconds, then continued. "I'm going to get her personal belongings out of the car just to be on the safe side, then we'll head back to the house. We ought to be there in twenty, maybe thirty minutes, but you don't need to wait up for us. You can meet her in the morning."

As he switched off the mobile phone and tucked it under his seat once again, Alison risked a glance in his direction. "Was that Ms. Francis?" She hadn't meant to worry the woman, but apparently—

"No," Bradford snapped, shifting the truck into drive and easing the vehicle forward, his eyes on the road.

"Well, excuse me for asking," Alison retorted. She'd tried to be nice. But the man was simply *impossible,* and she was getting fed up with his attitude.

"Look, Ms. Kent," he began in a more conciliatory tone of voice. "It's late. I'm tired, and I'm sure you are, too. I'm sorry we haven't gotten off to a very good start." He hesitated, as if carefully considering what he had to say next, then added, "Maybe we ought to call a truce for the time being, and try to sort things out in the morning."

"In other words, it would probably be best if we sat here and kept our mouths shut."

As he slowed the truck to a stop opposite her rental car, he turned and met her gaze. To Alison's surprise, he looked honestly apologetic.

"No offense meant, but under the circumstances, that sounds like a pretty good idea to me," he admitted quietly.

No offense meant? She stared at him for several seconds, more perplexed than ever. He seemed to realize that he was behaving badly, and he was obviously trying to make amends. Unfortunately, diplomacy didn't seem to be his long suit. But what could she possibly accomplish by giving him more grief?

She couldn't imagine what she had to sort out with *him,* but she wasn't about to ask. And she certainly didn't have any desire to go on sparring with him. With her luck, she'd end up saying something she'd regret, and she was already dealing with enough remorse to last a lifetime. She wasn't about to add to it by being rude to her hostess's hired hand.

"No offense taken," she murmured, lowering her gaze.

"Good." He nodded approvingly, then continued. "Have you got your keys?"

"Right here." She dug them out of her coat pocket and dropped them into his outstretched hand.

"Are your bags in the trunk?"

"Yes."

"Anything else you want out of the car?"

"Just my briefcase. It's on the front seat."

"I'll get it for you." He started to open his door, then turned back to her. "If you want more coffee, help yourself."

"Thanks."

Telling herself that he could be decent when he wanted, she refilled her cup as he crossed to the car and unlocked the trunk. Beside her, Molly sat up and stared out the windshield, whining softly as she kept an eye on her master.

"He'll be right back," Alison soothed, somewhat heartened by her behavior. No dog would be that devoted to anyone who was a complete curmudgeon.

Bradford stowed her suitcase, hanging bag and briefcase in the back of the truck. Then, with some cautious maneuvering, he managed to turn the vehicle around without sliding off the narrow road.

As if aware of her unspoken concern, he assured her that the car would be just fine until the next morning, when he'd round up some help and get it towed out of the ditch. Alison thanked him graciously. Then, as they'd agreed earlier, neither of them said anything more as they headed back to the ranch.

Initially, Alison welcomed the relative peace and quiet, especially since she was in no mood to carry on a conversation with the man. But after a while, much to her dismay, the silence stretching between them began to heighten her awareness of him in a most uncomfortable kind of way. Even with the dog between them, he suddenly seemed too...close. Shifting uncomfortably, she glanced at him, then quickly turned away when he met her gaze, his eyes cool and assessing.

What in the world was he thinking? And, more important, why on earth did she care?

When they finally pulled up in front of a long, low, adobe-style house, Alison heaved a quiet sigh of relief. Her ordeal was almost over, and not a moment too soon as far as she was concerned.

"Welcome to the Double B, Ms. Kent," Bradford offered quietly as he switched off the engine.

"Thank you, Mr. Bradford," she replied, forcing herself to turn and face him. "I'm...I'm glad to be here."

He held her gaze for one long moment, and suddenly Alison had a feeling that he was just as discomfited by her as she was by him. Considering how sure of himself he seemed to be, that struck her as rather odd. Surely he couldn't really believe she'd cause him any trouble. Even if she wanted to give him grief, which she didn't, she'd be too busy—

"Here, let me have that," he muttered, taking the empty cup from her.

He set it on the dash. Then, without another word, he opened the door and stepped out of the truck.

As the dog scampered after him, Alison wrapped her scarf around her neck, pulled her gloves on and slung her purse strap over her shoulder. By the time she managed to open the passenger door, he'd retrieved her luggage from the back of the truck and stood waiting to offer her a hand getting out. She accepted glady, then followed him up the snow-covered walkway.

To her surprise, he neither knocked on the front door nor rang the bell. Instead, he slid a key into the lock and swung the door open. Then he led her through the dark, silent house himself, as the dog, who'd squeezed in before he could stop her, trotted along beside them. Somewhere in the back of her mind, Alison had expected him to turn her over to a housekeeper. But then, she remembered the telephone call he'd made. That was probably who he'd talked to. And, of course, he'd told her not to wait up.

They passed through a neatly furnished living room, walked down a short hallway, then crossed a large, modern combination kitchen-breakfast room to a doorway that opened into a spacious bed-sitting room where a single lamp had been lighted.

To Alison, the room looked delightfully warm and inviting. Pausing halfway across the carpeted floor, she gazed at the sturdy old oak furniture, the lovely patchwork quilt and pile of pillows on the bed, and the easy chair and ottoman in front of the Franklin stove, complete with fire burning. She uttered yet another sigh of relief.

She couldn't have chosen a nicer place to stay if she'd tried. And, although the drive had been anything but enjoyable, she was glad she'd come straight to the ranch instead of spending the night in Santa Fe.

While she'd wanted to work with Ms. Francis, she'd dreaded having to travel the long distance to New Mexico. But she'd made it to the Double B in one piece. Why, she'd even driven a car for the first time in three years without a *major* mishap. Now all she needed was a good night's sleep. Then she'd be ready for just about anything her new employer had to throw at her.

"Something wrong?" Bradford asked, setting her suitcase on top of the cedar chest at the foot of the bed.

"Not at all," she answered, surprised that she'd given that impression. "The room is just . . . lovely."

"Glad you like it." He uttered the words almost grudgingly as he stowed her hanging bag and briefcase in the closet. "Bathroom's in here." He crossed to the open doorway to the left of the closet and switched the light on. "There are towels and soap and stuff in the cabinets. Just help yourself to whatever you need." Then he gestured toward the closed door on the far wall. "You can come and go whenever you want through there without disturbing anyone in the house."

Though Alison doubted she'd have either the time or the desire to go anywhere, she nodded her head agreeably. He obviously wanted to make her as comfortable as possible, and she really did appreciate his concern.

"Would you like something to eat?"

"No, thanks."

She'd grabbed a burger and fries at a drive-thru restaurant on her way out of Santa Fe, so she wasn't the least bit hungry. But she'd been on the road since early morning and the long day had definitely begun to catch up with her. At the moment, all she wanted was a hot bath and at least eight hours of sound sleep. But coming right out and saying so seemed rather rude.

"Well, then, I guess I'll say good-night, Ms. Kent." With a gentlemanly tip of his hat, he headed for the doorway that led into the kitchen.

"Good night, Mr. Bradford," she replied, oddly touched by his gesture. "And . . . thank you."

"For what?" He paused and glanced over his shoulder at her.

"For coming to my rescue," she answered, offering him a tentative smile.

"It was my pleasure."

For just an instant, he smiled, too, and Alison's breath caught in her throat as she realized what a truly attractive man he was. He had the most beautiful blue eyes she'd ever seen. And there was a teasingly sensual curl at the corners of his mouth that made her heart beat a little faster. But then, as if he'd read her mind and didn't much care for what she was thinking, his smile faded and he turned away, calling to the dog in a gruff tone of voice.

"Come on, Molly. You've got to go outside again."

"Oh, no...." Alison protested, frowning as she gazed at the dog. Molly had curled up in front of the Franklin stove and didn't seem the least bit inclined to leave. "It's so cold out there."

"You don't mind if she stays in the house?" he asked, making no effort to hide his surprise.

"Not at all."

"Well, then, it's all right with me. But see that she stays off the bed," he ordered as he strode out of the room.

Barely resisting the urge to snap off a smart salute, Alison agreed that she would. Then, aware that she'd let him get to her yet again, she crossed the room and closed the door behind him, muttering a choice word or two along the way.

Glad to be alone at last, she took off her coat and hung it in the closet, then opened her suitcase, dug out her long flannel gown, robe and slippers and headed for the bathroom. She filled the huge, old-fashioned bathtub with hot water, added a handful of the bath crystals she found in the cabinet next to the towels, and soaked until the last of the chill she'd caught had eased out of her bones.

Returning to the bedroom, she saw that the dog had moved from the floor by the Franklin stove onto the foot of her bed.

"Bad girl," she murmured as she slipped out of her robe, kicked off her slippers, then slid under the covers and switched off the lamp. "Bad, bad girl."

The dog whined softly and scooted closer to her.

"All right, so I'm a soft touch. Just don't tell *him,* okay?"

Him.

Turning onto her side, Alison stared at the flames flickering behind the glass doors of the Franklin stove. She had to get some sleep or she wasn't going to be worth a darn in the morning. But even though her body ached with weariness, her mind didn't seem to want to shut down. And, of course, all she seemed able to think about was Frank Bradford.

As she recalled all that he'd said and done during the short time they'd been together, she had the strangest feeling that she'd been wrong about him. Just as he'd been wrong about her.

She had no doubt that he'd been expecting someone named Alison Kent to show up at the Double B. But considering the way he'd reacted when she introduced herself, she was fairly sure that she hadn't been exactly *what* he'd been expecting. Maybe Orson hadn't been any more forthcoming about her when he'd talked to Ms. Francis than he'd been about Ms. Francis when he'd talked to *her.*

In any case, she'd come as a surprise to Frank Bradford. And for her part, she'd definitely misjudged him. Only time would tell how badly mistaken she'd been about him. But she already suspected there was much more to the man than she'd originally thought.

One thing for sure, he certainly wasn't any mere ranch hand. Perhaps he was related to Ms. Francis. He could be her nephew or maybe a cousin. He certainly knew his way around her house as if he were part of the family. And if he was, she was probably going to see quite a bit more of him than she'd anticipated.

Groaning softly, she rolled onto her back and stared at the shadows on the ceiling. She couldn't honestly say she dreaded the prospect of running into him again. And, unfortunately, *that* was what really worried her.

More than likely, most of the time she'd be too busy to do more than exchange a few words with him. Still, the less she saw of Frank Bradford, the better off she'd be.

She couldn't afford to allow herself to be distracted in any way while she was on the Double B. She'd come there to work with Ms. Francis, not get involved with some... cowboy. And she'd do well to remember that.

For his good as well as her own...

Hanging on to that thought, Alison closed her eyes, and after a while, finally drifted off to sleep.

Chapter Three

With a muttered curse, Frank tossed his blankets aside, swung his feet to the floor and stood up. According to the clock on the nightstand, it was almost one o'clock in the morning. He should have been asleep hours ago, but thanks to Ms. Alison Kent, he doubted he was going to get any rest at all.

Shoving a hand through his hair, he paced across the bedroom to one of the windows overlooking the backyard. Dressed in briefs and a short-sleeved T-shirt, he stood quietly for several seconds, staring out at the darkened landscape.

Though it was still snowing, the worst of the storm seemed to be over. With luck, the weather would clear by daybreak as the local forecaster had predicted, and he'd be able to tow the woman's car out of the ditch without any trouble. Unfortunately, he doubted that dealing with the rest of the worries he had concerning her was going to be anywhere near as easy.

Turning on his heel, he stalked across the room, grabbed the jeans he'd left on the rocking chair and pulled them on as he thought of his first meeting with Alison Kent. He couldn't recall the last time he'd run the gamut of emotions from anger to exasperation all in a matter of minutes. But that's exactly what he'd done with her.

Just as he'd feared, she'd run off the road. Then, heedless of the possible dangers, she'd left her car to walk the rest of the way to the ranch. When he'd caught sight of her stumbling through the snow, he'd been so infuriated by her foolhardiness that he'd wanted to shake the living daylights out of her. Luckily, by the time he'd climbed out of the truck and joined her on the road, he'd calmed down quite a bit. In fact, he'd been so relieved that she hadn't come to any harm that he'd been willing to forgive her rash behavior.

And then, about the time she'd introduced herself, he'd gotten his first good look at her. To say he'd been surprised that she was at least thirty years younger than he'd expected her to be was putting it mildly. And when he'd realized that the rather diminutive woman gazing up at him was also damned pretty, with her short dark hair, her wide brown eyes and her dauntless smile, he'd felt as if he'd been . . . bushwhacked.

Not that she was his type, he reminded himself as he headed for the kitchen and the bottle of bourbon he kept there for "medicinal" purposes. He'd always preferred tall, fair women with luscious curves and long, curly hair—women like Rebecca.

Still, he couldn't honestly say that he found Alison Kent unappealing. She couldn't be much more than five feet tall and probably weighed less than a hundred pounds dripping wet, yet she hadn't been the least bit intimidated by him.

She'd questioned him as if she'd had every right to do so. And when he'd responded in a churlish way, she'd stood her ground, giving as good as she got. Within a matter of minutes, he'd realized that she was a spirited little thing. And though he'd still thought she'd have been better off staying in her car rather than trying to walk to the ranch, he'd found himself admiring the hell out of her.

But then she'd mentioned Rebecca and really thrown him for a loop.

Standing at the kitchen counter, Frank poured half a glass of bourbon, recapped the bottle and set it aside, then eyed the closed door of Alison's room as he took a sip of the fiery liquor.

From the little Orson had told him about her, he'd thought that she would be closer to his father's age than his own. Because she'd lost her husband and son and no longer worked full-time for a publishing house, he'd simply assumed that she was in her sixties and semiretired.

Obviously, he'd jumped to the wrong conclusion about her. But what did it matter? He'd hired her to complete Rebecca's manuscript, and as long as she was capable of doing so in the time allotted, he couldn't really complain.

As he took another sip of his bourbon, Frank found himself wondering what had happened to her husband and son. Losing both of them must have been devastating for her. No wonder she'd quit her job. Yet she seemed to be doing all right now. But then, he'd already acknowledged the fact that the woman had courage. If he'd lost Jake and Joey as well as Rebecca, he wasn't sure he'd have chosen to go on living.

Which brought him back, albeit indirectly, to what Alison had said to him out on the road.

"...if I'm not mistaken, Ms. Francis is expecting me at the Double B."

Glass in hand, Frank turned and padded out of the kitchen, down the hallway and into the living room, where he stretched out on the sofa. Staring into the darkness, he mentally replayed the rest of the conversation he'd had with Ms. Kent just as he'd done off and on since he'd left her more than two hours ago.

She'd honestly believed that *Rebecca* was awaiting her at the ranch. As far as he could tell, she hadn't recognized his name at all. Nor had she seemed to realize that she'd come to the Double B at *his* request.

Granted, due to the limited information he'd gotten from Orson Hyde, he'd made some erroneous assumptions about *her.* But apparently Alison Kent had come to the Double B fully expecting to work with *Rebecca Francis.*

So what, exactly, had the agent told her about the job she'd been hired to do? And, more important, *why* hadn't he been completely honest with her?

Frank knew that if he'd questioned Alison earlier, he'd already have some answers, but he hadn't had the heart to push her. Though she'd put up a good front, she'd been more than a little leery of him. And after the kind of day she'd had, she'd looked about ready to drop.

He hadn't thought it would do her any good to find out that Orson Hyde had sent her to the Double B under false pretenses. Not when she was stuck there at least until morning. Frank had figured the least he could do was let her get a good night's sleep before he hit her with the fact that Rebecca was dead. He knew that kind of revelation would have rocked him back on *his* heels. And, unless he was gravely mistaken, he had a feeling Alison Kent wasn't going to be too thrilled with the news, either.

"Damn it, Orson . . . *why?*" he muttered as he raised his glass to his lips and swallowed the last of his bourbon.

The agent had gone out of his way to assure him that the woman wouldn't have any problem working with him on

Rebecca's manuscript. But then, he'd apparently had to dupe her into coming to the Double B. And there could be only one reason why he'd done that.

He'd believed that Alison Kent wouldn't have agreed to take the job if she'd been aware of the current state of affairs at the ranch.

But why send the poor woman all the way to New Mexico when there was a good chance she'd turn around and head back to New York just as soon as she could? Had Orson thought that she could be charmed into staying once she'd arrived? And if so, charmed by *what?*

Frank had to admit that he wasn't the easiest person to live with, even under the best of circumstances. And, in all honesty, having to hire someone to finish Rebecca's book, someone who'd turned out to be young and attractive, hadn't done much to improve his disposition.

And what about his father and the twins? He loved them dearly, but he couldn't say they'd be any help in winning her over. More likely than not, once she had an idea of what she'd walked into at the Double B, she'd walk right back out again. And, though he found himself wishing she wouldn't, Frank couldn't say he'd blame her in the least.

Five days ago he'd realized that he was ready to get on with his life, for his sons' sake as well as his own. But he couldn't do that until he'd seen to it that Rebecca's manuscript was completed. And for that he needed Alison Kent's help. If she refused to stay and work with him, he'd be back to square one.

Still, he had no choice but to be honest with her come morning. She'd been hoodwinked by someone she obviously trusted, and he doubted she'd be pleased when she found out. But he'd had no part in Orson's ruse, and he intended to make sure that she knew it. He needed her help, but not enough to prevaricate in any way. Maybe once she understood that, she wouldn't be quite so upset. And then maybe he could talk her into giving him a chance.

She hadn't struck him as being a heartless witch. In fact, she'd seemed kind of sweet underneath all the sass. She'd certainly taken to Molly, and she'd been honestly appreciative of the accommodations she'd been afforded. Anyone who had a soft spot for shaggy dogs and shabby furniture couldn't possibly convict one man for another's crime.

"So, think positive," he told himself as he stood and stretched, then headed back to the kitchen.

He'd talk to her first thing in the morning and let her know exactly what was going on. He'd apologize for Orson's artifice, and then he'd simply ask her to stay. The worst she could say was no. And, if she did, he'd take it from there.

For now, however, he was going to try to get some sleep. He might not be naturally charming. But if he was rested, he could probably convince her that he was reasonably agreeable.

Reasonably agreeable?

"Hah, who are you trying to fool?" he muttered, setting his empty glass in the sink.

He'd turn cartwheels if that's what it took to get Alison Kent to stay. And not only because he wanted to be done with Rebecca's book.

As he walked into his bedroom, he eyed the big, empty bed and realized just how lonely he'd been lately. Lonely for the sight, the sound, the very *scent* of a woman.

And, once again, he felt like a traitor.

He'd invited Alison Kent to come to the Double B for one reason, and one reason alone—to complete Rebecca's manuscript. And he could see no way that allowing himself to be sidetracked by a sweet smile would further that cause.

He owed it to Rebecca to concentrate on the task at hand. He'd vowed to see to it that *Hunter's Edge* made it to publication, and he intended to do whatever was necessary to keep his promise.

With that goal in mind, he knew he'd be wise not to think of Alison Kent as anything but a business partner. If she chose to stay at the Double B, they'd have to work together on a daily basis. Getting involved with her on a personal level would be a big mistake because somewhere along the line, someone would end up getting hurt. And that could very well have an adverse effect on Rebecca's manuscript.

He might be ready to get on with his life, but waiting until *Hunter's Edge* had been completed and Alison Kent had gone home shouldn't be all that hard to do. Then he'd have all the time in the world to think about taking care of his own wants and needs. For the time being, however...

Glancing at the clock on his nightstand as he stripped out of his jeans, Frank saw that it was now past two o'clock in the morning. No wonder he'd been thinking such crazy thoughts.

In the clear light of day he'd never have considered getting involved with a woman like Alison Kent. Never in a million years.

Or so he told himself as he crawled under the bed covers, buried his face in his pillow and tried, yet again, to fall asleep.

Who on earth was giggling?

Giggling?

Coming slowly, reluctantly awake, Alison opened her eyes and gazed at the clock on the nightstand. In the grayish gloom of early morning she saw that it wasn't quite six-thirty. Groaning softly, she closed her eyes again, sure that she must have been dreaming.

For all of thirty seconds, she thought about getting up. But she really wasn't ready to rise and shine just yet. Not after the kind of day she'd had yesterday. Surely, Ms. Francis wouldn't mind if she slept for another hour or two.

Burrowing a little deeper under the bed covers, she uttered a quiet sigh of contentment, then froze. From somewhere very close by came the whisper-soft sound of a young voice, followed by... giggles.

"What in the world...?" she muttered, rolling onto her back and pushing up on her elbows.

"Hi."

Two small boys with strawberry-blond curls and bright blue eyes had joined the dog at the foot of her bed. They were dressed in Ninja Turtle pajamas and had fuzzy Ninja Turtle slippers on their feet, and they gazed at her with angelic smiles on their cherubic little faces.

Twins, Alison thought, as she struggled to sit up. And one as full of mischief as the other, if she was any judge at all. But who were they? And, more important, why were they sitting on her bed?

Still feeling as if she was half asleep, she smiled tentatively. "Hi, yourselves." Then, having returned their greeting, she hesitated, unsure of what to say next.

"Are you Ms. Kent?" asked the boy sitting to her left.

"Yes."

They couldn't be more than five years old. About the age Nathan would have been if—

Raking a hand through her hair, Alison forced herself to veer away from that all-too-painful realization.

"Who are you?" she queried as cheerfully as she could.

"I'm Jake," the spokesman informed her. "And he's Joey."

"You're not as old as our grandpa." Frowning thoughtfully, Joey spoke for the first time. "You're not even as old as our dad."

"Your... dad?" Filled with a strange foreboding, Alison frowned, too.

"His name's Frank," Jake said.

"I . . . see."

So, these two were Frank Bradford's sons. And unless she was mistaken, they lived in Rebecca Francis's house along with their father and grandfather.

"Are you going to help our dad finish our mom's book?"

"Your . . . your mom's book?" As she gazed at first one boy, then the other, Alison felt a sinking sensation in the pit of her stomach.

Either she was having a really bad dream or everything was not as she'd thought it would be at the Double B. Or rather, as Orson Hyde had led her to believe it would be.

Damn the man—

"She died when we were three years old," Jake explained in a grave tone of voice.

"And our dad tried to finish writing her book," Joey added. "Only he couldn't."

"Then Mr. Hyde told him about you," Jake continued, then repeated his original question once again. "So, *are* you going to help our dad finish writing our mom's book?"

Gazing from one hopeful face to the other, Alison shook her head, at a total loss for words. No wonder Frank Bradford had looked so taken aback when she'd talked about Rebecca Francis as if the woman were alive. The poor man must have thought she was nuts.

Unless he'd been in on Orson's little scheme . . .

But no, he couldn't have been. She'd definitely thrown him off balance when she'd mentioned Rebecca's name. And although he hadn't said anything last night, he'd made a point of letting her know they'd sort "things" out in the morning.

Things . . .

She hadn't been hired by Rebecca Francis. She'd been hired by Frank Bradford, a widower with two young sons and an elderly father. But Orson Hyde had gone out of his way to make sure she didn't know it until she'd actually traveled to New Mexico. And Alison had a good idea *why*.

She was going to throttle him. Just as soon as she got back to New York, she was going to wrap her hands around his scrawny little neck and—

"Oh, please, don't say no," Joey pleaded, a woeful look on his face as he scooted closer to her. "Our dad's been so sad lately. But he'll be happy again once he's done with our mom's book. He *will*. I just know it."

"I...I suppose," Alison murmured, feeling as if she was caught between a rock and a hard place.

How could she say no to a little boy who seemed to want nothing more than for his father to be happy? Yet how could she deal with the emotional toll staying at the Double B would inevitably take?

She'd planned to spend the next few weeks with a reclusive woman, not two motherless children, their father and their grandfather. And that meant the dynamics of life on the Double B wouldn't be at all what she'd expected. She could try to maintain some distance between herself and the Bradfords, but she already felt herself drawn to Jake and Joey. And as for their father—

"You're not married, are you?" Jake asked, scooting a little closer, too.

"No."

"Do you like little boys?"

Did she like little boys?

For one long moment, Alison wanted nothing more than to gather the two of them into her arms and hug them close. She could only imagine how hard it had been for them to lose their mother. But she held back, knowing how dangerously easy it would be to allow them to fill the emptiness deep inside her.

"I like little boys a lot," she admitted, forcing herself to smile.

"How about our dad? Do you like—"

"I thought I told you two this room was off limits."

Startled by the deep, masculine voice that cut off Jake in mid-question, Alison shifted her gaze from the boys to Frank Bradford. He stood just inside the doorway of her room, his hands on his hips and a frown on his face. He wore a pair of worn, rumpled jeans and a plain white T-shirt. His feet were bare, his medium-length, reddish brown hair was mussed, and he hadn't bothered to shave yet.

In the daylight, without his hat shadowing his face, he looked even more rough-hewn than he had the night before. But to her dismay, Alison realized that she still found him attractive. And though he scowled as he met her gaze, his bright blue eyes flashed with a hint of amusement that made her heart beat a little faster.

Suddenly, all too aware that she was sitting in the middle of her bed, dressed only in a nightgown, she blushed to the roots of her hair. How long had he been standing there? And how much of her conversation with his sons had he overheard?

Feeling absurdly self-conscious, she fingered the buttons on the high neck of her flannel gown as she glanced at the boys again. Now sitting on either side of her, they turned to look at their father without the slightest show of apprehension.

"We weren't bothering her, Dad." Jake spoke on their behalf. "She *likes* little boys."

"I imagine she likes her privacy, too."

"You said she was going to be as old as Grandpa," Joey accused.

Wondering exactly what Orson had told Frank about her, Alison shifted her attention to him. He met her gaze for a moment and shrugged noncommittally. Then he eyed his sons sternly once again.

"Yeah, well, I was wrong," he admitted. "But that doesn't change the fact that I told you to stay out of here. Now, scoot, the two of you. It's almost seven o'clock and you're not dressed for school yet."

"But it snowed last night," Joey said.

"And they always close the schools when it snows," Jake added.

"Not always," Frank replied, his patience obviously beginning to wear thin. "The buses aren't running, but the schools are open. I heard it on the radio."

"But, if the buses—"

"Your grandfather's going to take you. So get a move on it. And take the dog with you."

Apparently realizing they'd pushed their luck about as far as they could, the boys clambered off the bed and scampered past their father, Molly close on their heels. But Frank didn't immediately turn and follow them out as Alison had hoped he would. Granted, they had quite a few things to sort out. But considering her current state of dishabille, she felt that she was at a distinct disadvantage.

"Ms. Kent..." He shifted uncomfortably as he tucked his hands in the side pockets of his jeans, seemingly at a loss for words.

"Mr. Bradford."

Though Alison sympathized with the man, she wasn't sure what to say, either. From what the twins had told her, she wasn't the only one Orson had misled. Apparently, neither she nor Frank had gotten what they'd bargained for. But she had no more idea what to do about it than he did.

"We need to talk," he said, not quite meeting her gaze.

"Indeed, we do," she agreed softly.

"I'll be waiting for you in the kitchen whenever you're ready."

"I...I won't be long," she murmured gratefully.

He started to turn away, then paused and glanced at her again. ''I'll understand if you want to go back to New York.''

She nodded her head, not quite trusting herself to speak. While she knew that was probably the best thing she could do, she'd acted impetuously once already. And no matter how untenable the situation at the Double B might seem at the moment, she wasn't about to make the same mistake twice. She'd talk to Frank Bradford first, then decide what to do next.

He stood in the doorway for several seconds, his eyes holding hers. Then, without another word, he walked out of her room, quietly pulling the door closed behind him.

With a groan of frustration, Alison flopped back on her pillows and stared at the ceiling. Somewhere in the back of her mind, she knew she'd end up being sorry if she stayed on the Double B. But when she considered all that Jake and Joey had said to her, she didn't see how she could live with herself if she left.

Had Orson told her that a widower with two young sons wanted her to come to his ranch to help him finish his wife's book, she would have refused. But now that she was actually here, now that she'd met Frank Bradford and his sons, turning around and heading back to New York seemed like a rather childish, not to mention churlish, thing to do.

Alison knew that only a man who had loved his wife dearly would go to such lengths to see to it that her last manuscript was completed. She couldn't help but admire him for that. Nor could she help but want him to be happy again, for his sons' sake as well as his own. And, unfortunately, that instinctive desire made it all but impossible for her to walk away without at least offering to give him the assistance he needed.

However, nowhere was it written that she had to get involved with Frank Bradford, et al, on a personal level. She'd come there to do a job, and as long as she conducted herself in a businesslike manner, she shouldn't be in any danger of having anyone, including herself, think of her as a part of the "family."

Surely Frank had made arrangements to keep his sons out of her way. And he'd have work of his own to do on the ranch, as well. Although she hadn't actually seen the partially completed manuscript for *Hunter's Edge* yet, Alison had a feeling she was going to have more than enough to keep her busy over the next few weeks.

If Rebecca's previous books were any indication, the manuscript she'd been working on when she died should be very good, indeed. The woman's writing had gotten progressively better, and Alison knew that living up to the standards Rebecca had set for herself would be no easy task.

Before she could begin the actual writing, she'd have to familiarize herself with the time period. She had no doubt Rebecca had done her research. More than likely, she had file folders full of pertinent information. Still, Alison was going to have to do a fair amount of background reading herself or risk ruining the basic integrity of the story.

Finishing Rebecca's manuscript was going to be a real challenge. But then, that just gave her one more reason to see the project through to completion, didn't it?

She was just perverse enough to want to prove to herself, as well as to Frank Bradford, that she could do it. Even though she wasn't as old as he'd expected her to be...

"Just wait till I get my hands on you, Orson," she grumbled as she sat up again and swung her legs over the side of the bed. The man was going to be sorry he'd played fast and loose with her. *Very* sorry.

She crossed to the pair of windows on the far wall and opened the blinds, then paused a moment, smiling appreciatively. Talk about a room with a view. Close by, sunlight sparkled on the snow-covered ground, while off in the distance mountain peaks reached up to touch the cerulean sky.

Sure that the storm's passing couldn't be anything but a good omen, she started to turn away, then stilled at the sound of high-pitched voices. An elderly man, who even at a distance bore a distinct resemblance to Frank Bradford, trudged across the yard to what appeared to be a garage, the twins spinning and sliding along behind him, chattering a mile-a-minute.

Though she couldn't hear what they were saying, their excitement was infectious, and Alison felt her smile widening. As she watched, the three of them opened the wide double doors, then disappeared inside the building. She heard the sound of an engine grinding, and a few moments later, an ancient pickup truck rolled out and headed down the drive.

Aware that if she wanted to talk to Frank alone she'd better get a move on it, she hurried into the bathroom. Then, wanting to set the right tone for the remainder of her stay, she dressed in a short, straight, black wool skirt, belted an oversized, pale peach cashmere turtleneck sweater over it, and added black tights and plain black flats.

She'd packed more casual clothes: a couple of pairs of well-worn jeans, some stirrup pants and leggings, several shirts and pullover sweaters, even some sweats. But this morning she was meeting with a client to discuss business, and she wanted to project just the right image. She was smart, savvy and sophisticated, and she wanted to be sure Frank Bradford knew it.

She styled her hair, put on makeup, even clipped on pearl button earrings. Then she quickly made the bed and straightened the room. She thought about unpacking, but decided that could wait until after her interview with Mr. Bradford. She'd been assuming that he wanted her to stay, but until they had their talk she couldn't be absolutely sure.

"So, go beard the lion in his den," she ordered softly as she glanced at herself in the mirror on the back of the closet door one more time. There was no denying she was grossly overdressed for a ranch house in northeastern New Mexico. But looking as good as she could always boosted her confidence.

Keeping that thought in mind, she took a deep, calming breath, crossed to the door leading into the kitchen and opened it. She'd talked to dozens of men and women about dozens of projects in the past. Frank Bradford was no different than any of them. No different at—

As she stepped into the kitchen, he turned from where he stood at the stove and gazed at her with such honest appreciation that Alison blushed for the second time in less than an hour. Though they were separated by almost the entire length of the room, she felt as if he'd touched her and awareness zinged through her in an unfamiliar, albeit not unwelcome, way.

He'd shaved and combed his hair, put on a red plaid shirt, navy blue sweater and a pair of boots. But he didn't appear any tamer than he had when he'd come to her room earlier. She could only imagine what he'd look like without any clothes on at all. *Downright uncivilized* were the first words that came to her mind.

His eyes narrowed as if he'd read her mind and hadn't approved of what she was thinking. Then he turned back to the stove and fiddled with the bacon frying in the skillet.

"Coffee, Ms. Kent?" he asked in an excruciatingly polite tone of voice.

"Yes, thank you," she replied, giving herself a firm mental shake.

She hadn't looked at a man twice in almost three years. Now, out of the blue, she was fantasizing about Frank Bradford in a blatantly sexual way. What in heaven's name was wrong with her? The man was still mourning his dead wife. And she never mixed business with pleasure. *Never...*

"Cups are on the counter next to the pot. Just help yourself."

Wordlessly, she did as instructed, hoping he didn't notice how badly her hands shook. Then, she crossed the Saltillo tile floor to the long wooden table and sat in one of the ladder-back chairs. Hanging on to her cup, she stared at his rigid back and tried to recall all the reasons why she wanted to stay on the Double B.

She reminded herself that the happiness of a widower and his two young sons was at stake. And she reflected once again on the basic challenge of completing Rebecca's manuscript in a way that would stand up to even the most assiduous scrutiny.

Yet, as she took a tentative sip of her coffee, Alison thought that hightailing it out of there as fast as she could was still the wisest thing to do.

Chapter Four

Trying desperately to gather his wits about him once again, Frank poked at the bacon strips sizzling in the pan on the stove. So much for thinking straight in the clear light of day. Seeing Alison Kent sitting in bed, all sleepy-eyed, had been bad enough. But then, she'd stepped into the kitchen a couple of minutes ago dressed in a short black skirt and a soft, pale sweater, looking more feminine than he'd seen a woman look in a long time. And he'd had the damnedest urge to pull her into his arms and bury his face—

"How do want your eggs?" he snapped, grabbing a pan covered with a paper towel and transferring the bacon onto it.

"Eggs?" she murmured hesitantly.

Realizing that he'd taken out his annoyance with himself on her, he glanced over his shoulder at her as he added a little more solicitously, "Fried or scrambled?"

She met his gaze, her wide, dark eyes wary. Breakfast was obviously the last thing on her mind, too. But Frank had hoped that sitting down together to share a meal would help ease their initial uncertainty about each other.

After overhearing her conversation with the twins, he'd been reasonably sure she was going to stay and work on Rebecca's manuscript. However, he'd begun to have second thoughts when she'd finally joined him in the kitchen. Much as he admired her outfit, he'd have preferred to see her wearing jeans and a sweatshirt. As it was, she looked as if she was planning to go somewhere other than Rebecca's office, somewhere like New York City.

"Scrambled will be fine," she said at last, lowering her gaze as she raised her cup to her lips.

Turning back to the counter, he broke eggs into a bowl, added some milk, whisked the mixture together and poured it into a fresh skillet. Then, unable to bear the silence stretching between them any longer, he glanced at her again.

"I'm sorry the boys woke you," he offered.

"No harm done," she admitted graciously. "I'm usually an early riser, too."

"I . . . I heard some of what they were saying to you," he added cautiously, easing toward the subject of Rebecca. "So I take it you know about my wife."

He wasn't about to tell her that he'd eavesdropped on most of their conversation. He could have stopped them much sooner than he had, but he'd realized almost immediately that Alison had taken to the boys in much the same way she'd taken to Molly. And he'd figured that she would be much more receptive to what they had to tell her than she would have been if he'd been the one explaining the situation. So he'd allowed the twins to do his dirty work for him. But he wasn't exactly proud of it.

"I know that she's dead," she stated simply, not quite meeting his gaze.

"But you didn't know that when you agreed to come to the ranch. You thought you were going to be working with her."

"That's what Orson told me," she acknowledged. "But then, he misled you, too, didn't he? You thought I'd be older and, I imagine, more experienced."

"To be honest, he didn't tell me you were older. I just assumed as much when he said you were a widow and no longer worked full-time for a publishing house."

"My husband and son were killed in an automobile accident almost three years ago," she stated in a matter-of-fact tone. "I couldn't work at all for a while afterward. Then Orson talked me into working with one of his clients who'd been having problems with a manuscript and I began freelancing." She shrugged, offering him a wry smile. "Would it help if I told you sometimes I *feel* old?"

Appreciating her honesty as well as her attempt at humor, Frank returned her smile for a moment. But then, he thought of all she'd gone through, and he grew serious once again.

"I'm sorry about your husband and son."

"And I'm sorry about your wife."

"She died in her sleep eighteen months ago," he said as he turned back to the stove and stirred the eggs to keep them from sticking to the skillet. "She'd been having bad headaches for weeks, but she refused to go to the doctor. She kept blaming it on stress. She was trying to finish her manuscript and the twins were only three years old. Turned out she had an aneurysm in her brain."

"And you've been trying to complete her manuscript since then," Alison murmured.

"Yes."

"I wish Orson had told me. You must have thought I needed my head examined the way I was rattling on about *Ms. Francis* last night."

"You're right. I did." He grinned as he risked another glance at her.

"Gee, thanks."

"I wonder why Orson didn't tell you what was really going on around here," he mused, then turned to face her once again when she didn't answer. "Would you have come if he had?"

"I'm . . . I'm not sure," she demurred, staring at the cup in her hands. "I usually work only with women writers. . . ."

From the way she avoided meeting his gaze, Frank sensed that she wasn't being completely honest with him. But he had no intention of badgering her about it. By hook or by crook, she was here now. And he figured it would be wiser to avoid reminding her of why she might not have come in the first place.

However, he still felt obliged to let her know he'd meant it when he said he wouldn't blame her if she chose to go back to New York.

"Does that mean you've changed your mind about working on Rebecca's manuscript?" he asked, bracing himself for the worst as he filled two plates with eggs and bacon, then added a couple of biscuits from the pan warming in the oven.

"Not necessarily," she hedged. "Unless that's what *you* want."

Feeling somewhat relieved, he carried the plates to the table, set one in front of her and one at his place, then filled their cups with fresh coffee. *Not necessarily* wasn't exactly the kind of commitment he'd hoped she would offer. But at least she wasn't planning on driving back to Santa Fe as soon as they hauled her car out of the ditch.

"All I want is for Rebecca's manuscript to be completed," he said as he sat down beside her. "And since I can't do it myself, I'll take whatever help you have to offer."

"I'd like to read the manuscript before I make a final decision," she advised. "And I'd also like to know how much input you plan on having. I'm open to any suggestions you'd like to make, but I also hope you're willing to give me a little leeway to do what I think is best. I understand that completing your wife's manuscript means a lot to you. But unless you can trust me to do my job, there's no sense in us pursuing this any further."

"Sounds fair to me," he admitted somewhat grudgingly.

She certainly seemed willing to give Rebecca's manuscript her best shot. And she hadn't insisted he give her a free rein with it. Doctoring books was her business. Although Orson hadn't been totally up-front with either of them, he had made it clear that Alison Kent already had many satisfied customers.

They ate in silence for a few minutes, then Alison spoke again, her voice tentative.

"Would you mind telling me why you're so determined to see to it that your wife's book is published?"

"Why do you ask?" He glanced at her suspiciously, recalling Orson's assumption that he needed the money.

"Just curious. Having me here, paying my expenses as well as my usual fee . . ." She shrugged and shook her head. "It's not something many men would do unless they had a really good reason. She must have meant a lot to you."

"She did," he admitted, somewhat mollified. "And she still does."

"She must have been a wonderful person."

"She was."

He hadn't talked about Rebecca much at all since her death. Doing so had been too painful for him. But suddenly he found himself wanting to tell Alison about her. She seemed honestly interested, in a kindly way. And maybe if she had an idea of how much Rebecca had given up for him, she'd understand why finishing her manuscript was so important to him.

He wasn't going to have a chance to take his wife to all the exotic places she'd wanted to go. But with Alison's help maybe he could fulfill her dream of making the *New York Times*'s bestseller list.

"We met fifteen years ago," he began, setting his fork on his empty plate and sitting back in his chair. "I'd just finished college and was working on the ranch with my father. Rebecca was waiting tables at Ruby's Café down in Vernon, a small town about twenty miles south of here. She was only nineteen and she was working her way to California. She'd grown up in a foster home in Lufkin, northeast of Houston, but she'd never been very happy there. So she took off as soon as she graduated from high school. She wanted to see the world."

"But she ended up staying in New Mexico," Alison said, a soft smile tugging at the corners of her mouth.

"Yeah, she did."

Recalling the first time he'd seen her, Frank smiled, too. She'd been so cool and distant. But by the time he'd left the café, he'd managed to make her laugh. And somehow he'd known that he wanted her to be a permanent part of his life.

"We were married four months later," he continued. "We moved into a trailer a couple of miles down the road, and while I helped out around here, Rebecca worked at Ruby's and went to college part-time in Santa Fe.

"About eight years ago, my father decided he was ready to retire. Since my mother had always wanted to live in Santa Fe, they moved there, and we moved into the house. Rebecca had finished school by then. She'd quit working at Ruby's, too, and had been giving my mother a hand with the Double B's paperwork, so the transition was a smooth one.

"About that time she also sold her first book. One of her professors had gotten her interested in writing, and she'd been working on the manuscript for almost three years. Over the next four years, she sold three more books. She was working on her fifth when she found out she was pregnant with the twins."

"The two of you must have been so happy," Alison murmured.

"Not exactly," Frank admitted quietly. "We talked about having children, but Rebecca was never very enthusiastic. She'd been the oldest of several foster children placed at the home where she grew up. As a result, she'd ending up caring for the younger ones a good deal of the time. She hadn't enjoyed it at all, and for a long time, she firmly believed that she just wasn't cut out for motherhood.

"Over the years I wore her down. She finally agreed to try to get pregnant, but only because she knew how much it meant to me. For some reason, neither of us considered the possibility that she'd have twins even though they run in my family. When the doctor gave us the news, I was thrilled. But poor Rebecca was in a state of shock."

"But surely she felt better about it after a while, didn't she?" Alison asked, frowning as she put down her half-eaten biscuit and pushed her plate away.

"She seemed more resigned than anything. But when they were born..." Frank paused as he recalled the look of wonder and joy on his wife's face when she'd held her sons in her arms for the first time. "We were both crazy about them. Unfortunately, we were also overwhelmed, but my folks came back to the ranch to give us a hand, and after a few weeks we settled into a routine of our own."

"You must have really had your hands full," Alison mused.

Although a faint smile edged the corners of her mouth, Frank couldn't help but see the sadness lurking in the depths of her dark eyes. He knew she was thinking about the birth of her own son, the son she'd lost three years ago. For a moment he was tempted to say something solicitous. But he doubted she'd appreciate his intruding on her memories.

"We were busier than we'd ever been before, especially during lambing season. But we were happy." Standing, he picked up their plates, then crossed to the sink as he continued with his story. "However, when the twins were about six months old, my mother died unexpectedly. My father wasn't especially happy living alone in Santa Fe, so we invited him to come back to the ranch.

"He was a big help to both of us, but especially to Rebecca. She was so busy with the twins that she never had any time to write. But my dad loved looking after them, so she finally had a chance to go back to work on the book she'd started before they were born. She finished it, then began working on *Hunter's Edge*. And just after the twins had their third birthday, we started planning a trip to Australia.

"Rebecca had been headed there when we met. She'd also been working on an idea for a story set in the outback. With the twins old enough to travel without too much hassle and my dad here to look after the ranch for the three or four weeks we'd be gone, the timing seemed just right. And since she'd made my dream of having children come true, I wanted to make one of her dreams come true, too."

He finished rinsing the plates at the sink, then returned to the table with the coffeepot. As he refilled her cup, Alison glanced up at him, the sadness in her eyes replaced by sympathy and, more important, understanding. "But she died before you could," she said, her voice hushed.

"Yes." He refilled his cup, put the pot back on the burner and returned to his chair. "But she had another dream," he continued as he cradled his cup in his hands. "She wanted to make the *New York Times*'s bestseller list with one of her books." He paused, glancing at Alison again. "And that's why I hired you, Ms. Kent. I didn't have a chance to take her to Australia. But with your help, maybe *Hunter's Edge* will end up on the bestseller list.''

"I'll do the best I can," she murmured, resting her hand on his arm for just an instant. "The *very* best I can. Trust me."

Surprised by the warmth of her touch, Frank turned to look at her. "I do," he said, and knew that he'd spoken the truth.

"Thank you, Mr. Bradford. I won't let you down."

"Why don't you call me Frank? Unless you'd be more comfortable with Mr. Bradford." Since they were going to be spending several weeks together, using first names didn't seem out of order to him. But he had to consider her feelings, as well.

"If you'll call me Alison," she replied with a wry smile.

"Alison..." He smiled, too. Then, after a moment's hesitation, he brought up the one subject that was still of some concern to him. "Are you sure you won't mind staying here over Christmas if you haven't completed the manuscript before then? Orson said that you wouldn't. But if that's not really the case..."

"I won't mind at all," she hastened to assure him, though she didn't quite meet his gaze.

"You're sure you wouldn't rather be at home?" he pressed, sensing her ambivalence. "Because I'd be more than happy to pay your—"

"I wanted to get away from the city." She glanced at him for one long, quiet moment. Then, ducking her head, she added softly, "My husband and son were killed a few weeks before Christmas. I thought spending the holidays somewhere besides New York City might be a little easier."

Aware that he'd once again stirred up memories that distressed her, Frank stared at the cup he still clutched in his hands. He hadn't meant to upset her, but obviously that was exactly what he'd done.

He remembered all too well what a hard time he'd had getting through the holiday season without Rebecca last year, but at least he'd had Jake and Joey, as well as his father. They'd been some comfort to him. But according to Orson, Alison didn't have any other family.

Frank could only imagine how painful the past couple of Christmases had been for her. But if he had anything to do about it—and he *would*—this Christmas would be different. This Christmas she'd have the Bradford family to keep her company. And he'd see to it that they were *good* company. One way or another, he was going to make sure the next few weeks were as pleasant as possible for her. All things considered, it was the very least he could—

"You two still lollygagging over breakfast?" Bert greeted them as he walked through the kitchen door, bringing a blast of icy, wood-smoke-scented air with him.

"How was the drive to town?" Frank asked as he and Alison turned to face him.

Meeting his father's twinkling blue eyes, he returned the old man's smile. They'd exchanged only a few words earlier, but from the look on his face, the twins had obviously given him the lowdown on Ms. Kent on their way to school.

"Not too bad. They're already clearing Highway 3." Shifting his gaze to Alison, Bert nodded cordially as he stood on the doormat and stomped the snow from his boots, then unbuttoned his jacket. "Your car's right where you left it, missy."

"Alison Kent, meet my father, Bert Bradford," Frank introduced them, his smile widening as he saw the startled look on her face. He doubted anyone got away with calling her *missy* in New York City. Yet, she didn't seem to take offense. In fact, she was suddenly smiling, too.

"Mr. Bradford." Standing, she politely offered him her hand. "I've heard a lot about you."

"All good, I hope." He took her hand and held on to it far longer than Frank deemed necessary.

"Very good."

"Please, call me Bert." The twinkle in his eyes became downright mischievous. "My grandsons were right. You're a real pretty little thing."

"Thank you. I think," she murmured, blushing in that endearing way she had.

"You really made a hit with them, Ms. Kent." He winked at her, then added before Frank could intervene, "How about you, son? You gonna keep her?"

"Dad, please," Frank muttered, feeling his own face grow warm with embarrassment. He loved his father dearly, but sometimes he really wanted to throttle him. "Alison has agreed to take a look at Rebecca's manuscript. After that, it'll be up to her whether or not she stays."

"Alison, huh?" Bert nodded knowingly. "Sounds like you got off to a good start, at least."

Frank groaned inwardly. No telling what the old reprobate would say next. But Alison didn't seem angry or upset. In fact, she seemed somewhat amused as she smiled at his father in much the same way she'd smiled at his sons a couple of hours earlier.

As he stood and shoved his hands in the side pockets of his jeans, he found himself wondering how it would feel to have her smile at *him* with such obvious delight. And then he gave himself a firm mental shake.

He was pleased that she'd hit it off with his family. And he was relieved that she seemed moderately well-disposed toward him. But he had no right to expect anything else of her.

Hell, he didn't *want* anything else from her. Did he?

"Listen, Dad, why don't you let me get Alison settled in Rebecca's office?" he suggested, his voice a shade gruffer than it had been a few minutes ago. "We still have to haul her car out of that ditch. And I've got to ride out and check on Carlos, Benito, and the sheep."

Bert eyed him quizzically for several seconds. Then, with an all-too-knowing look on his face, he nodded. "Fine, fine." Turning back to Alison, he rested a gnarled hand on her shoulder and waggled his bushy white eyebrows. "We can get acquainted later. Right, missy?"

"Right, Mr. Bradford."

"Bert."

"Right, *Bert,*" she repeated dutifully. Her dark eyes glinting with amusement, she faced Frank once again. "Ready whenever you are, boss."

As he met her gaze, Frank had the strangest feeling that maybe he ought to run for cover. Ms. Alison Kent could end up being one hell of a handful if he let her. But that definitely wasn't part of his game plan. Not by any stretch of the imagination.

"Rebecca's office is just down the hallway," he advised, taking her by the arm and steering her toward the open doorway on the far side of the kitchen.

Wordlessly, she fell into step beside him, but out of the corner of his eye Frank saw her trading smiles with his father yet again. Barely quelling the urge to grab her and shake her, he lengthened his stride so that she had to hurry to keep up with him.

He gave her a rather cursory tour of the main house, pausing for a moment in the living room, then showing her where the bedrooms were located just in case she needed something during the night.

When they finally came to Rebecca's office, he hesitated, just as he had for the past eighteen months. But then, with a sense of determination that took him by surprise, he swung open the door and ushered Alison into the room.

"The manuscript is on the desk," he said as he crossed to the windows and opened the blinds. "There's also a fairly detailed outline in the blue folder underneath it. Rebecca never did like working without a net."

"I'm glad," Alison admitted with obvious relief. "Finishing a manuscript with nothing more than a handful of barely legible notes as a guideline can be a real pain."

"You've done that?" Frank asked, making no effort to hide his amazement.

"Once. And once, as the saying goes, was more than enough."

"Well, then, you shouldn't have any trouble at all with *Hunter's Edge.*"

"Don't be so sure. I've read Rebecca's other books. She was a wonderful writer. Living up to the standards she set for herself isn't going to be easy."

"But you think you can do it, don't you?" Frank prodded.

"I wouldn't be here if I didn't," she assured him. Then, gesturing to the shelves lining one wall, she deftly changed the subject. "She really loved books, didn't she?"

"She once told me that books were her best friends when she was growing up."

A soft smile curving the corners of her mouth, Alison nodded, as if she understood all too well, and Frank found himself wondering if she'd also had a lonely childhood. He was almost tempted to ask. But then he reminded himself that he'd pried into her past one too many times already, and had caused her pain in the process.

"She bought a lot of books about the era in which she set her story. They're all on the shelves. However, if you need specific information and can't find what you need in any of them, we can go to the library in Santa Fe. She also made a habit of taking notes when she did her background reading. They're filed according to subject in that cabinet." He gestured toward the two-drawer file cabinet doing double-duty as a lamp table alongside the love seat. "You're welcome to go through them whenever you want."

"Thanks."

"Any questions?"

"Not at the moment."

"Well, then, I guess I'd better let you get started."

"Yes," she agreed in a soft voice as she moved to the desk. Pausing, she rested a hand atop the stack of manuscript pages and glanced over her shoulder at him. For the first time since he'd come upon her on the ranch road, she seemed somewhat uncertain. "Do you . . . do you mind if I work in here?"

"Not at all." Originally, he *had* had some qualms about her using Rebecca's office. But now that he'd gotten to know her, having her there didn't bother him nearly as much as he'd thought it would.

"As long as you're sure . . ."

"I'm positive." He smiled, then added encouragingly, "Just make yourself at home. Bert and the boys have lunch around twelve-thirty. You're welcome to join them, but if you want something to eat or drink before then, help yourself. Supper's at six. We usually go to the grocery store in Vernon on Thursdays or Fridays. So if you want anything special, let one of us know and we'll put it on the list, all right?"

"All right," she agreed.

Unable to think of a reason to linger any longer, Frank crossed to the doorway. He had a full day ahead of him, as did Alison, and they were already getting a late start. Yet he wasn't all that eager to leave her on her own. Not because he had any concerns about what she would or wouldn't do, but because he'd honestly enjoyed her company.

Unfortunately, she hadn't come to the Double B for his personal benefit. And Margaret Locke's January 15 deadline loomed too close for comfort. The sooner he allowed Alison to get to work on Rebecca's manuscript, the sooner she'd be done with it. And that was all he really wanted of her. Wasn't it?

"Do you want me to close the door on my way out?"

"I'd just as soon have it open."

"Fine."

He paused on the threshold and glanced at her one last time. She'd already turned back to the desk, obviously more than ready to get started. And all he could do was stand there, thinking of how nice she looked in her short skirt and soft sweater.

Which meant the time had definitely come for him to be on his way.

"See you this evening," he muttered as he spun on his heel and stalked into the hallway.

"Mmm, yes, see you..." she replied rather absently, her sweet voice trailing after him as he headed for the kitchen.

Alone in Rebecca's office at last, Alison stared at the stack of manuscript pages on the desk in front of her and allowed herself a small sigh of relief as Frank's footsteps faded down the hallway. She'd begun to wonder if he'd ever leave.

Not that she found his company offensive in any way.

In fact, the longer they'd been together in that tidy little room, the more aware of his vibrant masculinity she'd become. And much to her dismay, she'd had a hard time keeping her mind on business.

But now that he was gone...

As she pulled out the desk chair, the sound of voices coming from the kitchen caught her attention. She heard Frank exchange a few unintelligible words with his father;

then a door opened and closed, and the house once again settled into silence.

Moving to one of the windows, Alison watched as Frank and his father climbed into Frank's truck. Probably going to haul her car out of the ditch. But how would they be able to get into it without the keys? Whirling around, she started toward the doorway, then paused in mid-stride. With a rueful shake of her head, she turned and walked back to the desk. She'd given the keys to Frank last night so he could get her bags out of the car, and he hadn't given them back to her.

Sighing pensively, she sat down in the comfortably padded chair. She really ought to get to work. But the house was so…quiet. While she was used to being by herself, at home she'd always had the sounds of the city to keep her company. The beep of a horn, the wail of a siren or the clatter of a garbage truck had constantly reassured her that she wasn't really alone.

But the Double B was out in the middle of nowhere. And though the ranch house was nice enough, it suddenly seemed as alien to Alison as a domicile on a distant planet would be.

What in the world was she doing there? And *why* was she planning to stay?

All right, so she'd *said* she would. But considering the way she'd been conned into coming there, who would blame her if she left? Not anyone who really mattered to her.

"Oh, please, give me a break," she muttered, more aware than she wanted to be that less than twenty-four hours after her arrival, she'd already begun to care about the Bradfords too much to walk out on them.

Of course, given her penchant for being a bearer of bad luck, *that* should have been enough of an incentive for her to hop on the next plane back to New York City. Still, she couldn't bring herself do it. Not when Frank had confirmed what she'd already begun to suspect before she'd stepped into the kitchen that morning.

No matter what it might cost him in the long run, he was determined to see to it that at least one of his wife's dreams came true. And without her help, he probably wouldn't be able to do it. To walk out on him would be unforgivable, regardless of how uncomfortable she was with the situation. As she most definitely was . . .

Oh, she had a lovely place to stay. And though Rebecca's office was still very much *Rebecca's,* working there wouldn't be a problem for her. What she found unsettling was the emotional toll she knew she'd end up paying. Frank Bradford and his family were so darned likable. And they'd made her feel so welcome. Even Frank had made a point of letting her know that he didn't mind having her around, if only until she finished Rebecca's book.

Why, if she wasn't careful, she could all too easily begin to believe that she belonged—

No, she couldn't, *wouldn't,* allow herself to do that. Not under any circumstances. She'd have to share meals with them. But otherwise, she'd remain as aloof as possible and concentrate on the job she had to do.

With that thought in mind, Alison riffled through the first few pages of the manuscript. She was relieved to see that they were neatly printed in letter-quality type, which would make the reading fairly easy. But she'd also be taking notes, and that would slow her down a bit. Still, she'd learned that the more time she took at the outset, absorbing a writer's tone and style as well as acquainting herself with the way he or she used words, the less time she'd have to spend rewriting her own additions so they blended smoothly with what had already been done.

She had a lot of work ahead of her if she wanted to have some sort of report ready for Frank by tomorrow afternoon, and the sooner she got busy the better. But first . . .

Glancing at the small, square, crystal-encased clock atop the desk, Alison saw that it was just after nine o'clock. Which meant it was just after eleven in New York. Pulling the telephone closer, she lifted the receiver and punched in Orson's office number. The rat owed her an explanation, and that was just for starters.

His secretary answered on the third ring and put her through immediately, leaving no doubt in Alison's mind that he'd been expecting her call.

"So, Alison, sweetheart, you made it to New Mexico in one piece, huh?" he blustered, using his hale-and-hearty all-good-cheer tone of voice.

"Which is more than I can say for the shape you're going to be in when I get my hands on you."

"Now, sweetheart, settle down and let me—"

"Stop calling me that," she snapped, then continued even more angrily. "Why, Orson? Just tell me *why* you sent me out here thinking that I'd be working with a reclusive old woman when all the time you *knew* that Rebecca Francis was dead?"

"Because you wouldn't have gone if I'd told you the truth," he admitted so quietly, so *contritely*, that Alison wasn't sure if she wanted to laugh or cry.

"Oh, Orson..."

"Frank Bradford was desperate. You were the only one I knew of who could help him." He paused, then added almost as an afterthought, "And I honestly thought a little change of scenery would do you good."

"So you lied to me."

"Not exactly," he hedged defensively.

"Oh, I see. You just *forgot* to mention the fact that the only ones awaiting my arrival at the Double B would be a widower, his five-year-old twin sons and his father."

"Well, no, but—"

"I rest my case," Alison cut in with the kind of righteous indignation that should have made her feel better, but didn't. While there was no denying Orson had purposely misled her, she knew he hadn't done so to hurt her in any way.

"Okay, I agree. I'm a real jerk," he stated pragmatically. "But there's no law saying you have to stay if you're unhappy with the situation out there."

"That's easy for you to say," she muttered, fingering the stack of manuscript pages as she sat back in the desk chair.

"Just tell Bradford you don't want the job and come on home."

"I can't do that, Orson. Not now that I'm actually here."

"Why not?"

Because Frank Bradford is a decent man who needs to put the past behind him so he can be the kind of father his sons need. And he's not going to be able to do that unless I stay here and finish his wife's manuscript for him.

"I...just can't," she repeated quietly, unwilling to admit aloud how deeply she'd already allowed herself to be drawn into the Bradfords' predicament. She'd always been a sucker for sob stories, and apparently she still was. But she didn't want Orson jumping to the wrong conclusion.

Though he hadn't said as much, she had an idea he'd had matchmaking on his mind, and the last thing she wanted to do was add fuel to that particular fire.

"Tell me, what's Bradford like in the flesh...so to speak?"

"Watch it, Orson. You're already skating on thin ice with me," Alison warned.

"I'm sorry," he replied, sounding as if he meant it.

"He's a nice man, and he *is* desperate."

"What about *Hunter's Edge?* Is there any hope for it?"

"I can't say for sure. I haven't had a chance to read it yet. But if it's anything like Rebecca's earlier books, finishing it in a way that will do her writing justice will be a real challenge.''

"Well, if anyone can do it, you can, and Margaret agrees.''

"You told Margaret Locke I was going to work on the manuscript?''

"About an hour ago. She was quite pleased.''

Though she was flattered by the editor's faith in her abilities, Alison found herself wondering if she really was up to getting the job done. As luck would have it, there was only one way to find out.

"Guess I'd better get busy, then. Living up to *her* expectations could take me a while.''

"You're going to do just fine. Remember, you're the best book doctor in the business.''

"Yeah, yeah . . .'' She paused, smiling in spite of herself. The man was exasperating, but he meant well. "As long as you remember flattery isn't going to get you anywhere. Your butt's still grass and I'm not done chewing yet.''

"Aw, come on, sweetheart. Give me a break. Is it really that bad out there?''

"No. . . .''

"Well then, relax and enjoy yourself. You know that's what Len would have wanted you to do.''

Taken aback by the unexpected mention of her husband's name, Alison said nothing for several seconds. Of course, Orson was right. Len *would* have wanted her to have a nice time with the Bradfords. Yet how could she, when she didn't dare let her guard down around them? She couldn't risk caring about them any more than she already did. Not when she thought of the kind of bad luck she'd brought upon everyone else she'd ever been close to.

"I'll try,'' she answered at last, though she had no intention of doing any such thing.

"And let me know how you're doing with the manuscript, too."

"I'll call you in a couple of weeks."

"Sounds good to me. Have fun, sweetheart."

"Oh, sure. Talk to you later."

She cradled the receiver, then stood and picked up the
manuscript, more than ready to get to work. She crossed to
the file cabinet next to the love seat, set the stack of pages
atop it, and returned to the desk for a legal pad and a handful of pencils.

As she glanced out the window on her way back to the
love seat, she heard Molly barking. Pausing, she saw
Frank's truck coming up the drive, followed by her rental
car. Both vehicles pulled to a stop, then Frank climbed out
of the car as his father hopped down from the truck. After
exchanging a few words, Bert headed for the house while
Frank strode off toward the barn, Molly frolicking at his
heels.

Several moments later, Alison heard the back door open
and close, followed by the hollow sound of footsteps on the
kitchen floor. Relieved that her car was all right and Bert
was back at the house, she curled up on the love seat and
eagerly reached for the first page of *Hunter's Edge*.

"Got your car out of the ditch without any problems,"
Bert announced from the doorway.

Startled, Alison glanced up at him, then smiled when she
saw the hint of mischief in his eyes.

"I saw you pull up. Thanks a lot."

"Anything for a pretty lady like you." He grinned teasingly, then added, "How about some coffee? I've got a fresh
pot brewing."

"Maybe later." She'd had three cups at breakfast. If she
drank any more now, she'd end up bouncing off the walls.
And she really did have to settle down and start reading.

"Just help yourself."

"I will."

"Thanks for staying. Your finishing that manuscript means a lot to all of us."

"I'll do the best I can with it," she vowed, more aware than ever of how much the Bradfords were counting on her.

"Let me know if I can do anything to...smooth your way around here. Anything at all."

"I will," she murmured.

He looked as if he wanted to say more, but much to Alison's relief, after a moment or two he nodded, turned and headed back to the kitchen.

Smooth her way around here?

Staring at the now empty doorway, she wondered what the old man was up to. No good at all, if she was any judge of his choice of words, not to mention the devilish glint she'd seen in his faded blue eyes as he'd said them. In fact, if she didn't know better, she'd think he was in cahoots with Orson Hyde.

Unless she was mistaken, Frank Bradford's father had matchmaking on *his* mind, too. And as far as she could see, all she could do was dissuade him as gently yet as firmly as possible whenever the opportunity arose.

She was there to work on Rebecca's manuscript, and when she was finished, she was going home. Period. And no one, *no one,* was going to cause her to deviate from that course.

When Frank Bradford was ready, he'd find someone to take Rebecca's place. But she wasn't going to be that someone. She'd loved and lost enough in her lifetime. And some risks just weren't worth taking anymore. Not when the odds were against her, as well as against anyone she allowed herself to love.

Chapter Five

Drawn into *Hunter's Edge* from the first page, Alison read steadily for the next couple of hours. She was vaguely aware of Bert, puttering around the house. But she was so engrossed in the story that the clatter of dishes, the hum of the washer and dryer, and even the muffled roar of the vacuum cleaner didn't really disturb her.

Rebecca's writing was as finely honed as Alison had expected it would be, while the tale she'd chosen to tell was fraught with intrigue and emotion. In addition, the characters were portrayed in such a way that they were not only sympathetic, but believable.

Though she tried to maintain a certain critical distance, Alison found herself rooting for the heroine, Lydia McCabe, as she struggled against the allure of Grady Hawkins, the notorious outlaw who'd vowed to make her his woman. Unbeknownst to her, she had an ally close by, but federal marshall Ben Griffin, masquerading as a ranch hand, didn't trust Lydia enough to tell her who he really was. Her father had allowed his ranch to be used as a hideout by Grady and his band, and Ben couldn't quite make himself believe that Lydia wasn't in league with him, as well.

Alison knew the two of them would get together eventually. But Rebecca wasn't making it easy for them, and Alison appreciated the deft way in which she kept the reader waiting. At the same time, she kept reminding herself that she'd be the one who would have to write those crucial scenes, scenes that would naturally come toward the end of the book. So she made a concerted effort to pause after every few pages and jot down a few notes that she hoped would help when she finally set about completing the manuscript.

Just after eleven, Bert appeared in the doorway again, holding a steaming mug of coffee in his hand.

"Thought you might be ready for a little pick-me-up about now," he said.

"Oh, yes, thanks." Smiling gratefully, Alison stood and stretched, then crossed the room to take the mug from him. "I meant to get some a while ago."

"Rebecca always used to lose track of time, too. But she didn't like anyone bothering her, even when it was time to eat. If you'd rather I just let you be . . ." He shrugged as he slid his hands into the back pockets of his faded jeans.

"No, not at all." She took a sip of her coffee, savoring the warm, rich taste of it, then added ruefully, "I can't remember ever being so involved in my work that I willingly missed a meal. So if I'm not at the table when you're ready to serve, come and get me. I promise I won't snap your head off."

Bert nodded approvingly. "I'll do that, missy." He gestured toward the manuscript pages scattered on the floor in front of the love seat. "How's it going?"

"Really well," she admitted. "Rebecca was a wonderful writer, and so far, I love the story."

"Think you'll be able to finish it?"

"I won't be able to say for sure until I read the rest of what she wrote and take a look at the outline, but yes, I do."

"Good." Again he nodded approvingly. "Well, I guess I'd better get going. I have to pick up the boys at school. Do you need anything from the store?"

"Not that I can think of."

"Then I should be back in thirty, maybe forty-five minutes. Grilled cheese sandwiches and tomato soup okay for lunch?"

"Mmm, sounds good to me."

"Thought you might be used to fancier fare," Bert commented, his eyes twinkling merrily.

"Oh, steak tartare and Caesar salad are all right occasionally, but nothing can hold a candle to good, old-fashioned comfort food," she replied with a smile.

"Comfort food, huh?" Bert chuckled.

"Meat loaf, stew, chicken 'n' dumplings, maybe even . . . pot roast," she elaborated.

"Ah, my specialties."

"I was hoping you'd say that. Although I'll probably end up gaining twenty pounds if you cook like that the entire time I'm here."

"Wouldn't hurt you, missy. Not a bit." He winked at her teasingly, then turned and headed down the hallway with a wave of his hand. "I'll be back shortly."

Warmed as much by the old man's company as the cup of coffee she cradled in her hands, Alison walked back to the love seat and picked up easily where she'd left off.

Lydia was wearing herself to a frazzle trying to nurse her ailing mother through a bout of pneumonia while keeping an eye on her hellion of a younger brother. Yet she refused to allow Ben to lend a hand with any of her household tasks. He'd finally had enough of her nonsense, and was about to put his foot down when Alison heard the kitchen door open.

A few moments later the sound of the twins' happy chatter wafted through the office doorway.

Much to her surprise, she realized that she'd been looking forward to their return. Oh, she'd been concentrating on the story well enough. But somewhere in the back of her mind, she'd been waiting for them to come home.

Tossing aside the page she'd been reading, she stood and crossed the room. She told herself that she was ready for a break. And, of course, she really ought to help Bert with the luncheon preparations.

Still, she knew that she was heading to the kitchen more to see Jake and Joey than for any other reason she could dream up. And though she knew that what she was doing wasn't wise, she didn't hesitate for a moment.

"So much for keeping your distance," she muttered, then smiled in spite of herself.

She could avoid being in the Bradfords' company only if she behaved like a boor. But she'd never been intentionally churlish to anyone, and she could think of no good reason to start now. Surely the next few weeks would be easier on everyone if she made an effort to be a part of the family, instead. And, of course, that meant she had a duty to help out around the house whenever she could.

"Hey, guys, how was school?" she asked, stepping into the bright, sunny kitchen.

"Pretty good," Jake replied as he and Joey hung their jackets on the pegs by the kitchen door. Turning in unison, they started to smile, but as they faced her, their shoulders sagged. Frowning, they looked at each other, then back at her, their eyes suddenly full of sadness.

"When are you leaving?" Jake demanded.

"Leaving?" She sat down in a chair by the table and gazed at them with confusion.

"You're all dressed up," Joey said, his lower lip quivering slightly. "Our mom only dressed up when she was going somewhere."

"And this morning you said you were going to stay," Jake reminded her with a boy-size scowl.

"I *am* staying," she reassured them. Then, when they didn't appear to be convinced, she added, "I dressed up today because I...I wanted to make a good impression my first day on the job."

"Did you?" Joey asked hopefully.

"Oh, wow, did she ever," Bert replied before she had a chance to voice her own "I think so."

"All right," the boys crowed, giving each other a wildly enthusiastic high five.

Glancing at Bert, Alison saw him wink at them. Then he met her gaze with mock innocence. Once again, she wasn't sure if she wanted to laugh or cry, or maybe just head for the Santa Fe airport as fast as she could.

"Well, in that case, maybe I'll change into something less formal after lunch." She stood and joined Bert at the counter. "In the meantime, why don't you let me help with the sandwiches?"

"You can cook?" Jake asked.

"Oh, yes, of course."

"Do you know how to make cookies, too?" Joey prodded. "Our dad doesn't have enough patience, and Grandpa always forgets about them and they get all burned."

"I most certainly do," she admitted.

"Oh, wow...." Both boys grinned with obvious delight.

She was digging herself in deeper and deeper, yet she couldn't seem to stop herself. Ill-mannered or not, she should have stayed in Rebecca's office...with the door shut. But then, hindsight always was twenty-twenty. And, anyway, neither spending a little time with Jake and Joey nor baking cookies for them constituted any kind of commitment. So, what could it hurt?

"Okay, you two, get your hands washed," Bert ordered, then turned his attention to Alison as she spread butter on a slice of bread. "You don't have to help with meals, you know."

"I know, but I was ready for a break. And I don't mind giving you a hand. Although I have to warn you, I haven't spent a lot of time in the kitchen lately."

"Dining out on steak tartare and Caesar salad, huh?" he teased.

"Actually, I heat up a lot of frozen dinners in my microwave," she admitted rather ruefully.

"But you weren't kidding about the cookies, were you?"

"Oh, no."

"So, you will make some?" he queried hopefully.

"Of course. What kind does everybody like best?"

"The boys are crazy about chocolate chip, and I'm kind of partial to oatmeal or peanut butter. Now Frank, he likes brownies best—the kind with chocolate chips and a little icing on top."

"Well, if you have everything I'll need on hand, I'll bake a batch of each over the weekend." She hesitated, flipping the sandwiches over on the stove-top griddle, then quietly voiced her one concern. "Unless you think Frank would object to my taking time away from Rebecca's manuscript."

The man was paying her to finish his wife's book, and considering the fee she was charging for her services, he might not want her doing anything else but that while she was there.

"I doubt he'd begrudge you taking some time off over the weekend, especially for such a worthy cause," Bert assured her as he ladled tomato soup into the bowls he'd lined up on the counter.

"All right, then, let's plan on doing it Saturday afternoon."

"Doing *what?*" Jake demanded as he and Joey returned to the kitchen and sat down at the table.

"Baking cookies," Bert said, setting a steaming bowl of soup in front of each of them.

"But only if all three of you will help," Alison added as she carried the plate of sandwiches to the table, then pulled out her chair.

"What about our dad? Can he help, too?" Joey asked.

"Well, sure," Alison agreed after a moment's indecision.

Making a point of excluding him would be rather crass. Anyway, with luck, he'd probably have something more important to do. In fact, Alison realized she was counting on his being too busy to bother with cookie baking.

While she could see no real harm in spending a little quality time with Jake and Joey and their grandfather, Frank was another matter altogether. She was already much too aware of him on a personal level, even though she'd already admitted that, for everyone's good, keeping their relationship businesslike was extremely important. She could only hope he felt the same way, and acted accordingly. Because if he didn't, she was going to have a hard time maintaining any kind of emotional distance at all.

Until today, she hadn't been aware of how much she still longed for the kind of close and loving ties she'd chosen to eschew after Len and Nathan died. But doing anything to assuage those feelings would be foolish.

Over lunch the twins talked about their day at school. Because of the snowstorm, over half the class had been absent, so they hadn't done any "real" work. And much to the boys' disappointment, they hadn't been assigned their parts in the Christmas program scheduled for December 20. Their teacher, Mrs. Dunn, had wanted to wait until the following day when most everyone would probably be back.

From what they said, Alison realized that Jake and Joey were not only very bright, but also eager to learn. At the same time, she gathered they could deal Mrs. Dunn a fit when they put their minds to it, especially since she apparently had trouble telling them apart. Alison found that hard to believe. To her each boy seemed to have his own very distinct personality. But then, she didn't have eighteen or twenty other children competing for her attention.

After they finished lunch, the boys helped Bert clear the table and load the dishwasher while Alison slipped into her room to exchange her skirt for a pair of black knit stirrup pants. By the time she returned to the kitchen, the three Bradfords had donned their jackets and were getting ready to go outside.

"We have to do our chores now," Jake said by way of explanation.

"Yeah, we have to clean out our horses' stalls and brush them and give them some feed," Joey elaborated.

"But we can't go riding because our dad's not here. We can only go riding with him or Grandpa. And Grandpa said it's too cold out there for him today." Jake paused, eyeing her contemplatively. "Do you like to ride?"

"I used to when I was a little girl. I learned while I was at camp. But that was a long time ago. I've probably forgotten how."

"Oh, no, you never forget how to ride once you learn," Joey assured her. "So, maybe you could take us riding today...."

"I don't think your dad would want me to do that. I'm not very experienced, and I don't know my way around the ranch, either," she hedged.

The boys gazed at each other wordlessly for several seconds, and Alison could almost hear their clever little minds cooking up some scheme to get her on horseback. But she had absolutely no intention—

"Next time we go riding with our dad you can come with us, okay?" Jake said.

"That way he can show you where we like to go, and you can get 'sperienced," Joey added.

"Well, maybe..."

She looked to Bert for a little help, but he merely smiled and nodded his approval at the twins' idea.

"We've got a real nice little mare that would be just right for you, missy. I'll talk to Frank about it."

"Gee, thanks," she muttered, not exactly pleased or displeased.

She'd decided to stay on the Double B because she'd been sure she could maintain some distance between herself and the Bradford men. Yet within the past hour she'd blithely agreed to bake cookies *and* go horseback riding with them. She was afraid to think of what she might allow herself to be lured into next.

Of course, she could have simply refused to involve herself in anything not directly related to the completion of Rebecca's manuscript. But as she'd realized earlier, that would have required a degree of heartlessness she had yet to attain. At least where two impish little boys and their crusty old grandfather were concerned.

"We'll be out in the barn for the next hour or so if you need anything," Bert advised as he herded Jake and Joey toward the back door.

"Don't worry about me. I'll be fine." She waved them off, shivering in the gust of icy air that slid through the open door, then headed back to Rebecca's office.

Finding the sudden silence somewhat oppressive, especially after the twins' happy chatter, she fiddled with the stereo receiver tucked in among the books on the shelves. It was tuned to a station playing classical music, but she soon found another featuring her favorite fifties and sixties rock and roll.

Though she'd been born at the tail end of the "baby boom" era, she spent her formative years tagging after her older brother. Since he'd been her hero, it was no surprise that she'd shared his taste in music. While her friends had been playing with their dolls, she'd been learning to boogie to the sounds of the Beatles and the Rolling Stones, Otis Redding and the Righteous Brothers.

She and Patrick had been so close—best friends as well as sister and brother. They'd always been there for each other, especially after their parents were killed. In fact, he'd wanted to resign his commission in the army so he could look after her, even though she'd been a college freshman at the time. But she'd known how much his career meant to him, and she hadn't let him do it. Eighteen months later, while stationed in the Middle East, he was killed during a terrorist attack.

Turning up the volume several decibels, Alison willed herself to focus on the task at hand. She knew better than anyone that she couldn't change the past. But if she made a concerted effort to complete Rebecca's manuscript, she could make the future a little brighter for the Bradfords.

With Roy Orbison keeping her company as he sang about his pretty woman, she curled up on the love seat again, and gladly went back to work.

She heard Bert and the boys come in around three o'clock, but she was so absorbed in the chapter she was reading that she merely paused to note the time before continuing on to the next page. However, when Jake and Joey appeared in the office doorway a half hour later, she set aside the manuscript and offered them a welcoming smile.

"Did you get your chores all done?"

"Yes, ma'am," they piped up together, moving a little farther into the room.

As they did so, Alison noticed that Jake held a large cardboard box full of blocks while Joey clutched a folded quilt in his arms.

"So what are you going to do now?" she asked, although she already had a pretty good idea.

"We're going to build a big fort with our blocks," Jake replied. "But we're not supposed to bother you."

"I see." She hesitated, trying hard not to laugh out loud. They were so obvious, but she had no intention of saying or doing anything to hurt their feelings. "And where are you planning to build your fort?"

Now standing no more than a foot or two away from her, both boys shrugged and shuffled their feet, not quite meeting her gaze.

"You know, it wouldn't bother me if you wanted to build it in here," she said, barely resisting the urge to put her arms around them and hug them close. "Just as long as you're quiet, of course."

"Oh, we'd be *real* quiet," Joey vowed.

"Yeah, you won't hear us at all. Especially with the radio on."

"In that case, why don't you go ahead and get started?"

"Okay."

Jake set the box down, then he and Joey spread out the quilt. They sat close together, dumped the blocks between them, and wordlessly began to dig through the mess, apparently looking for just the right pieces to serve as a foundation for their fort.

Alison watched them play for a few minutes, amazed at how well they communicated with no more than a look or a nod or occasionally a small hand signal. Finally, with a sigh of surprising contentment, she reached for the page she'd been reading.

"Can we ask you one question?" Jake queried a few minutes later.

"What's that?" She glanced at the boys curiously.

"Do you have a nickname?"

"A nickname?" she repeated, wishing she could just say no. But she'd never found it easy to lie, especially to children.

"Yeah, like Grandpa's name is Bertrand, but his nickname is Bert," Joey explained. "And our dad's name is Francis, but *his* nickname is Frank."

"And we're Jacob and Joseph, but Jake and Joey are our nicknames," Jake added.

"Our mom was the only one in our family who didn't have a nickname," Joey murmured sadly. "She liked being called Rebecca."

"Anyway, we thought it would be kinda neat if you had one, too," Jake continued. "We asked Grandpa first. He couldn't say for sure, but he thought maybe it might be Ali."

Ali...

Only Patrick and her parents had called her that. And then, Len had, too. But to all of her other friends and acquaintances she'd always been Alison. Thus, Ali had always seemed like more of an endearment than anything else; a special name used only by the special people in her life.

"Your grandfather was right. My nickname is Ali," she admitted quietly.

"Would you mind if we called you that?"

She eyed first one boy, then the other, wishing she could say that she did. But how could she when it seemed to mean so much to them?

She thought of what Joey had said only a few moments ago.

Our mom was the only one in our family who didn't have a nickname.

Only someone truly insensitive could miss the signal they were so obviously sending. In their five-year-old minds, having a nickname was a kind of talisman. Without one, you could die.

She'd never wanted to be Ali to anyone ever again, as much out of fear as anything. But for Jake and Joey Bradford's sake, she'd make an exception. It would only be for a few weeks. And she didn't have to allow it to mean anything to her. At least not in the same way she had in the past.

"I wouldn't mind at all," she replied, realizing as she said the words that she actually meant them.

"That's good," Joey said.

"Yeah, *real* good," Jake added.

Glancing at each other, they nodded happily. Then, smiling once again, they turned their attention back to their building blocks.

She really did need her head examined, she thought, staring blankly at the page she'd been reading. She was probably going to regret the cookie baking, the horseback riding and, especially, allowing them to call her Ali. But not nearly as much as she'd regret it if she upset them in any way.

Just because she was being kind to Jake and Joey didn't mean she was getting too close to them. Not at all. Why, she'd only been there one day.

With a heartfelt sigh of relief, Frank guided his horse across the deserted ranch road, then up the long, narrow drive toward the house. Normally, spending hour after hour in the saddle didn't faze him in the least, but he hadn't gotten much sleep last night. As a result, the day's ride into the northern foothills where his sheep were pastured had left him feeling a mite weary. He was more than ready for a hot shower and the hearty meal he knew Bert would have waiting for him.

Still, halfway up the drive, he reined Dusty in, pausing for a minute or two to admire the streaks of red and orange and gold that trailed across the western sky as the sun dipped below the horizon. While he'd lived on the Double B all his life, he still tended to be moved by the sheer beauty of the sun setting over his land, even when he was cold and tired.

Really cold, he amended, as a gust of icy air slid under the collar of his denim jacket. With a slight shiver, he turned in the saddle and whistled for Molly. She'd lagged behind to investigate something or other. But as he urged Dusty forward and turned his attention to the house, she came racing across the snowy ground to join him.

Even at a distance, he could see that the light was on in Rebecca's office. The gentle, welcoming glow reminded him of all the evenings he'd ridden home to find her there, working diligently at her desk. And though he knew better, for just a moment his heart beat a little faster as he imagined how wonderful it would be to find her waiting for him in that tidy little room.

But Rebecca wasn't in her office. Nor would she ever be again. Someone else was working there tonight.

Alison...

As he had at odd moments during the day, Frank recalled how she'd looked that morning, standing by Rebecca's desk. And, with more than a modicum of guilt, he realized that, deep down inside, he was actually looking forward to seeing *her*.

He told himself that he was merely anxious to find out what she thought of *Hunter's Edge*. He had a lot riding on her desire as well as her ability to finish the manuscript. And she hadn't made a definite commitment yet. But he knew he was only fooling himself.

From the moment he'd laid eyes on her last night, he'd been drawn to her in a way he recognized all too well. Not because he responded in a similar manner to most women he met, but because he didn't.

Maybe he'd simply been celibate too long, he reasoned, hunching into his jacket as another gust of wind whipped around him. However, that being the case, surely he'd have tried to hook up with one or another of the attractive, attainable women he'd met over the past few months. One of the weavers up in Santa Fe who bought his high-grade wool had certainly been ready and willing the last time he'd stopped by her shop. And the principal at the grade school in Vernon had indicated she was interested, as well. Unfortunately, neither of them had caught his attention in the way Alison had. And no matter how hard he tried, he couldn't seem to figure out why not.

He certainly couldn't say that Alison reminded him of Rebecca. In fact, she didn't resemble his wife in any way, physically or, from what he knew of her so far, emotionally. Had he been on the prowl, he doubted he'd have looked at her twice. But she'd been dropped in his lap, so to speak. And though he couldn't for the life of him understand why, he found her unaccountably... alluring.

In addition, she wasn't really available. Not in the true sense of the word. She'd be around for the next six weeks or so, but once she finished Rebecca's manuscript, she'd be going back to New York City. And with all the responsibilities he had here in New Mexico, he certainly couldn't go traipsing after her.

Of course, *that* could be why he found the thought of getting together with her so appealing. He doubted there was any chance she'd ever be a permanent part of his life, not the way Rebecca had been. So he could "dally" with her for a while, then send her on her way.

Only he'd never "dallied" with any woman. He wasn't that kind of man. Never had been and never would be. And he doubted Alison Kent was the "dallying" type, either. In fact, he had a feeling that even thinking she'd be interested in casual sex was doing her a grave disservice. Why, she'd all but admitted that three years after she'd lost her husband and young son she was still mourning them. Hopping into bed with a man had to be the last thing on her mind.

Bottom line, they were both decent people who'd never consider getting involved in any kind of temporary relationship. And that was the only kind of relationship Frank could foresee their having. Despite what his father had said when they'd gone to haul her car out of the ditch.

She's a mighty fine lady, son. Pretty as a picture and sweet as pie. Your sons think she shoots the moon, and I have a feeling you do, too. But it's gonna take some convincing to get her to stay. So, I'd advise you to get busy.

Only Bert would say something so outrageous after spending no more than five minutes with the woman. The hell of it was, the old man had not only been right about her, but about Frank's interest in her, as well.

Not that his odd infatuation with her would make any difference in the long run. He knew better than to think she'd give up her life in the big city to live on a ranch out in the middle of nowhere. Considering they'd known each other for less than a day, he had to be crazy to even be wasting time thinking about it.

He'd be better off making plans to spend a weekend in Santa Fe, getting to know the weaver—Melissa or Melinda or whatever her name was. Maybe, after that, Alison Kent wouldn't look quite so good to him.

"Yeah, sure," he muttered. "And if you believe that, there's a guy out there just waiting to sell you a bridge."

With a rueful shake of his head, Frank dismounted and led Dusty into the barn. He pulled the saddle off the horse's back, slipped the bridle over his head and turned him into his stall. Then, taking his time, he poured a measure of oats into the gelding's bin and filled his pail with fresh water.

Recalling how his father had tried to play matchmaker with him, he could only imagine what the old guy had said

to Alison once he'd had her all to himself. On the way to retrieve her rental car, Bert had gone on about the boys need-
ing a mother, then made a point of warning him about how
unhealthy it was for a man Frank's age to allow his "juices"
to back up over a long period of time. And although Frank
had warned him to let Alison alone before they'd gone their
separate ways, he had a feeling the old reprobate hadn't paid
him much heed.

There was no telling what he might have said to Alison,
but Frank figured he'd find out just as soon as he walked
into the house. At least his father hadn't driven her away
yet. The light *was* on in Rebecca's office. And when he'd
ridden up, Frank had also noticed that her rental car was
right where he'd left it that morning. Of course, that didn't
guarantee she wasn't planning to take off first thing tomorrow. But maybe, before then, he could take care of any
damage control that might be necessary.

He really did want her to stay. Actually, he *needed* her to
stay, even though they'd probably both be better off if she
didn't.

Not exactly relishing the thought of what might be
awaiting him at the house, yet aware that he'd avoided the
inevitable as long as he could, Frank finished with Dusty
and quickly checked on the other horses. Then, with Molly
trotting along beside him, he headed out of the barn and
across the yard, his boots crunching on the ice-crusted snow.

He stomped on the mat by the back door. Then, along
with Molly, he stepped into the brightly lighted, spice-
scented warmth of the kitchen. As he tossed his worn leather
gloves on the counter and shrugged out of his jacket, his
father turned away from the stove and eyed him with concern.

"It's about time you showed up. I was getting ready to go
out looking for you."

"The snowfall was pretty heavy up in the hills, so it took me a little longer than I anticipated to ride to the camp."

He knew that his father tended to worry about him when he was out on his own. However, Bert also understood, from years of experience, that riding alone over miles and miles of open land was part of the job when you were a working rancher. And he'd had Molly, as well as his trusty mobile phone, with him in case of an emergency.

"Everything all right up there?"

"Carlos and Benito seem to have the situation under control."

The two young men who rode herd on his sheep knew what they were doing. With the help of a couple of Molly's well-trained brothers, they'd kept the Double B's losses down to a minimum so far that winter. And that was all Frank really asked of them.

"You look beat." Somewhat mollified, Bert turned back to the stove, lifted the lid on one of the pots atop it and stirred the contents with a large wooden spoon.

"I am." Crossing the kitchen, he rested a hand on his father's flannel-clad shoulder for a moment and inhaled deeply. "Mmm, that smells like your three-alarm chili."

"In honor of Ms. Kent, I thought two-alarm might be more in order," Bert admitted with a soft chuckle.

"Good idea," Frank agreed, aware that she'd probably find his father's not-quite-so-highly-seasoned concoction more to her liking than the fiery stuff he usually cooked up. "So, how'd it go around here today?"

"Just fine."

Avoiding his son's gaze, Bert lifted another lid, stirred the pinto beans in the pot, then checked on the cornbread baking in the oven.

"No problems?" he prodded.

"Not a one."

He ought to be relieved, but he wasn't. The sly grin tugging at the corners of his father's mouth wouldn't let him. The old guy was keeping something to himself. But what?

Not sure that he really wanted to know, Frank asked instead, "Where are the boys?"

Usually about that time of day, they were bouncing off the walls. But, aside from the burble of the pots on the stove, the soft snores of Molly, curled up on her rug in the corner, and the faint strains of rock and roll music drifting down the hallway, the house was quiet.

"Last I saw, they were with Alison."

"I *told* them not to bother her." Spinning on his heel, Frank started toward the doorway, but before he'd taken more than a couple of steps, his father caught him by the arm.

"Just hold your horses a minute. They're *not* bothering her."

"How can they not be bothering her?" Frank demanded angrily. "She's trying to work."

"They're playing with their blocks. Have been for the past couple of hours. As far as I can tell, she doesn't seem to mind having them in there with her. And if that's the case, I don't think you should, either."

Frank had to admit that his father was right. But he didn't want Alison thinking he expected her to baby-sit his sons. That definitely wasn't part of her job description, and he wanted to make sure she knew it. However, going off half-cocked and hollering at his sons wasn't the way to do it.

"I'll talk to her later, let her know she doesn't have to give in to those two little scoundrels every time they cozy up to her, wanting something."

"You do that, son," Bert replied with an all-too-knowing grin. "But now, why don't you hop in the shower? Dinner will be ready in about half an hour, so you'll have time to shave, too."

"I don't feel like shaving," Frank groused as he continued across the kitchen.

"Just thought you might want to gussy up a bit for the lady."

"Do me a favor, will you?"

"What's that?"

"Stop pushing."

"Pushing? *Me?*" Though he sounded somewhat affronted, his eyes twinkled mischievously.

"Yes, *you.*"

"Not a chance."

"You know, you're wasting your time."

"We'll see."

"Yeah, we sure will."

Determined to make those his last words on the subject, Frank stalked out of the kitchen and strode down the hallway. The sound of the Beatles singing "A Hard Day's Night" grew louder with each step he took. Apparently, Ms. Kent liked golden oldies.

Glancing into the boys' bedroom, he saw that they'd picked up the toys they'd strewn all over the floor the night before. At least they'd done one thing he'd asked of them, he thought as he moved on toward the open doorway of Rebecca's office. But that didn't ease his displeasure over the fact that they hadn't stayed out of Alison's way. And he intended to let them know it as soon as he got them alone.

Pausing just outside the office, he braced his hands on his hips and took in the scene before him. Oblivious to his presence, Jake and Joey wordlessly added a plastic block here and there to the towering monstrosity they were building. Also unaware of him, Alison sat on the love seat, jotting notes on a yellow legal pad. Manuscript pages littered the floor by her feet, and beside her, at least half a dozen books lay open. Atop the desk, several file folders lay scattered haphazardly, as well.

Never, in all the years he'd looked through that particular doorway, had Frank seen anything quite like the sight now meeting his eyes. Nor had he ever heard anything but the softest strains of classical music coming from the stereo on the shelf, he mused, as "A Hard Day's Night" faded into the Rolling Stones's "Satisfaction."

He knew he ought to feel at least a small measure of resentment at the way Alison had taken over Rebecca's domain, completely making it her own. Yet what he really felt was gratitude. She'd made every effort to adapt to the working conditions he'd offered her. And she'd also been especially kind to his sons.

Bert was right. Jake and Joey needed whatever time and attention she was willing to give. And, apparently, she was generous enough to offer them much more than he had a right to expect. Still, he had no intention of allowing them to take advantage of her. Nor did he intend to do so himself.

"Hey, Dad, look what we're building," Joey called out.

"What is it?" he asked, stepping into the office.

"A fort," Jake advised in a disparaging tone of voice.

"Oh, I see."

He shifted his gaze to Alison again, noting for the first time that she'd exchanged her skirt for a pair of black knit pants that fit her trim figure in a most pleasing way. As her eyes met his, her mouth curved into a welcoming smile that eased his weariness even as it warmed his heart.

"How was your day?" he asked, moving a little closer to her.

"Productive." She waved a hand at the pages on the floor. "I just finished reading the manuscript and thought I'd make a few notes before taking a look at the outline."

"What do you think of it?"

"It's wonderful," she replied without hesitation, her simple words ringing true.

"Even the last fifty pages or so?" he prodded, wondering if she'd tell him what she honestly thought of *his* writing.

"Well, they need a little work," she hedged, a teasing look in her eyes.

"A *little* work?"

"Don't sell yourself short, Mr. Bradford," she chided softly. "The pages you wrote are very good. However, your basic tone and style are different from Rebecca's."

"But you can fix it?"

"Yes."

"What about the rest of the story? Do you think you'll be able to finish writing it?"

"I haven't looked at the outline yet, so I'm not exactly sure what Rebecca has planned for her characters. But I'm fairly certain I can follow through in a way that you'll approve of."

"So, you'll stay and work on it?"

"Of course she's staying, Dad," Jake piped up. "Otherwise, we couldn't bake cookies on Saturday like she promised."

"Oh, really?" Frowning, Frank eyed his son, then shifted his gaze to Alison. Her smile had faded.

"Bert didn't think you'd mind. But if you'd rather I didn't take time away from the manuscript..." Ducking her head, she fingered the edge of the legal pad in her lap and shrugged with obvious uncertainty.

More than likely, Bert and the boys had conned her into agreeing to bake cookies before she'd had any idea what they were up to. When they put their minds to it and banded together, the three of them were pretty good at getting their way with just about anyone but him. And while he didn't care what she did during the free time he fully expected her to have on the weekends, he didn't want her to feel obligated to spend it entertaining his children.

"Your weekends are your own," he stated in a matter-of-fact tone. "You can bake all the cookies you want, but only if that's what *you* really want to do."

"Oh, yes, it is." She smiled as she met his gaze again, her dark eyes bright with anticipation.

"You can help, too, Dad," Joey advised. "Ali said so."

Ali?

"I thought I asked you to call her Ms. Kent."

"She said we could call her Ali," Jake insisted. "It's her nickname."

"Well, I really don't think—"

"My having a nickname seemed important to them," Alison cut in quietly, something in her tone drawing his attention to her. "And I don't mind. Really, I don't."

"Yeah, since we all have nicknames, that kinda makes her one of the family, doesn't it?" Joey said, obviously pleased with his deductive reasoning.

And he'd thought his father was bad. Shoving his hands in the side pockets of his jeans, Frank studiously avoided Alison's gaze. However, from the corner of his eye he could see that her face was red. Evidently, she wasn't exactly thrilled with the tack their conversation had taken, either.

Not that he didn't want her to feel at home on the Double B. Because he honestly did. But having his father and sons all but throwing them together after only one day couldn't be something she relished any more than he did. He was going to have to find a way to get them to cease and desist, or risk having them run her off before...

Before she completed Rebecca's manuscript, he added, though surprisingly that hadn't been the first thought that had come to mind.

"Um, listen, I need to get a shower," he responded noncommittally, shifting from one foot to the other. "Dinner will be ready in about twenty minutes. Why don't you two put your blocks away and give your grandpa a hand setting the table?''

Not waiting for a reply, he backed out of the office, turned, strode into his bedroom, slammed the door closed and headed for the bathroom. He showered quickly and, against his better judgment, shaved, then dressed in a fresh pair of jeans and a navy blue pullover sweater he usually wore only when he went into town.

Feeling faintly foolish, he returned to the kitchen where Alison and his sons were busy helping Bert put the food on the table. His father gave him a knowing look, but Frank frowned warningly as he held out a chair for Alison.

Apparently taking the hint, Bert kept their conversation focused on ranch business as they dug into the hearty meal he'd prepared. For her part, Alison listened attentively, occasionally asking a question about one aspect or another of sheep ranching, while the twins seemed content to chatter quietly with each other.

In fact, Frank hadn't thought the boys were paying any attention to the adults' conversation at all until Jake spoke up during a lull.

"Did you find any Christmas trees up there, Dad?" he asked, reminding Frank of his promise to scout around for one while he was up at the camp.

"I sure did." He'd actually seen three or four trees that would be suitable in the small stand of Douglas firs near the trailer. "Since you already have plans for Saturday, we can ride up there Sunday and you guys can take your pick."

"Can Ali go, too?" Joey pleaded. "She needs 'sperience riding."

"She does, huh?"

Wondering how his son had come to that conclusion, Frank glanced at Alison questioningly. For one long moment, she met his gaze, a stricken look in her eyes. Then, ducking her head, she set her spoon by her bowl and folded her hands in her lap.

He'd intended to ask her if Joey had been correct in assuming that she not only needed, but wanted, experience riding, then invite her to go along with them if she did. But suddenly he wasn't sure what to say to her. He had no idea what had upset her, and he certainly didn't want to risk making bad matters worse.

"Yeah, Dad. She said she'd like to go riding with us the next time we went," Jake added.

Okay, so riding wasn't the problem. Staring at his now-empty bowl, Frank remembered that they'd been talking about getting a Christmas tree—

A Christmas tree...

Of course, that had to be it, he thought. When they'd talked earlier, she'd told him that her husband and son had been killed a few weeks before Christmas, and he'd had a feeling the holiday season had been hard for her since then. Granted, she'd seemed to be looking forward to baking cookies with the boys, but that activity wasn't strictly Christmas-related. However, selecting a tree to decorate with bright lights and ornaments most definitely was.

"Maybe Alison has already made other plans for Sunday," he said, giving her what he hoped would be an easy way out.

"Did you, Ali?" Jake demanded.

"Yeah, did you, Ali?" Joey repeated, as both boys eyed her pleadingly.

With obvious reluctance, Alison raised her head and gazed at Jake, then Joey.

"Now, look, you two, give her a break," Frank warned, aware that she was trying hard to conceal her distress.

"But, Dad—" they whined in unison.

"No buts," he ordered, letting them know by the tone of his voice that he'd just had the last word.

"Actually, I don't have any plans for Sunday," Alison stated softly, her voice wavering just a little. "So if your dad doesn't mind having a rank amateur riding one of his horses, I'd love to go with you to get your Christmas tree."

Turning to face her, Frank saw that she'd pulled herself together and was smiling at the twins once again. By what seemed like a sheer act of will, she'd set aside whatever painful memories their talk of getting a tree had resurrected in order to make his sons happy. She couldn't have done anything that would have warmed his heart more. But he had a feeling that if he said as much to her, she'd fall apart on him. She was still on shaky ground, and he certainly didn't want to cause her any embarrassment.

"Don't worry, I've got just the horse for you," he teased lightly as he stood and picked up their bowls.

"You talking about Shadow?" Bert asked, standing also.

"I sure am."

"The little mare I mentioned this morning," Bert offered Alison by way of explanation.

"You did say she'd be perfect for me." Picking up the basket of leftover cornbread, she stood, too.

"He's right." Frank turned from the sink and winked at her encouragingly. "She's a steady old girl, but she's still got a lot of spirit. I think you two will hit it off just fine."

"Sounds good to me. Now, what can I do to help here?" she asked as Bert took the basket from her.

"Not a thing."

For a moment, Frank thought she might protest, but she didn't.

"Well, then, since I still have to unpack, I think I'll say good-night," she said.

They all chorused "good night" as she crossed the kitchen and walked into her bedroom. Pausing for a moment, she smiled as she glanced at them over her shoulder. Then she closed the door with what Frank imagined could only be relief.

Sometime tomorrow he was going to have a long talk with his father and the twins. For now, however, he, too, was going to call it a night. Unless he got some sleep, he'd be useless tomorrow.

"You two help your grandpa with the dishes, then hop in the tub and hit the sheets."

"What are you gonna do, Dad?" Jake asked.

"I'm gonna go to bed." Turning on his heel, he headed toward the hallway.

"Sweet dreams," Bert called after him.

"That *would* be nice for a change," Frank replied, surprising himself as much as his father.

"That's my boy."

Shaking his head at the older man's foolishness, Frank walked down the hallway. He stopped for a moment outside Rebecca's office, then moved on into his bedroom. Catching sight of himself in the mirror over the dresser, he saw that he was smiling. He wished he could say it was for no reason, but he knew better.

In less than twenty-four hours, Alison Kent had unwittingly turned his world upside down. And, though he probably needed his head examined, in all honesty, he couldn't say he minded. Not one bit.

Chapter Six

Just before six Sunday morning, Alison reached for the little clock on the nightstand and switched off the alarm button. As usual, she had it set for seven o'clock, but she'd already been awake for a while. And with all she had on her mind that morning, she knew she wasn't going to fall asleep again.

Slipping out of bed, she crossed to one of the windows and opened the blinds. On the news last night, the weatherman had promised the day would be bright and sunny with a continuation of the warming trend that had begun on Thursday. From what Alison could see, he'd been right on the mark. Though the sun hadn't crested the horizon yet, the sky definitely appeared to be clear.

Somewhere in the back of her mind, she'd half hoped that the forecaster would be wrong. But the raging snowstorm she'd imagined hadn't materialized. Today was going to be a perfect day to ride into the foothills north of the ranch house and choose a Christmas tree, she thought as she returned to her bed and crawled under the covers once again. Barring any unforeseen difficulties, she'd be heading out with Frank and his family around nine o'clock.

As she had all too often since Tuesday night, Alison wondered what had prompted her to agree to go with them to get their Christmas tree. When the twins had mentioned it, her first inclination had been to refuse. As if it had been only yesterday, she'd recalled the last time she'd made similar plans, plans that had led, albeit indirectly, to the death of both her husband and her son.

Since that awful day, she hadn't wanted anything to do with the trappings usually associated with the Christmas season. But one look at the twins' earnest little faces had convinced her that she couldn't say as much to them.

Last Christmas had been their first without their mother, and Alison would lay odds that it hadn't been especially happy for them. But this year they were obviously looking forward to the holiday season with joyful anticipation. Spoiling their innocent pleasure by broadcasting her own lack of enthusiasm would be inexcusable.

Though Frank had made it easy for her to get out of going along with them, she hadn't had the heart to do it. Including her had seemed important to Jake and Joey, and she hadn't wanted to disappoint them. So she'd ordered herself to buck up and set aside her reservations, and as cheerfully as she could, she'd agreed to join them on their outing.

However, over the past few days, each time she'd thought of the commitment she'd made, she'd done so with an inexpressible dread. What if something horrible happened while she was with them? Considering all that had happened in the past, her presence alone could very well put a jinx on what would otherwise have been an uneventful excursion. Especially since she'd begun to care for the Bradford men much more than she knew she should.

For the past three years, she'd kept to herself not only because she couldn't bear to lose anyone else she loved, but also to guarantee that no one else came to harm because of her. Yet, as she'd come to realize within a day or two, that was all but impossible on the Double B. Despite her every intention to remain aloof, she'd allowed herself to be drawn into the Bradford family in a way that caused her increasing apprehension with each day that passed.

Mornings she'd had breakfast with Frank, his father and the boys. She'd been up, anyway, and it seemed foolish to wait and eat alone after they'd finished. Then she'd gone to Rebecca's office, where she'd worked until lunchtime. After lunch, which she'd shared with Frank, as well as Bert and the boys, the rest of the week, she'd go back to Rebecca's office where she'd work alone until Jake and Joey joined her as they had on Tuesday afternoon, keeping her company while playing quietly until suppertime.

Yesterday, of course, she'd had to change her routine slightly to accommodate the cookie baking she'd promised Jake and Joey. Along with Bert, they'd started right after breakfast with a double batch of the twins' favorite chocolate chip cookies, then gone on to bake oatmeal-and-peanut-butter cookies for Bert.

Frank had begged off, saying he had paperwork to do. But after lunch, he'd hung around the kitchen long enough to make sure they still planned to bake brownies, too. He'd returned at odd intervals until the finished product was ready to be sampled, then did so with such obvious appreciation that Alison had blushed with pleasure.

All in all, she'd had a really good time, and she thought that Bert and the boys had, too. She'd forgotten how enjoyable it could be to spend a day working with others at a relatively simple, yet rewarding task. And she'd also realized how quickly she could get used to doing it on a regular basis once again.

But then, all too quickly she'd remembered that was something she couldn't do. So she'd helped Bert clean up the kitchen, and saying she had some background reading she wanted to do, she'd fled to her room, where she'd remained the rest of the afternoon.

Evenings she'd been determined to spend alone in her room, and she'd done just that on Wednesday and Thursday. But Friday night and again last night, she'd somehow ended up watching television with Frank and his sons until it was time for the boys to go to bed. Then, sure that Frank would probably appreciate some time to himself, she'd pleaded weariness and excused herself.

Not that she would have minded being alone with him. Actually, she'd discovered that she enjoyed his company quite a bit. On Friday afternoon, they'd spent time together, one-on-one, going over the changes she'd made to the fifty pages he'd written, and she hadn't been the least bit uncomfortable in his presence. To be honest, she'd felt surprisingly at ease. He hadn't been nearly as grim or as gruff as she'd originally thought he would be. Instead, he'd been kind and considerate. And, much to her delight, he'd had a sense of humor, apparently inherited, at least in part, from his father.

Thinking of Bert, Alison couldn't help but smile as she rolled onto her back and stared at the ceiling. He obviously loved his son and grandsons, and she'd felt honored that he also seemed to approve of her. What made her uneasy, however, were his none-too-subtle attempts at throwing her and Frank together at every available opportunity.

He'd been the one who'd suggested they all watch television together in the living room. Then, after fifteen or twenty minutes, he'd disappeared, leaving her sitting on the sofa with Frank while the boys sprawled on a couple of pillows on the floor by their feet.

She knew Bert meant well, and she was flattered that he felt she'd be a suitable addition to his clan. But he had no idea the kind of bad luck she'd brought upon everyone she'd ever loved.

After less than a week, Alison knew that loving the Bradfords wouldn't be hard for her to do. Just thinking of Bert and the boys warmed her heart. And no matter how she wished she could deny it, whenever she was with Frank, he stirred a longing deep in her soul. A longing she'd sensed he felt, as well. When she'd shown him her revisions Friday afternoon, his hand had brushed hers and their eyes had met, and—

Stirring restlessly, Alison willed away the memory of those long moments when they'd stared at each other with dawning awareness. For just an instant, before he'd drawn away, his fingers had tightened around hers, and she'd been so... afraid. She'd known that she ought to pull away from him, yet she couldn't seem to make herself do it. In fact, she hadn't wanted him to ever let her go.

If anything happened to any of them because of her...

"But nothing will," she stated with determination as she tossed the covers aside and slipped out of bed. "Just as long as you aren't a permanent part of their lives."

And she wouldn't be. Not under any circumstances. In five weeks, she'd be on her way back to New York City. Her work on Rebecca's manuscript was going even better than she'd originally anticipated. She'd already revised the pages Frank had written, and he'd been more than satisfied with what she'd done. She had a little more background reading to do, but then, on Monday or Tuesday at the latest, she'd be ready to pick up where they'd left off on the manuscript on Friday afternoon.

Depending on how well the writing went, she could easily be finished just after the first of the year. And if she kept her mind on what she was doing, there was no reason why the writing shouldn't go very well, indeed. Rebecca's outline was so detailed that as Alison had read it, she'd almost felt as if all she really had to do was add the dialogue. In reality, she had a good deal more than that to do in order to finish *Hunter's Edge*. But she couldn't have asked for any better guidance on how to go about it than Rebecca had so kindly, albeit unknowingly, provided.

With her thoughts on how best to structure the next chapter—the one in which Ben would finally give in to his growing attraction to Lydia—Alison took a long, hot shower. Then, despite the weatherman's promise of temperatures in the mid-forties, she dressed as warmly as she could, layering tights and a long-sleeved T-shirt under her jeans, plaid flannel shirt and bright red pullover sweater, and tugging on a pair of thick wool socks before slipping into her black, flat-heeled boots. Frank had warned her that it would probably be colder up in the foothills, and the last thing she wanted to do was end up catching a cold. She couldn't afford to let anything like that slow her down. Not when her ability to work quickly and efficiently was in everyone's best interest.

She made her bed and straightened the room. Then, as ready as she'd ever be for whatever the day ahead held, she stepped into the kitchen.

To her surprise, she was the first one there. Usually Bert or Frank and the boys were already bustling around by the time she ventured out of her room. But it *was* Sunday, and it still wasn't quite seven yet.

Smiling to herself, she started a pot of coffee, hoping it would be strong enough to suit the men. Then, taking advantage of the opportunity, she gathered together the necessary ingredients and set about stirring up a batch of pancake batter. At breakfast yesterday morning, Jake and Joey had mentioned that pancakes were a favorite of theirs. But, unfortunately, they'd added, whenever their grandfather tried to make them, he always ended up burning them, just like when he tried to make cookies.

When she'd finished with the batter, Alison crossed to the refrigerator and pulled out a package of bacon as well as a carton of eggs. She'd learned that, more often than not, meals on the Double B were rather hearty affairs. Once she had the bacon sizzling slowly in a skillet on a back burner of the stove, she found another mixing bowl in one of the cabinets and reached for an egg to break into it.

Her thoughts drifting back to *Hunter's Edge,* she imagined Ben coming upon Lydia in *her* kitchen and finding her in tears. He'd put his hands on her for the first time and draw her slowly, gently into his arms—

"Looks like you've been busy."

Startled, Alison whirled around, almost dropping the egg she'd been about to crack against the side of the bowl. Frank lounged in the doorway, eyeing her assessingly, his arms crossed over his chest, one shoulder resting against the doorframe. He was dressed as usual in worn jeans, a flannel shirt and boots. Just as she'd pictured Ben, she realized with utter dismay, staring at him as if she were seeing him for the very first time.

"Um, yes," she murmured, trying desperately to gather her wits about her as she turned back to the counter and dispensed with the egg. She'd been thinking about Ben and Lydia. She *had,* she assured herself as she took a deep breath, then another and another.

She could almost feel Frank watching her as she reached for another egg, but though her heart was pounding, her hands were blessedly steady. She could only hope he hadn't realized the kind of effect he'd had on her, or more important, *why.* Surely he couldn't have any idea how her mind had wandered, and she had no intention of telling him. Not that she thought he'd take advantage of her unwitting attraction to him. She just didn't want him to think she was offering him any encouragement. Because she wasn't.

"Coffee's ready." She nodded toward the pot on the counter as nonchalantly as she could.

"You know, you don't have to—"

"I know," she cut in before he could remind her yet again that she was a guest, and as such, not expected to help with household chores. "But I was up and dressed, and it seemed kind of silly to just sit here, waiting to be waited on." Having regained her equilibrium, she risked a glance at him, then smiled wryly as she added, "Especially when I had a craving for pancakes, and I'm apparently the only one around here who can make them."

"We need to talk, Ms. Kent," Frank growled as he poured mugs of coffee for both of them.

"About what, Mr. Bradford?" she queried lightly, not the least bit put off by his gruff tone of voice. She'd seen the smile edging the corners of his mouth before he'd turned his attention to the coffeepot.

"About the fact that you don't have to consider my sons' every wish your command." Leaning a hip against the counter near where she stood, he offered her one of the steaming mugs he held.

"I don't," she protested, wiping her hands on a dish-cloth, then taking the mug from him, being careful not to let her fingers brush against his.

"You do," he returned evenly. "They wanted to play in the office in the afternoons, so you let them. They wanted homemade cookies, so you baked some for them. They wanted you to go along with us to get a Christmas tree, and even though I have a feeling you're anything but enthusiastic about it, you agreed."

He paused as if waiting for her to say something in her defense, but she simply shrugged and smiled laconically as she took a sip of her coffee.

"And now, you're up at the crack of dawn making pancakes for the little beggars," he continued with a glower. "I should have seen it coming, especially when that's all they talked about yesterday morning."

"I wanted to do it for them. Really, I did." Without thinking, she rested a hand on his flannel-clad forearm to emphasize her words. "Otherwise, I wouldn't have bothered," she added earnestly.

As he met her gaze, Alison saw the same awareness in his eyes that she'd seen Friday afternoon, and knew that she'd made a big mistake. Before she could pull away, however, he covered her hand with his, holding her still.

"What about going to get the tree today? I know you were upset when the boys asked you to go with us, and I can understand why, after what you told me about your husband and son. If you don't really want to go, it's not too late to change your mind. I'll run interference for you, if you'd like," he offered kindly.

An hour ago, she might have been tempted to take him up on his offer. Since then, however, she'd convinced herself that as long as her relationship with the Bradford family was only temporary, she didn't have to worry about bringing her bad luck down upon them. So, she was actually looking forward to the excursion.

In fact, after three long, lonely years of self-imposed isolation, she was more than ready to take another step toward rejoining the land of the living. Sharing a few Christmas traditions with Frank and his family would definitely be a step in the right direction. And she wouldn't be the only one to benefit. She'd also be bringing a little happiness into Jake's and Joey's lives, as well.

"Oh, no. I'd like to go," she assured him. "As long as you don't mind my tagging along. It really has been a long time since I last rode, so I may have a hard time keeping up with you guys."

"We don't mind at all. And I promise we won't let anything happen to you." He squeezed her hand gently as he met her gaze. "We'll just take it slow and easy."

Alison willed herself to say something funny and move away from him fast. But all she seemed capable of doing was standing where she was, staring up at him, as if mesmerized. She knew better than to think he was talking about anything other than horseback riding. Yet she couldn't completely discount the unwonted glimmer of desire that flickered in his bright blue eyes as his thumb gently stroked the inside of her wrist.

"Whatcha doing, Dad?" Jake asked as he and Joey clambered into the kitchen.

"Burning the bacon, if I'm not mistaken," Bert answered in a singsong voice as he, too, joined them.

"Oh, I forgot—" A hot blush spreading across her cheeks, Alison turned away from Frank and moved the skillet off the burner. Although the bacon did look a little more well done than usual, luckily it hadn't begun to char yet.

"Why don't you guys set the table?" Frank suggested, his voice sounding huskier than usual as he moved away from her to refill his mug.

"What are we having for breakfast?" Joey asked, carrying the plates Bert handed him over to the table.

"Pancakes, scrambled eggs and bacon," Alison advised, trying desperately to regain some of her composure.

"Very *crispy* bacon," Jake admonished as he set out the napkins and silverware.

"I admit that I didn't do so well with the bacon, but I was kind of distracted." Ignoring Bert's snort of laughter, she stirred milk into the eggs. "However," she added, "now that you two are here to make sure I keep my mind on business, the pancakes and eggs should be just fine."

And, if the heaping stacks of pancakes and mounds of fluffy eggs everyone polished off were any indication, they were. Even the bacon, which wasn't all that bad, disappeared in record time.

After they finished eating, Alison and the twins cleaned up the kitchen while Frank and his father went out to the barn to saddle the horses. By nine o'clock, bundled into heavy jackets, hats and gloves, the five of them were riding down the drive, Bert leading the packhorse that would carry their tree back to the house and Molly trotting along behind them.

The twins, looking perfectly at ease astride their shaggy, brown-and-white pinto ponies, chattered happily as they quickly took the lead. Several yards back, Frank and his father rode on either side of Alison, taking turns advising her on how best to handle the dainty gray mare they'd chosen for her.

Shadow proved to be as gentle and well mannered as the men had sworn she'd be, and Alison soon found herself relaxing in the saddle. Since most of the snow had melted, making the going fairly easy, she also had time to take in the wild, rugged beauty of the wide, open spaces surrounding them.

"So what do you think of the Double B, Ms. Kent?" Frank asked after a while, his deep voice slicing through the silence that had settled between them.

As they'd started the gradual climb into the foothills, Bert had gone ahead to keep an eye on Jake and Joey, leaving the two of them to follow at a more sedate pace.

"I've never seen anything like it in my life. It's...it's just awesome," she replied, then waved a hand toward the horizon. "How many acres do you own?"

"About twelve hundred," he said.

"That sounds like a lot."

"Actually, we're one of the smaller operations out here," he admitted, then added proudly, "but we go back a ways."

"How long has the ranch been in your family?" she asked with honest interest.

"My great-grandfather, Bertrand, and his twin brother, Bailey, settled out here just after the Civil War."

"Ah, so that's where the ranch got its name."

"Yeah, the Double B—Bertrand and Bailey Bradford. Unfortunately, Bailey wasn't in the best of health. They'd only been out here a couple of years when he died. My great-grandfather ended up running the place on his own. Apparently, he was a tough old bird, but he only had one son—my grandfather, Denton. He had two sons, my father and *his* twin brother, Bailey.

"As it turned out, Uncle Bailey wasn't too fond of sheep ranching. He joined the navy as soon as he graduated from high school, and although he comes back occasionally to visit, he was more than happy that my dad inherited the ranch. He retired several years ago and spends most of his time in Florida."

"And now you own the ranch?"

"When my parents were ready to retire, Bert deeded the place over to me. In return, he gets a part of the profit I make each year for as long as he lives. All things considered, it seemed like a good idea, and so far, it's worked out well for us."

"You really love the place, don't you?" she ventured, although she already had a fairly good idea what his answer would be.

"Yes," he replied without a moment's hesitation.

"I can see why," she murmured, gazing at the glorious vista before them, then added, "even though it's quite a bit different from anywhere else I've ever been."

"I guess that means you've never traveled through this part of the country before." He glanced at her with obvious curiosity.

"Actually, I've never traveled much at all," she admitted. "My parents were content to stay fairly close to home, and I guess their lack of wanderlust rubbed off on me."

She didn't add that the first real trip she'd ever taken, a trip she'd sworn she wouldn't miss for anything, had ended in their deaths. Fifteen years ago, during spring break in her freshman year in college, she'd driven to Florida with a couple of friends, even though she hadn't been feeling well for several days. When she'd ended up in the hospital with a bad case of the flu, her parents had insisted on flying down to be with her. Their plane had crashed on takeoff, and though there had been many survivors, her mother and father hadn't been among them.

"So you've always lived in New York City, then?"

"Not always. I grew up in a nice neighborhood in Philadelphia. Every summer I spent three weeks at a girls' camp in Minnesota, and the family spent the month of August at a cottage on the New Jersey shore. I went to a small liberal arts college in Connecticut, then moved to New York after graduation to work for Norville Press."

"Sounds like you've been a few places, after all," he teased.

"A few," she agreed, offering him a wry smile.

"What did your parents do?"

"My father worked for an advertising agency and my mother worked part-time at the local library." She paused a moment. Then, hoping to stave off any further questions about them, she continued quietly. "They died several years ago."

"I'm sorry."

"Me, too. I still miss them."

"Were you an only child?"

"I had an older brother. He . . . he died a short time after my parents."

Glancing at Frank, she saw the questioning look in his eyes. He had to be wondering what had happened to her family. But he was too polite to come right out and ask her.

For just an instant, Alison was tempted to tell him exactly how they'd died and, more important, why. Then she certainly wouldn't have to worry about him developing any serious interest in her. Once he knew the kind of bad luck she could be, she had no doubt he'd not only give her a wide berth, but see to it that everyone else in his family did the same. Yet she couldn't seem to bring herself to say the words that would surely spoil what was turning out to be one of the nicest days she'd had in a very long time.

"Bert mentioned that you have twin sisters," she said instead, trying to change the subject as deftly as she could. "Are they older or younger than you?"

"Five years younger," he answered after a moment's hesitation. Though he must be aware of how she was dissembling, much to her relief, he seemed willing to let her get away with it.

"How often do you get to see them?" she prodded, determined to steer their conversation as far away from herself as possible now that she had the chance.

"They were here in August. I'd hoped they'd be able to come for Christmas, but they've both got a lot going on in their lives right now."

"Your father said that Ellen's in the navy."

"Yeah, my sister, the lieutenant commander." His smile held more than a hint of pride. "She graduated in the top ten percent of her class at Annapolis, and since then, she's been all over the world. Right now, she's stationed in San Diego. Apparently, she's going through some sort of intense training to qualify as the first female member of one of the navy's elite special operations' teams."

"Did your Uncle Bailey have anything to do with her career choice?"

"Actually, my dad suggested she apply to Annapolis. She was always talking about wanting to see the world, and he knew the military had been good to his brother. Bailey did write a recommendation for her, but she also had the grades and the gumption necessary to qualify for the academy."

"What about your other sister?"

"Elaine's a much quieter, gentler soul than her sister. She owns a small bookstore in Seattle that specializes in mystery novels."

"How did she end up there?"

"Ellen was stationed at the Bangor Naval Base a couple of years ago. Elaine went to visit her and fell in love with the area."

"Does she have any interest in writing herself?" Alison asked, recalling that many of the booksellers she'd met did.

"Not that I know of. But I gather she *is* interested in *a* writer. Unfortunately, there seems to be something keeping them apart. Elaine wouldn't say exactly what, but the last time I talked to her, I got the feeling she's hoping they'll be able to work out the problem, whatever it is."

"Sounds like you're pretty close to each other even though you live kind of far apart," she mused rather wistfully.

"Yeah, we are." He smiled as he met her gaze. "I think you'd like them, and I *know* they'd like you. Especially Elaine. She's always been fascinated by anything that has to do with books. She'd really get a kick out of meeting an editor from New York City."

Gratified that he so obviously approved of her, Alison returned his smile. "Do you think they'll ever move back to New Mexico?"

"Much as I wish at least one of them would, I seriously doubt it. Neither of them was particularly fond of living on a working ranch. Like my Uncle Bailey, they both took off as soon as they could, and they come back only occasionally. After the places they've been and the things they've done, they find it awfully dull around here. From what they've said, I gather Albuquerque and Santa Fe don't hold much appeal for them, either. But I guess you can understand that after living in a big city yourself." He eyed her once again, his expression rather pensive. "You've been here less than a week, but I guess you're already getting kind of tired of this place, aren't you?"

She considered his question for a moment or two, then responded with utter honesty. "Actually, I like it here. It's so peaceful." She risked another glance at him, then added teasingly, "And I've got more than enough to keep me busy. If I'm not working on *Hunter's Edge*, then I'm baking cookies or going to get a Christmas tree...."

"Give it a couple more weeks," he growled, though a smile once again tugged at the corners of his mouth. "You'll be ready to climb the walls."

"Maybe," she conceded. After all, she hadn't experienced any of the trials and tribulations associated with life on a working ranch yet. "But I honestly don't think so."

"No *maybe* about it. You will."

"You sound like you'll be disappointed if I'm not," she teased.

"Surprised, but not disappointed," he replied, his tone matter-of-fact. When she glanced at him, he held her gaze, a searching look in his eyes as he added, "Not disappointed at all."

As she had when they'd been alone together in the kitchen, Alison had a feeling he was saying more to her than his simple words seemed to imply. And the underlying message she sensed he was sending warmed her heart in a way she knew she shouldn't allow it to do.

Whether or not she liked living on the Double B shouldn't make any difference to either one of them. Yet it seemed to matter to Frank, and knowing that opened up a whole world of possibilities Alison found herself wanting to explore. But how could she, when she firmly believed it would be best for both of them if she took herself back to New York just as soon as she could?

"Rebecca must have been very happy here," she said, deeming it wise to remind them both of why she was there.

Only the sound of the horses' hooves clicking against the stony ground broke the silence that settled between them once again. But Alison could almost feel Frank watching her, and she sensed that he wasn't smiling anymore.

"For a long time she thought of the ranch as a kind of haven. She'd always wanted what she considered a 'real' home, and she had that here," he answered at last. "But like my Uncle Bailey and my sisters, she'd always wanted to see the world. I think, after a while, she missed being able to just pick up and go, especially when first Ellen and then Elaine struck out on their own. I've often wondered whether she would have come back to the Double B with me if we'd actually gone to Australia. Maybe that's why I kept finding reasons to put off the trip until it was too late."

"Of course she would have," Alison hastened to assure him. She'd wanted only to quash her own foolish hopes. But, had she known how Frank would react, she'd have kept Rebecca out of the conversation. Stirring up any lingering doubts and insecurities he had regarding her was the last thing she'd intended to do. "As you said, the ranch was the first real home she'd ever had. That had to mean a lot to her. And, from what you've told me about her, she doesn't sound like the kind of person who would abandon her family on a whim."

"You're right," he conceded. "But sometimes I feel so damn guilty for not having tried harder to make her dreams come true. She not only worked hard to help me keep the ranch going, but to succeed at her writing, as well. And she was a good mother to the twins. Looking back, I realize how much I took for granted, and I wish I hadn't been quite so selfish.''

Alison understood all too well how he felt. Yet, as far as she could see, he had no reason for such self-reproach. Basically, he was a very kind and generous man. He'd given Rebecca two things she'd wanted but never had—a home and a family. He'd also been much more supportive of her career than most men would have been. And from what he'd told her, he had no reason to blame himself for her untimely death, either.

''I think you're being too hard on yourself. Under the circumstances, you did the best you could with what you had, and that's all any of us can ask of ourselves.'' She hesitated, then continued in a lighter tone. ''And unless Rebecca was a lot more malleable than you've led me to believe, I have a feeling that if she'd really wanted to see the world, she wouldn't have let you or anyone else stand in her way.''

''She certainly wasn't *that*. Not by any stretch of the imagination,'' he admitted, laughing fondly.

''Well, then, stop beating yourself up, okay?''

''Okay.'' They rode in silence for a few minutes, then he added quietly, ''Thanks.''

''For what?'' She glanced at him curiously.

''For listening. You really helped me put things in perspective.'' He paused, then turned to meet her gaze. ''Let me know if I can ever do the same for you.''

''I will,'' she answered, looking away.

More than anything, she wished that she could. But she knew in her heart that she never would. Not if she wanted to maintain the rapport she'd established with Frank and his family for the duration of her stay on the Double B.

She said nothing more as they continued along the trail. But a short while later, as they crested the ridge of the hill they'd been climbing, she exclaimed with childlike pleasure, "Oh, it's so beautiful."

Before them spread a wide valley cut by a meandering stream that sparkled in the sunlight. In the distance, off to their left, hundreds of sheep gazed under the supervision of two men on horseback, aided by a couple of dogs that looked a lot like Molly.

"That was the original ranch house."

As they guided their horses down the gentle slope, Frank gestured toward the charred remains of what appeared to be a cabin. Nearby, tucked into a stand of fir trees, stood a relatively new travel trailer, and in a little clearing off to one side Alison saw what appeared to be a small, three-sided barn with an old jeep parked next to it.

"What happened to the house?"

"While my grandparents were living there, the place was struck by lightning, and pretty well burned to the ground. Since they had to rebuild completely, my grandmother talked my grandfather into doing so closer to the main road. She'd never liked being quite so isolated. After the fire, they decided to use adobe instead of wood."

"I never realized you had so many sheep," she said, her gaze drawn back to the herd that seemed to be moving slowly, yet inexorably, toward them.

"About eight hundred, but that's not really a lot compared to some of the larger operations in the state. However, the Double B is known for producing especially fine wool. And we also have a reputation for breeding top-quality lambs."

"And you only have two men to ride herd on them?" she asked, eyeing him quizzically.

"And the dogs," he pointed out with a teasing grin.

"Ah, yes, the dogs." She smiled and shook her head. "Goes to show what *I* know."

"Actually, sheep don't need a lot of looking after until lambing season. Before then, we'll have moved them to the pasture just south of the house so Bert and I can help Carlos and Benito keep an eye on them."

"When *is* lambing season?"

"Our first lambs are due toward the end of January, but just to be on the safe side, we'll probably move the herd within the next couple of weeks, depending on the weather."

To her surprise, Alison was disappointed that she'd be gone before the lambs were born. But then, she realized that most of them would probably be sent to market, and admitted she'd have found that particular aspect of sheep ranching rather hard to bear.

"What's wrong?" Frank asked, his voice suddenly full of concern.

"Oh, nothing," she hedged, wishing he weren't quite so attuned to her feelings.

"Thinking about the lambs?"

"Well, yes...."

"Actually, we raise quite a few, then sell them to other ranchers who want to improve their herds," he said as they came to a halt just outside the barn.

She turned to face him, smiling gratefully, but before she could say anything more, Jake and Joey ran out to meet them. Along with Bert, they'd arrived at the camp a few minutes ahead of Frank and Alison, and had just finished feeding their horses a measure of grain.

"You sure were riding slow, Dad," Jake commented, bracing his hands on his hips in a stance that was an exact imitation of his father's.

"Yeah, we wanted to head back and tell you to hurry up, but Grandpa wouldn't let us. He said you and Ali needed a little privacy," Joey added.

"Well, your grandpa was right," Frank replied, then caught Alison by the arm as she shifted in her saddle to dismount. "Stay put a minute, okay?"

"Okay," she agreed, watching as he swung out of his saddle with consummate ease.

"Now, hop down," he said as he stood beside her horse and offered her his hand.

Though she was sure she could have managed on her own, Alison put her hand in his and slid out of the saddle. The moment her feet hit the ground, her knees buckled and she stumbled against him.

"Oh, my . . ." she murmured, leaning against him gratefully.

While all the walking she did kept her in fairly good shape, riding Shadow had exercised an entirely different set of muscles, all of which seemed to have turned to jelly.

"Are you all right?" Frank asked, a hint of laughter in his voice as he steadied her with a hand at her waist.

"Just a little wobbly." She smiled up at him, and once again, awareness zinged through her. She wanted nothing more than to rest her head on his shoulder and stay right where she was. Instead, she slipped her hand free as she took a step away from him. "But I'll be fine once I walk around a bit."

"Can we pick out a tree now, Dad? Can we, *please?*" Joey asked.

"Why don't you put Shadow in the barn, loosen her girth and give her some feed first?" Then you can take a look at the trees out behind the trailer and choose the one you like best."

"What are you gonna do?" Jake demanded.

"I'm going to ride down and talk to Carlos and Benito. When I get back, we can eat the lunch your grandfather packed for us. After that, we'll chop down our tree and head back home." He paused, eyeing his son with amusement. "Unless you have any objections."

"No, sir."

"All right, then." As Jake and Joey led Shadow into the barn, Frank turned his attention back to Alison. "If you get cold or tired while I'm gone, go on in the trailer and make yourself at home."

"I will," she assured him, then stood back and watched admiringly as he swung into the saddle once again and set off at a brisk trot.

"A fine figure of a man, if I do say so myself," Bert said, coming to stand beside her.

Wondering if he realized he'd been voicing her sentiments exactly, Alison blushed. "He seems to be a very accomplished rider," she murmured, not quite meeting the old man's gaze.

"That he is, missy. That he is," he agreed. "But I imagine that's to be expected. His mamma used to say the same thing about me. 'Course, she wasn't talking about how I sat in the saddle...."

"Oh, Bert, you really are incorrigible," she chided, trying, unsuccessfully, not to laugh.

"I am, huh? Is that good or bad?"

"Bad. Very, very bad."

"Really?" he asked, sounding quite pleased with himself.

"Yes, really."

"Okay, Grandpa, we took care of Shadow. Can we *please* go look at the trees now?" Jake pleaded.

"Yes, we can go look at the trees now." Turning to Alison, Bert asked solicitously, "Would you like to go with us or would you rather wait in the trailer?"

"I'll go with you."

"Well, then, come right along."

Grinning approvingly, he offered her his arm, and Alison gladly looped hers through it as they started toward the stand of fir trees, rustling in the gentle breeze.

By the time Frank returned, they'd all agreed on a stately six-footer with unusually full branches and a nicely tapered shape that Bert thought would fit quite well near one of the living room windows. Upon inspection, Frank gave it his seal of approval, as well.

After a lunch of sandwiches, chips, homemade cookies and juice that they shared in the surprisingly tidy little trailer, Frank took an ax from one of his saddlebags and, with Bert and the boys shouting instructions and Alison laughing at their antics, made short work of chopping it down.

They arrived back at the ranch house late in the afternoon, and though they were all tired, they were also in high spirits. Frank suggested that they wait until the following evening to decorate the tree, but the twins insisted on doing it right away. When they went so far as to agree to help with the horses, he finally acquiesced.

Sent to the house to warm up, Alison put on a pot of coffee and made hot chocolate for the boys. Then, humming happily to herself, she filled several casserole dishes with an assortment of leftovers and popped them in the oven to warm. In another hour or so everyone would probably be hungry, and they'd be able to have a hot meal without a lot of hassle.

The day had turned out to be so much nicer than she'd ever imagined it would be. She'd had a good time with Frank and his family. And, much to her relief, they'd all made it back to the house safe and sound. She was going to be awfully sore tomorrow, but none of the rest of them seemed to be any the worse for wear. In fact, when she thought of everything that could have gone wrong and didn't, she was almost tempted to believe she'd finally left her bad luck behind. But then, her relationship with Frank and his family wasn't all that close. They were just friends, really. And nothing bad had ever happened to anyone she'd thought of as just a friend.

Frank had gotten out the tree stand, lights and several cardboard boxes of decorations yesterday afternoon, so they wasted no time getting started when he finally brought in the tree. Again with Bert and the boys issuing instructions, Frank managed to get the tree upright in the stand. The five of them spent the next thirty minutes unraveling several strands of multicolored lights, checking for burned-out bulbs as they did so. Then, with Alison's help, Frank looped them around the tree, working carefully from top to bottom.

They took a break after that to eat the leftovers Alison had heated up, quickly cleaned up the kitchen, then returned to the living room to finish decorating the tree. Claiming he was fading fast, Bert sat on the sofa, unwrapping the ornaments stored in one of the boxes and handing them, one at a time, to the twins while Frank and Alison worked out of another box.

At first, as they handled the ornaments Alison assumed Rebecca had collected over the years, they were all rather quiet. And, once again, Alison realized that she wasn't the only one who had sad memories associated with the season. From several things the twins had said, she had a feeling they hadn't had a tree last year. So the last time they'd unpacked the lovely ornaments stored in the boxes, Rebecca had been there with them.

As she hung a clothespin Rudolph on one of the branches, Alison also found herself thinking of the boxes of Christmas decorations she'd stuffed into a closet at home. She hadn't really planned to use them again. Yet she hadn't been able to give them away, either. Now she was glad that she hadn't. Instead of bringing back painful memories, decorating her own tree next year would remind her of the happy times she'd shared with Frank and his family on the Double B. And Christmas would no longer be such a sad season for her.

Little by little, everyone's earlier exuberance returned, and finally, much to the twins' dismay, the last of the ornaments had been hung. However, at the bottom of the box Frank and Alison had unpacked was another, smaller box. As Frank lifted it out and opened the lid, Jake and Joey came to stand on either side of him, bright smiles on their little faces.

"Our stockings." Joey sighed happily, taking his from the box and holding it up so Alison could see it.

"To hang by the fireplace," Jake added as he did likewise.

Each one was embroidered with an identical little blond, curly-haired angel standing under a sprig of mistletoe.

"Oh, they're just darling." Alison smiled with delight. "But then, they ought to be since they look just like you."

"Do you really think so, Ali?" Joey asked, beaming proudly.

"Oh, yes."

"Here's Dad's and Grandpa's." Jake took two more stockings from the box and showed them to Alison. Frank's had a jolly Santa embroidered on the front, while Bert's featured a fat Frosty the Snowman. "And Mom's, too," he added quietly, holding up a stocking with an equally jolly Mrs. Claus on the front.

"They're all lovely," Alison said around the sudden lump in her throat, then asked with a lightness she didn't really feel, "Did your mom make them?"

"Yes," Frank answered, taking Rebecca's stocking from Jake and wrapping it in a piece of tissue paper. "Let me get a hammer and some tacks so we can hang them on the mantel, okay?"

Still holding Rebecca's stocking, he walked out of the living room. When he returned a couple of minutes later, he had only the hammer and a box of tacks in his hand.

"All right, how do you want to hang your stockings?" he asked as he halted next to the fireplace.

Though made of adobe to suit the pueblo-style house, the fireplace also sported a narrow wooden mantel above the arched opening of the firebox.

"How about yours first, Dad? Then mine and Joey's and Grandpa's," Jake suggested. "But leave a space in the middle for Ali's." He turned to her, frowning slightly. "You *do* have a Christmas stocking, don't you?"

"Well, yes, but I . . . I forgot to bring it with me," she admitted.

"Oh." Jake's frown deepened as he looked a his father. "Do we have an extra one?"

"Yeah, Dad, do we?" Joey asked hopefully. "Because Ali *really* needs one."

"I don't think so," he admitted, eyeing her with obvious dismay as he shifted from one foot to the other.

"No problem," she hastened to assure him. "I'm sure I can get one in Vernon."

"That's right. You can," Frank agreed, shooting her a look of gratitude, then turning back to the mantel.

Apparently satisfied that she wouldn't be left out, the twins dug into the not-quite-empty box that had held their stockings.

"Look, here's the star for the top of the tree." Grinning, Joey held up a large, intricately-wrought, gold-and-silver star that glimmered with surprising warmth in the lamplight.

Alison had never seen anything quite so beautiful in her life. She had no doubt it would look absolutely stunning atop the tree. And instinctively she also knew that it had a very special significance for Frank and his family.

"Great-great grandma's star," Jake stated proudly, as if he'd read her mind. "Brought all the way from Ohio a long, long time ago. Can I *please* put it on the tree, Dad?"

"No, I want to do it," Joey said, clutching the star to his chest as he backed away from his brother.

"I'm the oldest, so I should be the one to do it," Jake insisted.

"But I'm the youngest, so *I* should," Joey retorted.

"Dad—" both boys cried in unison.

"Give it to me. Now," Frank said sternly, holding out his hand.

Apparently, the long day had finally caught up with the twins. Alison had never heard them argue over anything, but according to the clock on the mantel it was almost eight-thirty, and their eyelids were definitely beginning to droop. Trying not to smile, she glanced at Frank and saw that he was watching her, his eyes glinting with good humor.

"I think we ought to let Ali have the honor of putting the star on top of our tree this year," he said. "What about you, Dad?"

"Oh, I think so, too," Bert heartily agreed.

"How about you guys?" Though he spoke to his sons, he continued to hold her gaze.

"Okay."

"Yeah, okay."

"Want to step up here?" Frank asked, offering her his hand as he nodded toward the stool they'd taken turns using to reach the higher branches of the tree.

Ali. He'd called her *Ali,* she thought, stunned by how gently his deep, rich voice had wrapped around her name, making his usage of it sound so right as he drew her even more deeply into the heart of his family. She wanted to run to her room and hide. But all she seemed capable of doing was standing there, staring at him as if mesmerized by the kindness in his brilliant blue eyes.

"Come on, Ali," Joey urged, taking her hand and all but dragging her across the living room. "We want you to put the star on the tree."

"Yeah, we *really* do," Jake insisted, hopping from one foot to the other with renewed energy.

Giggling, Joey placed her hand in his father's. "There you go."

Oh, yes, there she went, she mused as she allowed Frank to help her onto the stool, then took the star from him without meeting his gaze. Straight down a road that could very well end in ruin if she wasn't careful.

Still holding on to Frank's hand for balance, she reached up and slipped the open base of the star over the tip of the topmost branch of the tree. Then she hopped off the stool and slid her hand free as Jake and Joey exclaimed over what a good job she'd done.

"All right, you two, off to bed," Bert ordered, putting an arm around the boys' shoulders and herding them toward the hallway. "As for you two..." He grinned rakishly and waggled his eyebrows. "Light a fire in the fireplace and relax for a while."

"Umm, I'd better go, too," Alison murmured, her face flushing as she backed away from Frank. The *last* thing she dared do was relax with him in front of a fire. But if he took her hand in his again, and drew her close, she wouldn't have the strength to resist him. "I...I had a wonderful time today. Thanks." Shoving her hands in the side pockets of her jeans, she spun on her heel and headed for the doorway.

"Ali?"

"Good night, Frank."

Ignoring the hurt and confusion she'd heard in his voice, she quickened her pace. By the time she closed her bedroom door, her heart was pounding. Why, she wasn't quite sure. He'd let her go without another word. But, oh, how she wished he hadn't, she thought, as she sat on her bed and switched on the lamp.

"Don't be silly," she chided softly, her sore muscles protesting as she pulled off first one boot, then the other.

She did *not* want Frank Bradford pursuing her. Not at all. She wanted to finish Rebecca's manuscript and go home. And she wasn't going to allow herself to be sidetracked again. Not as she had been today.

Nowhere was it written that she had to act as if she were a part of the Bradford family. If she tried, if she *really* tried, surely she could find a way to keep her distance without hurting anyone's feelings. And starting tomorrow, that was exactly what she intended to do. She *was*. Because walking away from Frank tonight had used up just about all the willpower she possessed.

Chapter Seven

"**I** bet Alison wouldn't mind giving you a hand with that if you asked her," Bert said as he crossed the kitchen and set his empty mug in the sink. It was late Thursday evening.

"Well, I'm not asking," Frank muttered, frowning as he eyed the patterns spread out on the table, then shuffled through the instruction sheets Mrs. Dunn had sent home with the twins on Tuesday.

Surely he ought to be able to assemble elf costumes for them in time for the Christmas program scheduled for December 20. He had almost two weeks. He knew how to use his mother's old sewing machine. Or at least he had several years ago. And how hard could it be to cut out a couple of little vests, two pairs of knickers and some curly-toed shoe covers, and stitch them together? Most of the rest of the things they needed—turtleneck shirts, matching tights and knit hats—he could buy at the store.

As far as he was concerned, he didn't need Alison's help. Considering she'd gone out of her way to keep her distance since Sunday night, it was just as well.

"What happened between you two the other night?"

"Nothing."

"I kinda gathered *that*," Bert retorted sarcastically.

"Look, Dad, she's here to finish Rebecca's book. Expecting anything else of her isn't really fair. She's been nice to the twins, and I appreciate that. She'd also made an effort to fit in around here, and that's been a help to all of us. But she doesn't seem to want to be quite as involved in our lives as she was over the weekend. And I honestly can't say I blame her."

He could also understand why she'd been so aloof lately. She'd lost everyone to whom she'd ever been close, and he knew how deeply that kind of loss could hurt. He hadn't had an easy time of it after his mother's death. And losing Rebecca had been totally devastating.

Had he been in Alison's position, he probably would have been inclined to keep to himself, too. A little bit of heartache went a long way, and she'd suffered more than her fair share. That she seemed to be shying away from a situation that could lead to even more didn't really surprise him.

"Seems to me she enjoyed being a part of the family," Bert said. "At least until I left the two of you alone in the living room. Are you *sure* you didn't say or do anything to upset her?"

"I didn't say or do anything at all after you left," he growled. "She didn't give me a chance. She took off like a scared rabbit."

He'd gone over the events of the past weekend more often than he liked to admit, trying to figure out where he'd gone wrong. But for the life of him, he didn't have a clue. She hadn't seemed to mind spending time alone with him on the ride up to the camp. She'd talked a bit about herself, and listened with sympathy as well as understanding to what he'd had to say. But then, that had been the only time they'd been together on their own.

Back at the house, she'd seemed more than happy to help with decorating the tree. Her good spirits had been contagious, and as a result, he'd found it relatively easy to focus on the present rather than dwell on the past. And she'd handled the business of the Christmas stockings in such a sensitive way that he'd found himself wanting to hug her.

In fact, up until the moment he'd slipped and called her Ali, she'd seemed to be having a wonderful time. After that, she'd looked almost afraid.

He wasn't sure why he'd used her nickname. Certainly not to upset her. He'd just felt so comfortable with her. And, thanks to Jake and Joey, he'd been thinking of her as Ali for days.

"So, you didn't put any moves on her, huh?" Bert prodded.

"No, I didn't."

Unless that's what you called holding on to her hand a little longer than absolutely necessary whenever he'd had the chance, he added silently. He'd definitely been guilty of *that* several times since Friday afternoon. But, as far as he was concerned, compared to what he'd *thought* about doing, that wasn't anything at all.

"Well, if you don't get on the stick, she's going to end up going back to New York, you know."

"Of course she's going back to New York. She has a life there, and I seriously doubt anything I say or do is going to convince her to give it up."

Actually, he had a feeling his "getting on the stick" would only end up causing her to work that much faster on the manuscript so she could get away from him even sooner than she'd planned. As it was, she'd already been putting in overtime since Monday, going back to Rebecca's office right after dinner and staying there until after midnight. He knew because he hadn't been able to fall asleep as long as she was just across the hall from him.

He'd wondered if she was really working, or simply using the manuscript as an excuse to avoid spending any time alone with him. He'd finally come to the conclusion that it was probably a combination of the two. He'd noticed that she headed for Rebecca's office whenever there was even a remote chance that they might end up alone together anytime day or night.

"Oh, I don't know about that," Bert retorted. "I've seen the way the two of you look at each other. Seems to me, if you stopped tiptoeing around her and let her know you wouldn't mind having her around on a permanent basis, she'd think twice about going back to the big city."

"Oh, yeah, I can just see her giving up everything to live on a ranch out in the middle of nowhere with me, my five-year-old sons and my slightly addlebrained old man."

"Hey, you might be surprised."

"I doubt that very much."

"Well, what could it hurt to let her know how you feel? You know the old saying—nothing ventured, nothing gained."

Frank had to admit that his father might be right. But, at the same time, he also knew that neither he nor Alison needed any more complications in their lives than they already had. Especially since he wasn't exactly sure how he felt about her.

Granted, he found her physically attractive. He'd known that almost from the first moment he'd seen her standing in the snow. And he was truly touched by the kindness she'd shown Bert and the boys. Even though she gave *him* a wide berth, she was still spending quite a bit of time with them.

He also found it hard to think ahead to the time when she'd be gone for good. He really liked having her on the

Double B. And, when he thought about it, he knew he wouldn't mind her being a permanent part of his family.

But he'd known her less than two weeks. Not that he didn't believe in love at first sight. He'd fallen in love with Rebecca the moment he'd laid eyes on her, hadn't he? But he was older now, and hopefully, wiser. And he couldn't think only of himself anymore. If he made a mistake where Alison was concerned, the two of them wouldn't be the only ones who'd end up paying for it.

Maybe he was just horny as hell, and since she was handy— But no, he'd already determined that wasn't the case. Over the past few months, he could have taken care of his physical needs on several occasions, but he simply hadn't been interested. Yet, whenever he was with Alison, he found himself wanting to pull her into his arms and make slow, sweet love to her.

Not have sex. Make *love*...

That's what really worried him. He was already finding it hard to imagine not having Alison around. What if he got even more involved with her, and she still chose to go back to New York when she was finished with the manuscript?

"You don't have anything to say to that?" Bert asked, obviously exasperated by his son's silence.

"What would you like me to say?"

"That you're not going to let Ali get away."

"You're assuming an awful lot, you know," Frank replied, eyeing his father steadily.

"Just putting two and two together and coming up with four." He crossed to the table and rested a hand on Frank's shoulder. "You know, I wouldn't have brought this up if I didn't have everybody's best interests at heart, including Alison's. We need her, and unless I'm sadly mistaken, she needs us, too. So, at least give some thought to... getting together with her."

"Believe me, I have been. And I will."

"Good enough." He gave Frank's shoulder a squeeze, then headed toward the hallway. "Well, I'm bushed. Guess I'll see you in the morning."

"Yeah, see you in the morning," Frank said, turning back to the instruction sheets without much enthusiasm.

For all his earlier bravado, he wasn't really sure where to begin. While he knew how to mend a rip, he was afraid stitching together something that actually resembled a vest and a pair of knickers might be beyond his limited capabilities. But the twins had been so excited about being chosen to play the parts of Santa's elves that he was determined not to let them down. One way or another, he'd have them outfitted according to Mrs. Dunn's specifications for the program on the twentieth.

He'd best make a list of what he'd have to buy at the store, he thought, jotting down items on a blank piece of paper as he read through the instructions yet again. Cotton fabric in red or green for the vest and knickers, matching felt, buttons, zippers and thread—

At the sound of footsteps in the hallway, he glanced at the clock on the wall above the refrigerator. Just past ten-thirty. A little early for Alison to be calling it a night, but maybe the long hours she'd been putting in over the past few days had finally caught up with her.

She walked through the doorway, head down, her attention on the sheaf of papers she held in her hands. Then, as if sensing his presence, she paused and glanced up at him. For several seconds, she stared at him wordlessly, her eyes wide with surprise. Apparently, she hadn't expected to come upon him there. And, if the look of dismay on her face was any indication, she wasn't exactly thrilled that she had. In fact, he had the distinct impression that she was seriously considering a hasty about-face.

That she didn't actually turn and run gave him a small measure of satisfaction. He didn't want her feeling that she had to avoid him at all cost. He wasn't about to force himself on her. Not in any way. He'd respected her decision to put some distance between them, and he'd continue to do so as long as that seemed to be what she wanted.

However, there was no reason why they couldn't spend a little time together, discussing business, now that the opportunity had presented itself, he decided.

"So, how's the manuscript coming along?" he asked with what he hoped she'd interpret as no more than casual interest.

"Umm, so far, so good," she murmured, a tinge of pink creeping up her cheeks as she lowered her gaze. "I should have the next chapter ready for you to read by the weekend."

He couldn't understand why she seemed so embarrassed. But then, he remembered the chapter she was working on was supposed to be the one in which Ben and Lydia had their first sexual encounter, and he knew exactly how she felt. That had been one of the major reasons why *he* hadn't been able to get past the fifty pages he'd written.

Rebecca had been known for her sensual love scenes. One reviewer had even suggested that her fans might consider donning "asbestos gloves" before delving into her last book. He also recalled how Rebecca had shut herself away for long hours at a stretch, several days in a row, when she was writing those scenes. She'd been cool and distant, too, as if all her emotion had to be channeled into what she was writing.

Maybe that was why Alison had been avoiding him. Not because she didn't want anything to do with him, but because she didn't want to be distracted.

"Are you pleased with what you've done so far?" he prodded curiously.

"Oh, yes, very pleased," she assured him as she glanced up again, then away, her face growing even redder.

She knew that *he* knew what she'd been working on, and that knowledge was definitely making her uncomfortable. Yet, to Frank's surprise, she didn't plead exhaustion and hurry into her room as he expected her to do. Instead, she edged a little closer to the table.

"I'm sure I will be, too," he replied.

"You are?"

"After the way you revised what I wrote, I have every confidence in your ability to complete Rebecca's manuscript to everyone's satisfaction."

He'd been amazed at how she'd softened his rather terse writing style with the addition of a word here or the elimination of a sentence there.

"I really appreciate your saying that."

Still, she stood her ground, eyeing the patterns spread out on the table, and Frank found himself wondering what she had to tell him. He could think of no other reason why she'd linger in the kitchen when she was so obviously ill at ease. And from the way she seemed to hesitate, he had a feeling that whatever it was, he wasn't going to like it.

"Are these the patterns for the twins' costumes?" she asked at last, fingering one of the stamped sheets of brownish tissue paper. She'd been at the dinner table the other night when the boys had first mentioned their parts in the program.

"Yes."

"Too bad they couldn't have been angels. You could have draped a white sheet over each of them and cut out a couple of pairs of cardboard wings."

"That would have been a lot easier," he agreed with a rueful chuckle. "As it is, I have to make two vests, two pairs of knickers and some felt shoe covers."

"Felt shoe covers?" She eyed him quizzically, a smile tugging at the corners of her mouth.

"To transform their sneakers into elf boots."

"Ah, I see." Her smile widened for a moment. "Do you have a sewing machine?"

"An old one that belonged to my mother."

"Do you know how to use it?"

"I did once." He shrugged as nonchalantly as he could. "I imagine I'll be able to figure it out again."

"You know, I wouldn't mind giving you a hand with the costumes," she said, not quite meeting his gaze.

"You wouldn't?" He stared at her in surprise. He hadn't intended to ask for her help, but if she was offering...

"I haven't done any sewing for a while, but I made most of my clothes when I was in college. Whipping up a couple of vests and two pairs of knickers shouldn't take me long at all."

Not when she already knew how to put pieces of fabric together so they came out looking like something somebody could actually *wear,* he thought.

"In that case, yes, I'd be delighted to have your help."

She studied the patterns again, then gestured toward the instruction sheets he'd laid out in front of him. "Why don't you give me a list of what I'll need, and I can buy the stuff while I'm in Santa Fe on Saturday."

She risked a quick glance at him, and Frank realized that was what she'd been working up to all along. She'd been planning on going to Santa Fe on Saturday, and though she'd been hesitant to do so, she'd felt obligated to tell him. He wasn't sure why. He'd already let her know that her weekends were her own and she was free to do whatever she wanted.

"Santa Fe, huh? I told you you'd be going stir-crazy around here sooner or later," he teased.

"I was afraid you'd think that. But really, I'm not," she protested. "I just want to do a little Christmas shopping and maybe some sightseeing."

"I should do some shopping, too." He paused, thinking of what his father had said earlier. *Nothing ventured, nothing gained.* Still, he hesitated. She'd made it clear that she didn't want to be alone with him. But they'd just be sharing a ride. Once they reached the city, they could each go their separate ways if that was what she wanted. "We could drive up there together," he suggested, then added in a matter-of-fact tone, "but I'll understand if you'd rather go alone."

As she met his gaze, Frank could sense her indecision. Yet he took heart when she didn't automatically say no.

"Were you planning to go to Santa Fe on Saturday?" she asked at last.

"Not really," he admitted with a grin. "But when you mentioned Christmas shopping, I realized that if I don't get started on mine, Santa's going to come up short again this year."

"Well, as long as you're not going out of your way..."

"Not at all."

"All right, then, I guess we might as well go together."

"We can make a day of it. Hit the mall first, then walk around the plaza. If you want..."

"That sounds fine to me." She smiled slightly, then turned away. "Well, good night."

"Good night," he called after her as she continued across the kitchen and into her room, then closed the door without a backward glance.

He knew better than to make too much of her relatively easy acquiescence. After all, she hadn't been exactly bursting with enthusiasm, he reminded himself as he folded the patterns and stuffed them back in the envelopes. But at least she'd ended up agreeing to spend some time with him, and he intended to make the most of it.

She'd seemed like a different person last weekend. Whether she'd been baking cookies with the twins or hanging ornaments on the tree, she'd honestly seemed to be enjoying herself. And being a part of his family had had a lot to do with that. Why, she hadn't even minded being alone with him while they were riding. She'd only shied away when Bert had all but thrown them together, and he couldn't blame her for that.

What he could do on Saturday was let her know that she had nothing to fear from him. He wasn't interested in rushing her into anything. He just wanted to be with her so he could do his damnedest to prove to her that the two of them, on their own as well as with the other members of his family, could have a good time together.

Because, unless *he* was sadly mistaken, having a good time was what she really needed right now.

For the life of her, Alison couldn't imagine what had come over her Thursday night. She'd known the moment she set foot in the kitchen and saw Frank sitting at the table that she'd be wise to keep right on walking. Still, not wanting to seem rude, she'd made the mistake of stopping to exchange what she'd meant to be only a few words with him. Of course, one thing had led to another, as "things" tended to do. Before she knew it, she'd not only offered to help him with the twins' elf costumes, but agreed to go to Santa Fe with him.

Now, sitting beside him in his truck early Saturday morning as he guided the vehicle down the drive, she admitted for the umpteenth time that she really did need her head examined.

Once she'd put her mind to it, she hadn't found it all that hard to avoid him. In fact, she'd gotten the feeling that he'd not only been aware of what she was doing, but had been willing to go along with what she'd seemed to want.

But then, her mind had begun to wander in the worst possible way.

One moment, she'd been deeply involved in Ben's sweetly sensual seduction of Lydia, and the next moment, she'd found herself thinking of Frank and the way he'd looked at her Sunday night when Bert had left them alone. She'd known better than to indulge in such wayward thoughts. Yet she hadn't been able to stop herself from doing so.

Quitting work earlier than usual Thursday evening had seemed like her only sanity-saving alternative. She'd gotten nothing done in the three hours she'd been in Rebecca's office after dinner. The increasing sense of restlessness she'd been fighting all week had her ready to crawl out of her skin. She'd realized that she had to get away for a day or two, and as she'd headed down the darkened hallway, Santa Fe had seemed like as good a place as any for her to go.

She'd known that she'd have to tell Frank about her plans. While she didn't feel obligated to apprise him of her whereabouts, she was a firm believer in common courtesy. And common courtesy dictated that she do so—Saturday morning, preferably as she was on her way out the door.

She'd been in the midst of calling herself a coward when she'd come upon him sitting at the kitchen table. And, unfortunately, it had been all downhill from there.

When she'd seen the patterns spread out on the table in front of him, she'd known what he was doing, and her heart had gone out to him. He'd seemed so determined to make the twins' costumes himself, yet he'd obviously been at a loss as to where to begin. And she simply hadn't been hard-hearted enough to let him muddle along on his own. Not when she knew she could whip up the vests and knickers they needed in a tenth of the time it would take him to do it.

So she'd offered to help him with the costumes. And then, not knowing when to leave well enough alone, she'd casually mentioned her plans to go to Santa Fe.

Though she hated to admit it, somewhere in the back of her mind she'd known that he'd probably offer to go with her. Yet as soon as the opportunity presented itself, she'd mentioned her trip. And though she'd tried to tell herself that she wasn't thrilled with the idea of their going together, she hadn't put up much resistance, either.

Which meant that she was back to square one where Frank Bradford was concerned, she mused, as they came to a stop at the intersection of the ranch road and Highway 3. She might want to believe that she was determined to stay away from him. But here she was, about to spend the day with him, and, much to her dismay, looking forward to it more than she had any right to.

"You've been awfully quiet since we left the house," Frank said, turning to face her.

"Just thinking about what I want to get at the mall," she replied, not quite meeting his searching gaze.

She didn't like lying to him, but how could she admit all she'd really had on her mind since they'd set off down the drive was *him?* She didn't want him getting the wrong idea about why she'd agreed to go to Santa Fe with him. She might be looking forward to spending the day with him, but she'd really rather he didn't know it.

"You didn't make a list?" he asked as he pulled onto the highway.

Since there was no telling when either one of them would have a chance to make another trip to the city, he'd recommended that she do so just to be sure she didn't forget anything she thought she might need over the next few weeks.

"Well, yes. But I left it on the dresser."

"Good move." He glanced at her again, a teasing grin tugging at the corners of his mouth.

"Yeah, wasn't it, though?" She offered him a wry smile. "What about you? Did you remember to bring the list of stuff we need for the twins' costumes?"

"Right here." His eyes on the road once again, he patted the pocket of his black leather bomber jacket.

She murmured approvingly, then turned to gaze out the window. And found herself thinking, as she had earlier when she'd first seen him standing at the kitchen counter, how different he looked today.

He'd dressed in fashionably pleated black wool pants, a white shirt with black pinstripes, a burgundy crew-neck sweater and black boots instead of the faded jeans, worn work shirt and battered brown boots he usually wore. And, in addition to the leather jacket, he'd added a stylish black Stetson with a feather band circling the base of the crown.

Anyone seeing him for the first time would automatically assume he was a prosperous rancher. And, of course, they'd be right.

As for her... She'd found him awfully appealing in jeans and a work shirt. But now she understood just how irresistibly attractive he could be when he really put his mind to it. Not that she thought he'd dressed up to impress her. They were going to the city, after all, and he certainly wasn't any country bumpkin. Of course he'd dress appropriately, she reasoned.

Just as she had.

Her tailored gray wool pants, creamy cashmere turtleneck sweater and calf-length black wool coat would take her through the day and, thankfully, into the evening, as well. She'd assumed they'd probably return late in the afternoon. But as they were on their way out the door, she'd heard Frank tell his father not to expect them for dinner, adding that they probably wouldn't get back to the ranch until late that night.

Bert hadn't seemed to mind at all. In fact, he'd nodded approvingly, a teasing glint in his eyes as he'd clapped his son on the back and told him to have a good time. Even the twins had seemed quite happy to see them go. Alison had thought they'd beg to come along, but they'd appeared to be perfectly content to stay at home with their grandfather.

And though she didn't like to admit it, Alison was glad. She'd told herself that she'd prefer to have their company. But, to be honest, she hadn't been all that disappointed that Bert and the boys had opted to spend the day on the Double B. No matter how she tried to convince herself otherwise, she liked the idea of having some time alone with Frank. Considering all they were really doing was sharing a ride to Santa Fe, what could possibly be wrong with that?

Nothing at all, she assured herself, trying, unsuccessfully, to ignore the little niggle of guilt that insisted on lingering in the back of her mind. Unfortunately, she could only fool herself some of the time.

"Does your father have anything special planned for today?" she asked, making a conscious effort to curb her wandering thoughts.

"He and the boys are taking Molly to the vet in Vernon. She's due for her annual checkup. And I imagine they'll stop at Ruby's Café for lunch."

"How far is Vernon from the ranch?"

"About twenty miles south on Highway 3. Instead of turning right as we did this morning, you turn left off the ranch road." He glanced at her questioningly. "You haven't been there yet, have you?"

"No, not yet. But I'll probably ride in with Bert one day next week. I have a couple of things that need to go to the dry cleaners, and he mentioned that there's one on Main Street."

"Along with a couple of grocery stores, a five-and-dime, a hardware store, feed store, a pharmacy and three or four other shops selling clothes and shoes. Besides Ruby's, there's also a steak house and a burger shack. And there's a grade school as well as a high school. Also, about a year ago, a couple of doctors opened a minor emergency clinic there. That's been especially helpful since the nearest hospital is in Santa Fe."

"Sounds like Vernon's a pretty nice place," she said with some surprise. She'd assumed the town had much less to offer than it actually did.

"For a small town, it is. But it's also twenty miles away," he added, reminding her once again of how isolated the Double B really was.

As she gazed out at the acres and acres of gently rolling ranch land, bounded by the rugged, snow-capped mountains curving along the northern horizon from east to west, she found herself wondering what it would be like to live there permanently. Getting to the nearest town, and a small town at that, would mean a twenty-mile drive, one way, while Santa Fe, the nearest big city, was over seventy miles away. And, though she'd noticed a couple of narrow roads veering off the highway, she hadn't seen any other houses since they'd left the ranch. Granted, they had passed a few cars, but not many.

Would she miss New York after a while? She couldn't say that she had anytime during the past two weeks. She'd honestly enjoyed the peace and quiet as well as the overwhelming sense of security she had on the Double B. But how would she feel after two months or two years? Would she end up climbing the walls as Frank seemed to think she would?

She *had* been feeling restless the past few days, but she knew that had much less to do with where she'd been than the company she'd been keeping. Or rather, *hadn't* been keeping. Of course, if the Double B were her home, then Frank would be her husband, and she wouldn't have to avoid—

"How close are your nearest neighbors?" she asked, aware that her thoughts were once again taking a dangerous turn.

"The Camdens are about fifteen miles to the east of us on the ranch road. They're an older couple, friends of my father's. Their youngest son has been working the ranch for them, but he and his wife live in Vernon, where she teaches at the high school. The Ramirez family lives about the same distance north of us. They're in their mid-forties, and have four kids. Their oldest son, Carlos, has been working for me for about a year, earning money for college."

"Do you see them very often?"

"Not as often as I'd like. We run into each other in Vernon occasionally, and we usually get together once or twice during the summer for a barbecue."

Out here, there would be no running next door to share a cup of coffee and some idle chatter with a friend, Alison mused. Visiting a neighbor would take almost as much time and energy as a trip to town. But then, how often had she gone downstairs to see the Albertsons or the Morgans? She thought of them as friends, but she'd hadn't seen them much lately. Yet she couldn't say she'd missed having their companionship. With Frank and his father and the boys to care for, she'd—

"What's it like living in New York City?" Frank asked, his deep voice drawing her out of her reverie.

"Compared to the Double B, it's downright frenetic," she said, smiling as she thought of the noise and the crowds of people and the constant activity going on all around.

"And you love it, don't you?"

"I did, but . . ." She hesitated, wanting to elaborate. Yet she wasn't exactly sure how. She'd been perfectly content with her life in the big city. Until she'd come to the Double B.

"But what?" he prodded gently, meeting her gaze for a moment.

"I can't honestly say I'd rather be there right now," she admitted with unwonted candor, then blushed when she realized what she'd said. Mentally chastising herself, she turned to look out the window again.

Considering the way her mind had wandered since they'd left the ranch, she shouldn't be surprised that she'd finally spoken her thoughts aloud. But she'd never been one to run off at the mouth. The fact that she'd suddenly done so with Frank disturbed her greatly.

"I'm really glad to hear that," he said, obviously gratified by her simple statement.

"Oh, well..." She shrugged, then waved her hand dismissively as she added lightly, "By mid-January, I'll probably be more than happy to go back."

She seriously doubted that would be true. But given the circumstances, what else could she say? She had no intention of leading him on. And allowing him to think there was a chance she'd ever be a permanent part of his life would be just as mendacious.

After several moments of silence, Alison risked another glance at him. He eyed her narrowly, making no effort to hide his skepticism.

He must think she was nuttier than a fruitcake. Not only had she made a point of letting him know how much she liked living on the Double B, but she'd just finished telling him she didn't particularly miss New York City, either. Then she'd turned around and blithely insisted that she'd be ready to go home when the time came.

She waited for him to question her obvious equivocation, wondering what kind of lie she'd have to tell to put him off. Instead, he turned his attention back to the road, and after a few moments, asked in a casual tone, "Do you live in Manhattan?"

Feeling as if she were on safe ground again, Alison told him about her third-floor apartment in the elegant old brownstone on the Upper West Side. Aware that he was listening attentively, she went on to describe the neighborhood, explaining that everything she needed, from corner grocery to deli to French bakery, as well as a myriad other small shops and stores, was located within a five-block radius of her building.

"And you walk everywhere?" he asked with astonishment.

"Unless the weather's bad. Then I take the bus."

"You're not afraid to go off alone like that?"

"I know my way around the city, I never carry a purse or wear expensive jewelry, and I usually dress as casually as I can so I won't attract any attention. To be honest, I was probably in more danger of freezing to death out on the ranch road my first night in New Mexico than I've ever been of squaring off with a mugger in New York City."

"Well, making the drive from Santa Fe to the Double B in the middle of a snowstorm wasn't the smartest thing to do," he muttered.

"I realize that now," she admitted with a laugh. "I had no idea that once I got a little ways from the city, there would be nothing around for miles. But I certainly know now. And I'll always be grateful that you came to my rescue."

"Couldn't risk letting anything happen to you. Not after Orson swore you were the best book doctor in the business," he teased.

"And you *had* paid my airfare, after all," she added with a wry smile.

"Yeah, I wanted to be sure I got my money's worth." He glanced at her, his eyes twinkling. "Which reminds me... have you finished chapter 17 yet?"

"Umm, yes, I finished it yesterday afternoon. But I wanted to read over it one more time before I gave it to you," she hedged, pretending a sudden, intense interest in the scenery outside her window.

She hadn't really wanted to talk about Rebecca's manuscript today. That was one of the reasons why she'd waited to give him the chapter to read. But not the major reason, she reminded herself. While she'd had no qualms at all about the content or the quality of what she'd written, for some reason she couldn't quite define, she hadn't wanted Frank reading those sweetly sensual, yet sexual, love scenes right before they went off alone together.

"Did you end up having a problem with it?" he prodded, seemingly unwilling to let the subject drop.

"Not at all."

"I was just curious."

As she had Thursday night, she knew that he knew what she'd had to include in chapter 17. Unfortunately, unlike her, he didn't appear to be the least bit uncomfortable talking about it. But then, why should he be? He'd read his wife's books, and although *she* was finishing *Hunter's Edge*, she was supposed to be doing so as Rebecca would have. That's why she was there. And, of course, he'd want to know how she was progressing.

"I'll give you the chapter pages when we get back to the ranch," she offered quietly, suddenly feeling like a fool.

"No rush," he assured her. "We won't be getting back until late, so I probably won't get around to reading them until sometime tomorrow, anyway."

"Sounds like you have a lot planned for today," she said, welcoming the chance for another change of subject.

"Thought we might as well make the most of our day away. But we can head back whenever you're ready," he offered generously. "Just say the word."

"Oh, no, I'm not in any hurry. I'd like to see and do as much as possible because I probably won't have an opportunity to come back again." She gestured toward the houses, most of them pueblo-style adobes, that had begun to appear with increasing frequency since they'd turned onto the interstate highway. "Looks like we're getting close."

"We should be at the mall in about fifteen or twenty minutes." He glanced at her and grinned. "Last chance to make a list."

"You and your lists." She shook her head in exasperation.

"You'll thank me when we get home and you realize you won't have to make this drive again for a while because you actually remembered everything you absolutely *had* to have."

"Oh, all right."

Smiling in spite of herself, Alison opened her purse, pulled out a small notebook and pen, and tried to recall all the things she'd originally planned to get while she was in Santa Fe. As she did so, the worries and fears that had lingered at the back of her mind since they'd left the ranch slowly began to recede. Much to her surprise, her mood lightened considerably, and finally she allowed herself to look forward to the day ahead.

She'd always loved to go Christmas shopping, especially with a good friend. The past few years, she hadn't had the heart for it. But today... Today, she could see no reason why she couldn't have a good time. Nor could she see any reason why she couldn't enjoy the company of the man sitting beside her.

She thought she could honestly say that over the past couple of weeks they'd become friends. *Just* friends, of course, but friends, all the same. And, as long as she kept that fact in mind, what could it hurt to relish whatever time they had together?

No harm at all, she told herself. No harm at all...

Chapter Eight

After parking on the mall lot, Frank and Alison went to the fabric store together. Frank had gone through the twins' closet yesterday afternoon and found that each boy already had a red-and-white striped turtleneck shirt. Alison had then suggested that they use green fabric and felt for the vests, knickers and shoe covers, and buy red tights and red knit caps to complete their costumes. Frank had readily agreed.

They found the fabric and the felt they needed without any trouble. Then, as they'd decided earlier, they went their separate ways, agreeing to meet in a couple of hours at the mall entrance closest to where they'd parked.

Since she had to go to the department store for a few things on her list, Alison offered to get the tights and knit caps while she was there. But first, as Frank headed for the toy store, she stopped in the card shop.

She'd had her mail forwarded to the ranch, and along with the usual assortment of bills and a couple of requests

for her help with a manuscript, she'd already received quite
a few Christmas cards. Since she hadn't sent cards herself
for several years, she'd been surprised at how many friends,
acquaintances and business associates still took the time to
remember her. And she'd decided that the time had come
for her to let everyone know how much she appreciated their
thoughtfulness by returning the favor.

She bought three boxes of cards along with some wrapping paper, ribbon and bows. Then, humming along to the
strains of ''White Christmas'' drifting through the mall, she
walked the short distance to the department store.

She found two pairs of red tights and identical red knit
caps in the children's department, paid for them and went
on to the men's department. She wanted to get Christmas
gifts for Frank and his father, just a couple of things she
knew they could use. She didn't want to embarrass them by
giving them anything too expensive. Or, in Frank's case, too
personal. So, after much thought, she settled on pile-lined
work gloves and navy-blue plaid wool mufflers for both of
them.

Finally, sure that Frank had finished at the toy store, she
reentered the mall and, weaving through the growing, yet
friendly, crowd of shoppers, made her way there.

Jake and Joey had spent most of yesterday afternoon sitting on the floor in Rebecca's office, pouring over a toy
catalog that had come in the mail. Alison had pretended to
be busy working, but she'd actually been eavesdropping,
making a note whenever they showed special interest in one
thing or another. Last night, alone in her room, she'd
browsed through the catalog herself and decided which of
the toys they'd mentioned Frank probably wouldn't mind
their having.

She'd considered talking to him about it, but she'd had a
feeling he wouldn't approve of her spending a lot of money
on his sons. And she'd wanted to get them something really

special that they'd be able to enjoy long after she'd gone back to New York.

Luckily, the store still had two of the radio-controlled, futuristic-looking race cars, as well as a finely detailed pirate ship, in stock. And according to the clerk at the checkout counter, the tall man in the black leather jacket and black hat hadn't bought anything similar when he'd been in about an hour earlier.

Weighted down with shopping bags, yet feeling quite satisfied with herself and her purchases, Alison wandered slowly back to their meeting place. Seeing that Frank wasn't there, she found a place to sit and went over the list she'd made one more time, assuring herself that she'd remembered everything she'd wanted to get at the mall.

She'd forgotten how much fun it could be to go out and buy gifts for people you cared about. She'd really had only Orson and his wife the past few years, and she hadn't been able to rouse herself to do more than have a case of their favorite wine and a huge poinsettia sent to them. This year, however, she wanted to get them something special, maybe a unique piece of pottery, a pen-and-ink drawing or a small painting at one of the art galleries near the plaza. Not only had Orson and Deborah stood by her through the worst time of her life, but if Orson hadn't conned her into coming to the Double B—

"I can't believe you finished before me," Frank muttered, sitting down beside her on the bench. He was even more loaded down with shopping bags than she was. "You must have raced from one end of this place to the other."

"Not really. I'm just organized." She offered him a smug smile as she waved her list at him, then stuffed it in her purse before he could get a good look at it.

"So, you're ready to go, then?" Scooting a little closer to her, he eyed her packages, making no effort to hide his curiosity.

"All ready. And no snooping," she warned as she grabbed her shopping bags and started toward the door.

They drove the short distance to the historic downtown area, parked in a lot near the convention center and walked to the plaza. For Alison, it was love at first sight. She was enchanted by the weathered adobe buildings, some nearly two hundred years old, that crowded along the narrow, winding city streets. Most now housed art galleries, clothing boutiques, bookstores, gourmet shops, or jewelers, as well as a wide variety of restaurants. There were also several museums, a library, a movie theater and, right on the plaza, a five-and-ten that, amazingly enough, didn't look the least bit out of place.

At Frank's suggestion, they had lunch at a little Mexican restaurant favored by the locals. Then they wandered up one street and down another, stopping at a gallery here or a boutique there.

At one store, Alison bought an exquisite metal sculpture of an Indian shaman decorated with bits of fabric, beads and feathers for Orson and his wife, knowing it would appeal to the Hydes' eclectic tastes. And at another, she splurged on a calf-length, crushed velvet, accordion-pleated emerald-green skirt, with a white silk shirt and burgundy-and-green tapestry vest to wear on Christmas Day. A pair of silver earrings—three finely wrought feathers dangling from a half moon—caught her eye, as well. But she managed to resist the temptation to indulge herself any more than she already had.

However, she did buy the sleek leather belt with the elegantly styled, hand-crafted silver buckle Frank had spent several minutes admiring. She hadn't intended to get him anything quite so extravagant, but when he wandered off to look at the boots displayed at the back of the store, she handed the clerk her credit card and asked him to wrap it up for her without a moment's hesitation.

Being with Frank and his family over the past couple of weeks had gone a long way toward restoring her joy in the Christmas season, and she wanted him to know how much his kindness and consideration had meant to her. The belt would be her way of showing her appreciation. She'd wait and give it to him right before she left, she decided. As a thank-you for allowing her to be a part of his family at a time when she needed, more than anything, to *belong*.

After a last stop at a little candy store to buy gummy bears for Jake and Joey and butterscotch drops for Bert, as well as a gingerbread house baking kit that Alison couldn't resist, she and Frank walked back to his truck. It was after five by then, and twilight was falling. All too soon, their lovely day would fade completely into what promised to be a clear, cold night, and they'd be on their way back to the ranch.

"Tired?" Frank asked as he unlocked the door.

"Not really," she admitted after a moment's thought. Despite all they'd done already, she felt oddly exhilarated.

"Feel like doing a little more walking?" He stowed her packages, then glanced at her, a questioning look in his eyes.

"Oh, yes," she agreed eagerly. Then, just in case he'd had enough, she added, "If you do."

"I thought we'd go up to Canyon Road," he said as they made their way back to the plaza. "They'll be lighting the *farolitos* and I want you to see them, but it's best done on foot."

"*Farolitos?*"

As they walked along one side of the plaza, he gestured toward the small brown bags lining the sidewalks running through the little park in the center. "Each bag holds a candle anchored in a couple of inches of sand. At night, as part of the holiday tradition here, the candles are lighted." As he explained, a man moved from one bag to another with a glowing taper. "Those are *farolitos,* too," Frank added, nodding toward the rows of lights outlining the tops of many of the buildings. "However, those bags are made of plastic and little light bulbs are used instead of candles."

"They really are lovely," she murmured, gazing up at the glowing lights appreciatively.

"Wait until you see Canyon Road," he said, taking her hand in his as they turned onto a quiet side street.

"I'm looking forward to it." Weaving her fingers through his as if it were the most natural thing on earth she could do, Alison took a deep breath, savoring the tangy scent of wood smoke that clung to the cold air.

She was having the most wonderful time, and she knew she had Frank to thank for it. She'd have enjoyed walking the streets of Santa Fe on her own. But not nearly as much as she had with him. All afternoon he'd pointed out places of interest, saying they could return here or there another day when they had more time. And, though she knew in her heart that they probably wouldn't, she'd allowed herself to believe that anything was possible. Just as she was doing now, walking along beside him, her hand clasped warmly in his.

The *farolitos* along Canyon Road really were something to see. Nearly one hundred galleries, shops and restaurants lined the narrow road. And most of the owners had decorated their sidewalks, walls or rooftops with the little flickering lights.

"You're right. It's just beautiful," she said, making no effort to hide her awe as they paused at the bottom of the road. "Thanks for bringing me here."

"I thought you'd like it."

Letting go of her hand, he put his arm around her shoulder, and without hesitation, Alison slipped her arm around his waist. He *was* a friend, after all. Just like Orson. And Orson sometimes put his arm around her, too, she justified.

"It's kind of quiet tonight," he continued. "But on Christmas Eve the road is usually jammed with people."

"I think I like it better this way."

"Yeah, me too," Frank agreed, his voice husky as he hugged her close for just an instant.

They walked about halfway up the road, then retraced their steps back to the plaza. There they opted to have dinner at a classy old café that, to Alison's delight, featured several of her favorite Greek dishes.

As they sat side by side in a booth near the front window, Frank told her a little more about the city and surrounding area. Once again, Alison found herself wishing she could stay longer than she'd originally planned. In fact, from the way Frank talked, she had the strangest feeling he was tempting her to do just that.

According to him, the skiing was great in January and February, the desert absolutely stunning when it bloomed early in the spring, the Santa Fe opera a real treat, and the Indian market days in August an experience not to be missed.

But she wasn't going to be there for any of it. She *couldn't* be. She had a life of her own in New York City—a solitary life, but a good one, all the same. One she had to go back to if she really cared about Frank and his family.

They lingered over coffee and chocolate cream pie, but finally they seemed to have no choice but to head back to the ranch. They drove most of the way without saying much, each lost in thought. All too soon, it seemed, they were pulling up in front of the house.

"Did you have fun?" Frank asked as they carried the last of their packages into the kitchen.

According to the clock on the wall, it was almost midnight, and except for the light above the sink that Bert had left on for them, the house was dark, and very quiet.

"Oh, yes, I had a lot of fun." As Frank locked the door, Alison set her bags on the table and shrugged out of her coat. "Thanks for a wonderful day."

"You're very welcome." He tossed his hat on the table and hung his jacket over the back of a chair. "Sure you remembered everything?" he asked with a teasing grin, nodding toward her pile of packages.

"Everything I had on my *list*," she retorted.

"What about a Christmas stocking?"

"Oh, no—" She clapped a hand to her forehead. "The twins are going to have a fit. I promised I'd get one as soon as I had a chance. They must have reminded me about it half a dozen times yesterday, and I had it on my original list, but I completely—"

"Forgot?" he supplied, his amusement more than evident.

"Yes," she muttered with disgust.

"Not to worry." Looking much too pleased with himself for her liking, he pulled a long, narrow box out of one of his bags and offered it to her.

"What's this?" she asked suspiciously.

"Open it and see."

Frowning, she slid off the red ribbon tied around the box and lifted the lid. "Oh, Frank, it's beautiful," she murmured, gazing at the Christmas stocking nestled in a froth of tissue paper.

Embroidered on the front was an old-fashioned Christmas scene. A woman wearing a long Victorian gown stood on a stool, setting a star atop a decorated tree while a man, four small children and a dog looked on. Across the top, against a background of white satin, *Ali* had been stenciled in dark green script that matched the velvet backing.

Blinking back a sudden rush of tears, Alison ran her fingers over the intricately detailed design. "You shouldn't have," she said, knowing the stocking must have cost a fortune. Then, smiling up at him, she added softly, "But I'm so glad you did." She would treasure it always. Always...

"So am I." Reaching out, he touched her cheek with the tip of his finger, catching the single tear that had somehow managed to slip from the corner of her eye. Then he turned and crossed to the counter. "Come on. Let's go hang it by the fireplace," he suggested as he opened a drawer and took out the hammer and box of tacks he'd used Sunday night.

Wordlessly, Alison followed him out of the kitchen and down the dark hallway. She wanted to tell him so many things. But she was afraid that if she tried to express her gratitude, she'd reveal the other, wholly inappropriate feelings he'd somehow managed to stir in her all-too-lonely heart.

Just inside the living room doorway, he flipped the wall switch, turning on the lights on the Christmas tree. Glancing at her, he smiled, then grabbed her by the hand and led her across the room. He took a tack from the box, hammered it into the mantel in the place the twins had insisted they leave for her, then set the hammer and box aside.

"Do you want to do the honors, or should I?" he asked.

"You."

He took the stocking from her, fit the loop over the tack, then shifted it a bit until the stocking hung just so.

"Perfect," he pronounced, his smile widening as he studied his handiwork.

"Absolutely," she agreed, her voice barely above a whisper, her eyes on him rather than the stocking.

"Sure you like it?" Turning, he took the empty box from her and tossed it on the sofa.

"I love it." Smiling, she reached up and rested a hand against his cheek. "You know, Frank Bradford, you really are a very nice man."

"Why, thank you, ma'am," he drawled, a teasing glint in his eyes.

"No, seriously—" she began.

"Yeah, seriously," he interrupted quietly, catching her hand in his as she started to draw away.

And before she quite realized what he had in mind, he bent his head and ever so tentatively brushed his lips against hers. Instinctively, she sighed and closed her eyes, and as if that were all the assent he needed, he put his arms around her, pulled her hard against him and kissed her with a sudden hunger that sent desire coursing through her hot and fast.

Whimpering softly, she wrapped her arms around his neck and opened her mouth for him, welcoming the sensually possessive thrust of his tongue against hers. Somewhere in the back of her mind, she knew she should push him away. But she simply couldn't make herself do it. She'd forgotten how good it felt to be held by a man, to be kissed by him . . . and caressed. . . .

As if he'd read her mind, he slid his hands up her rib cage until his fingers brushed the sides of her breasts. Then, for what couldn't have been more than one long, soul-searing moment, he rubbed his thumbs over her already taut, tingling nipples, and she shuddered with a wanting so intense she could hardly keep from crying out.

"Ali?" Her name a whisper on his lips, he raised his head, a questioning look in his eyes.

Gazing up at him, Alison knew that all she had to do was say the word, and he wouldn't stop again until they'd finished what they'd started. She was tempted, so very, very tempted. A soft word, a smile, a simple nod of her head, and—

"I . . . I don't think this is a good idea," she murmured, bracing her hands against his chest.

"I got just the opposite impression a few moments ago." He hesitated, a frown creasing his forehead as he stared at her with obvious confusion. "Tell me something. Are you afraid of me? Because I'd never do anything to hurt you, Ali. Never."

"Of course not," she hastened to assure him, then put the lie to her words by trying, unsuccessfully, to slip out of his embrace.

She was afraid, all right. Afraid *for* him. But how could she tell him that? He'd think she was certifiable.

"Then why are you running away from me again?" he demanded in a bewildered tone of voice.

"I'm not." Tipping her chin up, she eyed him steadily, and added in the haughtiest tone of voice she could dredge up, "I'm just not interested in having an affair."

"Well, that's good, because I'm not interested in having an affair, either," he retorted, his gaze equally unwavering.

Somehow Alison had known that all along. He wasn't the kind of man who'd settle for anything less than happily ever after. But actually hearing him say it... She wanted to cry out with joy. Yet, at the same time, she wanted to weep. She'd stopped believing in happily ever after years ago, and she'd done so with good reason. Still—

"But what else *could* we have?" she asked, hating the way her voice quavered.

"Whatever we want. But only if you'll give us a chance."

His sincerity tore at her heart. Yet she couldn't let herself hope. "Please, Frank, I just can't—"

"Can't what? Give in to what's been building up between us since we first laid eyes on each other down on the ranch road in the middle of a snowstorm? *Something* is going on between us, Alison, and I think we owe it to ourselves to find out exactly what it is."

"We just haven't... been with anyone for a while. Or, at least, I haven't," she muttered, ducking her head.

She was grasping at straws, and she knew it. But at this point she was willing to say just about anything to put him off. She cared for Frank, truly cared for him in a way she'd vowed she would never care for anyone again.

But she'd lost everyone she'd ever really loved. She couldn't bear to lose him, too. And if he, or anyone in his family, came to any harm, because of her—

"I haven't, either. But then, until now, I haven't wanted to be," he growled, grasping her chin in his hand and tilting her face up, forcing her to meet his gaze. "And I'm not the only one who's wanting here, am I?"

She wished she could tell him he was wrong, but that would be a lie, and he'd know it. She'd responded to him with an ardor she couldn't deny without demeaning him. And he deserved much better than that from her.

"No, you're not," she whispered, resting her cheek against his chest and savoring the delicious sense of security she felt in his arms.

Now, if only she could believe that he, too, would be safe...

Maybe, just maybe, he would be, she thought, as he held her close and murmured her name, his breath warm against the nape of her neck. Maybe she no longer had any reason to be so superstitious. Maybe her luck had changed, and she could finally care for someone without somehow putting him in danger.

For so long now, she'd been terrified of allowing herself to get close to anyone. But what if she no longer had any reason to be? More important, what if she was actually *meant* to be with Frank and his family all along? What if all the anguish she'd endured had been necessary so that she could finally find true and lasting happiness here with them?

Of all the places in the world she'd ever imagined she would end up, she'd have to say a sheep ranch in New Mexico was among the last. Yet here she was, standing in the arms of a man with whom she could easily spend the rest of her life. All things considered, *that* had to be fate, if anything was. They certainly hadn't sought each other out. They'd simply come together through a series of unusual circumstances. And now...

As he'd said, didn't she owe it to herself to at least be open to the possibility that something wonderful could come of it?

"So, does that mean you'll give us a chance?" he asked, putting his hands on her shoulders and taking a step back.

Meeting his gaze, she nodded her head. "But I *am* afraid," she admitted. "Not of you, but of... of..."

Believing I'm not bad luck anymore and being wrong, she thought.

"Hey, I'm kind of scared, too." Smiling ruefully, he smoothed a hand over her hair. "I haven't courted anyone in quite a while, and I want to do it right. What do you say we just take it slow and easy, and see what happens?"

"All right," she agreed, touched by his unwonted sense of gallantry.

"If you want me to back off, just say so."

"As long as you promise to do the same," she replied only half-teasingly. She knew they'd be better off not rushing into anything, but suddenly found herself wanting to fulfill the promise of tomorrow *tonight.*

"Somehow I don't think I'm going to have to worry about that."

"Oh, you might be surprised, Mr. Bradford," she retorted with a lightheartedness she hadn't felt in years.

"I'll be looking forward to it, Ms. Kent." He bent his head and kissed her long and hard, as if sealing a pact. Then he set her away from him with a muffled groan." If we're going to take it slow and easy, I think maybe I'd better see you to your room and say good night."

"I think so, too," she agreed somewhat breathlessly, her pulse pounding once again.

Slipping his arm around her shoulder, he walked back to the kitchen with her, then helped her gather up her packages. At the door to her room, he kissed her cheek and, as good as his word, said good night.

When she was finally alone, Alison sagged down on the side of her bed and waited to be overwhelmed by remorse. Instead, much to her amazement, what she felt was anticipation.

For the first time in a very long time, she wanted to believe that the best was yet to come. And though she knew that believing in something wouldn't necessarily make it so, she suspected that having a little faith was often half the battle when it came to making your dreams come true.

And that was exactly what she intended to do over the next few weeks. Have a little faith as well as a little hope that she'd once again have someone to love. This time, for always...

Much to his chagrin, Frank realized he'd come to the end of the chapter Alison had given him after breakfast that morning. Setting the last page atop the others stacked beside him on the love seat in Rebecca's office, he tipped his head back and stared at the ceiling. He wanted the next chapter, and he wanted it *now*. And, if nothing else, that was a pretty fair indication of just how good a book doctor Alison Kent really was.

Granted, he'd been impressed by the way she'd cleaned up the pages he'd done, but the chapter she'd written entirely on her own was even better than he had thought it would be. Somehow she'd managed to absorb Rebecca's unique style, and as a result, the pages Alison had written moved the story forward with a seamlessness that left him utterly in awe.

Yet, at the same time, Alison's writing was imbued with the kind of warmth and sensitivity that could only have come from *her* heart. In fact, Frank had found the intimacy, both physical and emotional, of the love scene between Ben and Lydia wonderfully reassuring. He hadn't imagined Alison's passionate response to him last night. Not by a long shot.

He'd really enjoyed being with her yesterday. She'd seemed so relaxed and happy, and they'd had such a good time, laughing and talking as if they'd been together forever. Still, he hadn't planned to end up kissing her. Not really.

But after he'd hung her stocking by the fireplace, she'd looked at him in such a way that he'd thought maybe, just maybe, she'd begun to care for him as he'd begun to care for her.

Then he'd wanted to kiss her more than anything, but just once. A chaste overture to let her know that he thought of her as someone very special. But then he'd put his hands on her and brushed his lips against hers, and she'd responded in a way that had all but destroyed his self-control.

He hadn't realized just how much he wanted to claim her as his own until she'd put her arms around him and arched against him, unconsciously offering him all that she had to give. He could have taken her then and there. She'd been ready, so ready, and so had he. But she'd been caught up in the moment, and he would only have been taking advantage of her. Afterward, she would have realized it, and more than likely, she'd have never forgiven him for it.

When he made love to her for the first time, Frank wanted her with him all the way, without reservations or the possibility of regrets. And, for that, he was willing to wait.

As he'd told her, he wasn't interested in having an affair. What he had in mind was a hell of a lot more permanent. Yet sitting there, alone in Rebecca's office, he had a feeling Allison could very well find *that* totally out of the question.

She'd said that she didn't miss life in the big city all that much, but she'd been on the ranch only a couple of weeks. And, for the most part, Bert and the twins had been in good spirits, the weather had been reasonably nice, and while he always seemed to have enough work to keep him busy, he'd been able to spend some time with her.

But how would she feel when his father and sons no longer deemed it necessary to be on their best behavior twenty-four hours a day? The three of them could be downright ornery when they put their minds to it, and they tended to be so all at the same time.

The weather wasn't always quite so agreeable, either. How would she like being stuck in the house for days on end after a snowstorm? And what about the summers there? Could she stand month after month of sweltering in the heat?

And what about the times when he'd be too worn out to do more than kiss her on the cheek and fall into bed? She'd never been through lambing season or a sheepshearing. Nor had she been left alone with two little boys and a crotchety old man while her husband went off for several days to buy or sell stock.

He was probably crazy to even imagine she'd ever agree to stay with him on the Double B.

Still, after the way she'd responded to him last night, he could almost believe she needed him as much as he needed her.

Not only had she lost everyone she'd ever loved, but for the past three years she'd lived a solitary life. Yet beneath that cool and distant facade she'd tried so hard to maintain with him beat the heart of a warm, sensual, vibrantly alive and loving woman. He'd sensed her joy and contentment whenever she was with Bert and the boys. And last night, as he'd bent his head and kissed her lips, he'd seen the longing in her eyes.

Damn it, they belonged together. He knew it in his heart. Now all he had to do was convince Alison of it, too. He couldn't promise her their life together on the Double B would be easy. But then, nothing worthwhile ever was. He could, however, make sure she understood how very much she meant to him and to the rest of his family.

He'd loved Rebecca, and a part of him would always miss her. In a way, they'd grown up together, sharing their youthful hopes and dreams. But now, as he thought of the years ahead, he found himself wondering what it would be like to have Ali there by his side.

He'd always thought that eventually he'd find someone to take Rebecca's place, for the twins' sake if nothing else. He'd also figured that when he did, he'd experience a certain amount of self-reproach. But in a very short time, Alison had made her own special place in both his heart and his home, and he felt good about it rather than guilty.

There was nothing he could do to bring Rebecca back. He'd accepted that fact long ago. And she'd never had a grudging bone in her body. She'd have wanted him to be happy, and with Alison he knew he could be.

Now all he had to do was find a way to get her to stay. He wanted to believe that with a little bit of luck, and a hell of a lot of patience, anything was possible. But only time would tell, and unfortunately, he had very little of that. Still, he'd promised her they'd take it slow and easy, and he was a man of his word.

At least she hadn't seemed to have had a change of heart since last night. He'd been more than half afraid that once he left her on her own, she'd start having second thoughts. But when she'd come into the kitchen that morning, her smile had been so warm and so astonishingly inviting that he'd taken heart once again. In fact, if Bert and the boys hadn't been there, too, he'd have hauled her into his arms and kissed her senseless.

For the time being, however, he figured it would be wise to keep their change in relationship as much to themselves as possible. He didn't want Bert badgering either one of them. Nor did he want the twins getting any more attached to Alison than they already were. They'd had a hard time dealing with Rebecca's death, and they already cared about Alison quite a bit. But they seemed to accept the fact that she'd be leaving in a few weeks. Until she actually agreed to stay and marry him, he thought it best not to rock that particular boat.

From what he could determine, Alison seemed to feel the same way. She hadn't said anything about what had happened between them last night. But she hadn't avoided him as she'd done most of last week, either. She'd given him the chapter after they'd finished breakfast. Then, at his invitation, she'd gone out to the barn with him and the boys to help with the horses. They'd taught her how to muck out a stall as well as how to saddle Shadow. And when they'd finished their chores, they'd gone for a ride down the road.

That evening, after dinner, he'd left her in the kitchen, cutting out the patterns for the twins' costumes. He'd had paperwork to do, but somehow he'd ended up in Rebecca's office, reading Alison's chapter. And now...

Now he realized that he'd better call it a night. The clock on the desk read eleven-fifteen. Bert and the boys had come in to say good-night well over an hour ago. And Frank imagined Alison had gone to bed, too.

He gathered up the manuscript pages, tucked them into the folder and put them on the desk, then headed out of the office. Bert had locked up earlier, but as Frank started toward his bedroom, he saw that someone had left the Christmas tree lights on. Their cheerful twinkling brightened a patch of the otherwise darkened hallway just outside the living room doorway.

Making a mental note to remind Bert and the boys to be sure to turn off the lights when they left the living room, he turned and walked down the hallway. He paused just inside the doorway, but as he reached out to flip the switch, a flash of color caught his eye. Still wearing the red sweater and jeans she'd had on earlier, Alison sat on the sofa, her legs curled up under her, a mug of something steamy cradled in her hands.

"I thought you'd probably gone to bed already," he said, more pleased than he believed possible to find her there.

"I'd planned to, but I wasn't very sleepy. I found some chamomile tea in one of the cabinets and thought it might help." She lifted her mug, her smile so enticing that it was all he could do to stay where he was. "I hope I didn't disturb you by coming in here and turning on the lights. I thought I was the only one still awake."

"I was in the office reading the chapter you gave me this morning."

"Oh?" She lowered her gaze, staring into her mug as if it held something infinitely more interesting than chamomile tea. "Was it . . . was it all right?"

"It was wonderful, just wonderful."

"So, you liked it?"

"Very much," he assured her.

When she glanced at him uncertainly, he finally moved toward her. But he didn't dare sit on the sofa. Considering the way his mind had been wandering, not to mention the way his body had responded to just the sight of her, if he actually got close enough to put his hands on her—

Instead, he hunkered down on the floor in front of her, facing the tree as she did, and rested his back against the sofa's seat rail.

"Your chapter blended perfectly with the rest of Rebecca's story," he continued. "If I hadn't known differently, I would have thought she'd written it. And yet . . ."

"What?" Alison asked, her voice full of concern.

He glanced over his shoulder at her. "There was something of you in those pages, too."

"I didn't realize—" She frowned and shook her head. "I'm really sorry. I'll do whatever I can to fix—"

"Don't you dare," he warned, reaching out and taking her hand in his.

"But—"

"Your vibrancy, or whatever, doesn't distract from Rebecca's style. As far as I'm concerned, it enhances it."

"Thank you for that."

"I think I'm the one who should be thanking you." He squeezed her hand gently, then turned away again. "Among other things, I really appreciated your help out in the barn today. And I can't even begin to tell you how grateful I am that you're making those costumes for the twins."

"Don't be silly." For just a moment, he felt her fingers brush against his hair. "I'm having the time of my life here."

"You've got to be kidding." He caught her hand again and pressed his lips against her palm.

"I've never been more serious in my life."

"Bad thing to say."

"Why's that?"

"Remember what happened when you started talking seriously last night?" he teased.

"Mmm, yes," she said, the barest hint of laughter in her voice as she ruffled her finger through his hair once again.

He was tempted to pull her onto the floor with him. But he knew the odds that he'd be able to stop before he finished what he'd be starting were slim to none. And, no matter what she said, she wasn't ready for that yet.

"I don't know about you, but I think that's my cue to say good night." Reluctantly, he stood and shoved his hands in the back pockets of his jeans.

"Mine, too," she agreed with a soft sigh, uncurling her legs and standing, too.

"Not that I *want* to," he muttered, barely resisting the urge to reach for her.

"Me, neither." She gazed up at him, a searching look in her eyes. "But I guess it would be best, wouldn't it?"

"I'm afraid so."

She nodded gravely, then turned toward the doorway. "Well, then, good night, Frank."

He managed to let her take all of two steps before he caught her arm and whirled her around to face him. "Good night, Ali," he muttered, then bent his head and kissed her with a thoroughness that left them both breathless.

For the space of a heartbeat, he hugged her close. Then, taking a deep breath, he stepped away from her and gently turned her toward the doorway.

"You go on," he urged quietly. "I'll get the lights on my way out."

"All right." She hesitated, and for just an instant, he was afraid she wouldn't leave. Finally, however, she moved away from him. "See you in the morning."

"Sleep well."

"You, too." Glancing over her shoulder at him, she smiled winsomely, then turned away again.

"Fat chance," he muttered as he spun around and paced to the fireplace.

Resting a forearm on the mantel, he counted to twenty, giving her time to get down the hallway, across the kitchen and into her room. Then he crossed to the doorway, switched off the lights and headed for his own room, sure that he wouldn't get any rest at all. Unless, of course, he treated himself to a cold shower.

Groaning inwardly just at the thought of standing under a spray of icy water, he sat on the edge of his bed and pulled off his boots. Finally, however, giving in to the inevitable, he strode into the bathroom, shucked his clothes, stepped into the shower stall and with a muttered curse, turned on the tap.

Chapter Nine

"So, Orson, how's life in the big city been treating you lately?" Alison asked as she sat back in the desk chair in Rebecca's office and wound the telephone cord around her index finger.

"I can't complain," he said, then continued with obvious concern. "How about you? I thought I'd hear from you sooner. When I didn't, I began to worry."

"You shouldn't have," she hastened to assure him. "I'm just fine. Anyway, I told you I'd call in a couple of weeks and I am."

"Alison, sweetheart, you've been out there almost *three* full weeks," he pointed out, making no effort to hide his exasperation.

"Oh, right." Glancing at the little calendar on the desk she realized it was Friday...again. "I guess I kind of lost track of time."

"Does that mean you're having fun, as in time flies when . . . ?" he prodded.

"Well, actually, I am," she admitted. "More fun than I've had in a long time."

"Really?" He sounded honestly amazed. "I never would have thought you'd like living on a sheep ranch in New Mexico."

"Then why did you con me into coming out here?"

"Frank Bradford needed your help, and you needed to get away for a while," he replied without the slightest hint of remorse, then added almost as an afterthought, "how's the manuscript coming along?"

"Umm . . . fine, just fine," she hedged.

In truth, she hadn't gotten nearly as much done on the story over the past few days as she'd originally planned. Instead of working on *Hunter's Edge,* she'd spent more and more time with Frank and his family. But, looking back, she didn't regret it one bit.

She'd ridden into Vernon with Bert Monday morning, and they'd had a fine old time together, running errands, then shopping for stocking stuffers for Frank and the twins. To her surprise, he hadn't said anything about her relationship with his son. But when they'd stopped at the school to pick up Jake and Joey, and he'd introduced her to their teacher as "our Ms. Kent," the mischievous twinkle in his faded blue eyes had assured her that he knew exactly what was going on, and heartily approved.

Tuesday and Wednesday she managed to get a little writing done. But yesterday Frank had taken her and the twins riding after lunch. They'd gone to visit John and Louise Camden, taking the back trails rather than the ranch road, which shortened the distance by more than five miles. Alison had enjoyed meeting the older couple, and appreciated the warm welcome they offered her. In their own quiet way, they'd let her know how happy they were that she'd come to the Double B, and how much they hoped she would stay.

Off and on during the week, she'd also worked on the twins' costumes and helped them learn the words to the songs they were supposed to sing in the Christmas program. With their eager assistance, she'd also done the baking for the gingerbread house they were going to put together tomorrow. And, of course, she'd sent out her Christmas cards and wrapped the gifts she'd bought.

Evenings she'd spent with the Bradford men, watching television or playing board games until Bert hustled Jake and Joey off to bed. Then, Frank would light a fire in the fireplace, and with the lights on the Christmas tree twinkling, they'd curl up on the sofa in the living room, sometimes talking, sometimes just sitting quietly, their arms around each other.

Last night, however, as if neither of them could hold back any longer, they'd gone beyond the tentative kiss or two they'd allowed themselves to share the other evenings. Way beyond, Alison mused, smiling dreamily. Though, by mutual agreement, they'd stopped long before things had gotten too far out of—

"Earth to Alison, earth to Alison. Come in, please," Orson demanded reproachfully.

"I'm sorry," Alison murmured. Her face warming with embarrassment, she wondered if Orson had any idea how her mind had wandered. She could only hope not. "Did you say something?"

"I asked if you thought you'd have the manuscript finished by January 15."

"Yes, of course," she assured him.

Actually, she could have it finished much sooner than that, but she intended to take her time. Once she completed the manuscript, she'd have to determine whether or not to go back to New York. And she'd rather wait as long as she could to make that particular decision. She wanted to stay, and she was moving steadily in that direction. Yet she couldn't quite dispense with the fear she'd lived with for so long.

"How are you getting along with Bradford?"

She hesitated a moment, then replied as blithely as she could, "Just fine."

"So, everything's *fine.*"

"Well, yes...."

"You don't sound too sure of that."

"Oh, Orson..."

She wanted to tell him how she'd begun to feel about Frank, but she wasn't sure how he'd react. Granted, he'd played matchmaker on more than one occasion, but he'd also been Len's best friend.

"Tell me, sweetheart?" he urged, his voice full of concern once again. "Is he acting like a horse's ass, or what?"

"No, not at all." She hesitated, then took a deep breath and asked quietly, "I was just wondering what you'd say if I told you I was thinking about...about staying out here?"

"That depends. What do you mean by 'here,' and for how long?"

"On the Double B until...until death us do part."

"Are you in love with him?"

"Yes."

"And the feeling's mutual?"

"I think so."

"Has he asked you to marry him?"

"Not in so many words, but he's indicated that's what he has in mind."

"And what about you?" Orson prodded. "Is marriage what you have in mind, too? Marriage to a sheep rancher with five-year-old twin sons?"

"And an elderly father who sometimes tends to be a bit crotchety," she added with a laugh.

"You didn't answer my question," he reminded her gently. "Do you want to marry Frank Bradford?"

"I want to, but..."

"But what?"

"I'm not sure I should."

"Why is that?"

"I haven't had a lot of luck with close personal relationships," she replied, blinking at the unexpected sting of tears in her eyes. "Everyone I've ever really loved has died. Sometimes..." She hesitated, then forced herself to finally voice her deepest fear. "Sometimes I think I'm jinxed, and if that's true, then the best thing I could do for Frank and his family is get out of here just as fast as I can."

"Alison, sweetheart, you are *not* jinxed. You weren't flying the plane when your parents were killed. You didn't set off the bomb that took your brother's life. And if you think Len would have let you make your own way home from the airport during that damn blizzard three years ago, then you didn't really know him at all.

"Blaming yourself for any of their deaths is almost as foolish as running away from the first real opportunity you've had to have some joy in your life again. If you love Frank Bradford and he loves you, then take a chance. Len would have wanted you to be happy. And, the way I see it, the odds are in your favor. You're definitely due some *good* luck for a change."

"Oh, Orson, thank you."

As she brushed the tears from her cheeks with her fingertips, Alison couldn't help but smile. He'd known all the right things to say, things she'd needed to hear. And he'd said them with such total conviction that she found herself believing the future really did hold a wealth of possibilities for her, after all.

"Yeah, well, you deserve to have something good happen. But don't rush into anything out there unless you're sure it's what you really want. You know, you could just as easily fall in love with a stockbroker here in New York as a sheep rancher out in New Mexico," he teased.

"I don't think so," she replied with absolute certainty.

"Then be happy, sweetheart."

"I'll try."

"And don't forget to let me know what's happening. With the manuscript *and* with Bradford."

"I promise I'll keep you posted."

"Good enough. I'll talk to you—"

"Oh, wait. I almost forgot," she interrupted, remembering why she'd called him in the first place. "I wanted to tell you I had a little something shipped to you and Deborah for Christmas, something I found while I was shopping in Santa Fe. So be on the lookout for it, okay?"

"You actually went Christmas shopping this year?" he asked, making no effort to hide his amazement.

"Hey, that's nothing. I've also baked dozens and dozens of cookies, helped decorate the tree, sent out about fifty cards and made elf costumes for the twins for their school program," she stated proudly. Then she added, "Tomorrow we're putting together a gingerbread house."

"I knew conning you into going out there was a wise move," he said in smug tone of voice.

"The way I see it, you're darn lucky the whole thing didn't blow up in your face. I could have hated it out here."

"Yeah, I guess I am. But I'm not the only one. Right, sweetheart?"

"Right, Orson," she agreed unequivocally.

After promising to call again in a week or so, Alison said goodbye. She was so glad she'd talked to him. She'd always trusted his judgment in the past, and she could see no reason not to do so now.

Realizing that she'd better get to work if she wanted to get any writing done at all, she switched on the computer. The twins had only three days of school next week. Then they'd be off until just after the first of the year. She'd wanted to be able to spend a little more time with them then, but she wouldn't be able to justify it unless she completed quite a bit more of the manuscript than she already had.

She shuffled through her notes, read over what she'd written yesterday, then stared at the blank screen for several minutes. Finally, accepting the fact that she simply wasn't ready to settle down yet, she picked up her mug and headed for the kitchen. Maybe a little hot coffee would help.

To her surprise, she heard Frank's voice as she walked down the hallway. The twins had squabbled with each other from the moment they'd gotten out of bed that morning, and they'd ended up missing their bus. Frank had left about an hour ago to take them to school, but he'd planned to run some errands and do the grocery shopping before he headed back to the ranch sometime later in the afternoon.

She couldn't make out what he was saying, and by the time she reached the kitchen, Bert was the one doing the talking.

"Well, I really think I ought to go along and give you a hand," he said. "Especially if that storm's moving this way as fast as you seem to think it is."

"But what about the boys? We can't take them with us, and we can't expect Ali to look after them on her own for the next couple of days. She's doing so much around here already." Hands on his hips and a grim look on his face, Frank stood by the sink and stared out the window.

"What's going on?" Alison asked as she crossed to the counter and reached for the coffeepot.

From what she'd overheard, she already had a pretty good idea. Frank was going to have to move the sheep sooner than he'd planned under less-than-optimum conditions. Yet he didn't want to ask for her help. Considering how their relationship had changed over the past week, she figured she had a right to know why.

"Seems that big snowstorm they mentioned during the weather forecast last night, the one that was supposed to bypass us well to the north, shifted to the south during the night," Bert replied. "Frank heard the revised forecast on the radio on his way into town. He went straight to the grocery store to stock up on supplies, then headed back here so we could get started moving the sheep down to the lower pasture."

"Not *we*," Frank growled as he turned away from the window and eyed his father. "I'm riding up to give Carlos and Benito a hand while *you* stay here and look after Ali and the twins. And that's all there is to—"

"I beg your pardon," Alison cut in mildly. "But I'm more than capable of looking after myself. And if you need Bert's help, I wouldn't mind looking after Jake and Joey, too."

She didn't add that if she was going to be a part of the family, then she expected to pull her weight. But something about her expression as she met Frank's gaze must have clewed him in to how she felt.

"I really could use his help," he admitted after a moment or two. "We won't be able to start moving the sheep down until early tomorrow morning, and we're really going to have to hustle because the storm's supposed to roll through here late in the afternoon. But we're going to have to head up to the camp as soon as we can, and we'll probably be gone until late tomorrow night or early Sunday morning."

"I'm sure I can manage on my own for that amount of time," she assured him.

She doubted she'd have any problems with the twins. The three of them would have lots to do to keep busy. Nor was she afraid to be alone with them in the house. She'd never felt as safe anywhere as she did on the Double B.

"I'll leave Molly here with you," Frank offered.

"I'd appreciate that," she admitted with a slight smile. The little dog was fiercely protective, allowing no one near the house she didn't know.

"We'll have the mobile phone with us, and we can leave the neighbors' numbers, too," Bert added. "John and Louise Camden would be more than happy to help you out if you run into any problems. So would Juan and Rosa Ramirez."

"Well, then, what are you guys waiting for?" Alison teased. "Head 'em out."

As it was, it took them more than an hour to get ready to go. While they packed their gear, Alison made sandwiches, wrapped cookies and fruit in plastic bags and filled several thermoses with hot coffee. She also jotted down telephone numbers and other bits of important information either Frank or Bert thought she might need while they were gone.

The twins were supposed to ride the bus home from school, so around eleven-thirty she'd walk down to the end of the drive to meet them. Otherwise, she wasn't planning on going anywhere. Still, Frank gave her the keys to his truck, insisting she use it rather than her rental car if she had to do any driving.

"Are you sure you're going to be all right here on your own?" he asked as he took the saddlebags from her.

Bert was already out in the barn, tying the last of their gear onto the backs of their saddles. Once Frank joined him, they'd be on their way.

"I've been on my own in New York for almost three years," she reminded him.

"Yeah, but you had neighbors right downstairs. It's a lot more isolated out here."

"Trying to scare me, Mr. Bradford?" Tipping her chin up, she gazed at him steadily.

"Just giving you the facts, ma'am."

"Well, thanks. I think," she quipped, smiling up at him.

"Damn it, I hate going off like this and leaving you alone," he muttered, slinging the saddlebags onto the counter, then catching hold of her and pulling her into his arms.

"We're going to be just fine." Maybe if she said it enough times she'd finally begin to believe it, she thought as she put her arms around him and rested her cheek on his chest.

Despite her talk with Orson, she hadn't been able to ignore the little niggle of fear that something might happen, either to the twins while she was alone with them, or to Frank and his father while they were away. In fact, as she'd made sandwiches and jotted down notes, she'd had to beat back all sorts of awful imaginings.

Now, however, she couldn't allow her anxiety to get the better of her. Not when Frank so obviously needed her help.

"This is a hell of a way to be courting you," he grumbled. "Dumping my kids on you for two days along with everything else. By Sunday, you'll probably be packing your bags."

"Well, no, not Sunday. I promised I'd finish *Hunter's Edge,* and I always keep my word. So, I'd have to stay until at least Monday or Tuesday."

"You're that close to being finished?" he asked, momentarily sidetracked.

"Not really," she admitted. "I'd have to work like the dickens, and to do that, I'd have to have the right incentive."

"Two days alone with Jake and Joey ought to do it."

"Hey, they aren't *that* bad."

"They've been on their best behavior the past three weeks, but after this morning..." He shrugged and shook his head.

"They were up later than usual last night, trying on their costumes," she reminded him. "They were probably just tired."

"I hope so. Maybe they'll go to bed early tonight and give you a little peace." He hugged her close, then bent his head and kissed her slowly, sensuously.

As she clung to him, kissing him back, Alison wanted to beg him to stay. But she knew she couldn't. He had work to do, the kind of rough work necessary to keep his ranch running profitably. And, much as she'd like to keep him out of harm's way, it simply wasn't possible. All she could do was hope that he'd come back to her safe and sound.

"You've got the numbers we gave you?" he asked, easing away from her.

"The paper's taped to the door of the refrigerator."

"Then I guess I'd better get going." He stroked her back, making no move to leave.

"Mmm, yes, I guess you better." Rising up a little, she kissed him on the chin. "Be careful. Please..." she murmured as she pressed her lips against the hollow at the base of his throat.

"I will," he promised, taking her mouth once again, swiftly yet surely, then releasing her. "We'll be back late tomorrow night or early Sunday morning." He grabbed the saddlebags off the counter, slung them over his shoulder and started toward the door.

"Take care," she said, gripping the counter with one hand to stop herself from going after him.

"You too, Ali." Glancing over his shoulder at her, he eyed her steadily, as if memorizing her features. Then he turned and walked out the door, closing it quietly behind him.

Alison stood by the sink, gazing out the window until Frank and his father rode out of sight down the drive. She puttered around the kitchen for a few minutes, tidying up. Finally, giving herself a firm mental shake, she walked back to Rebecca's office. She didn't have to meet the twins' bus for over an hour, and she knew she'd be a lot better off spending that time sorting out Ben and Lydia's problems than making herself sick with worry about everything that could possibly go wrong over the next couple of days.

Sooner or later, she was going to have to trust that she wasn't really some sort of jinx. And now seemed as good a time as any to start. If she couldn't dispense with her paranoia, she'd be better off living alone. And she didn't want to do that, not when she had a chance to be part of a warm and loving family once again.

She managed to get quite a bit of work done in the next hour. Then, feeling rather proud of herself, she put on her jacket, scarf and gloves, and, with Molly gamboling along beside her, headed down the drive.

She loved the way the warmth of the sunshine blended with the crisp, cold air. To look at the clear blue sky above her, she wouldn't have thought a major snowstorm was coming their way. But off in the distance, she could see clouds massing along the horizon. And she had no doubt that all too soon the weather would be changing.

Right on schedule, the bus halted at the foot of the drive and the twins jumped off. After waving to the driver, Alison bent and gathered them into her arms for a hug.

"How was school?" she asked, smiling as she looked from one of them to the other.

"Okay," Jake said.

"Yeah, okay," Joey agreed, then asked with obvious concern, "Where's Grandpa?"

"He rode up to the camp with your dad to help Carlos and Benito with the sheep. We're supposed to have a big snowstorm tomorrow afternoon, and they wanted to move them out of the foothills before then."

"We could have helped, too," Jake grumbled.

"Our dad said we were getting big enough," Joey added, sounding equally irritable.

"Well, maybe next time," Alison offered brightly.

As they had that morning, both boys seemed awfully cranky. And they certainly weren't as energetic as usual. Instead of skipping along beside her, they trudged up the drive as if it were all they could do to put one foot in front of the other.

Just tired, she told herself as they walked into the house. Even normally bouncing-off-the-wall little boys wore down occasionally.

After a lunch of soup and sandwiches that they only nibbled at, Alison went out to the barn with them to check on the horses. Frank and his father had cleaned the stalls before they left, but she'd promised that she and the boys would make sure the animals had feed and fresh water.

Back inside again, she asked if they wanted to start on the gingerbread house instead of waiting until the next day, but neither of them displayed much enthusiasm. She also failed to interest them in playing a game or listening to a story. So, after helping them arrange their quilt on the office floor, then hauling their box of building blocks in there for them, she went back to work.

They seemed to be playing for a while, but then Alison realized they were unusually quiet. Glancing over her shoulder, she saw that they were both asleep. With a sigh of relief, she turned back to the computer. Surely they'd feel better after they had a nap.

If anything, however, they woke up even grouchier than they had been that morning. They argued so vociferously over who would build what part of their latest fort that even with the radio playing rock and roll music, Alison couldn't concentrate. Giving up on getting anything else done, she decided to start dinner.

As they had at lunch, Jake and Joey just picked at their food, even though she'd made their favorites, meat loaf and macaroni and cheese. When she suggested they might want to take their baths and put on their pajamas, they nodded almost gratefully, and by seven-thirty, they were tucked into their beds, sound asleep.

As the silence settled around her, Alison let Molly in the house to keep her company while she finished cleaning up the kitchen. Then she made a cup of tea for herself and went back to the office to work on the manuscript a little more.

Frank called on the mobile telephone just after eight to make sure she and the boys were all right. They talked no more than a minute or two, but she felt relieved as she cradled the receiver, knowing he and Bert were safe for the night.

Around ten o'clock she finally decided to call it a night. As she crawled into bed, she realized that the day had gone quite well, all things considered. After a good night's sleep, Jake and Joey would be their old selves again. And since she'd finished another chapter of *Hunter's Edge,* she could justify spending all day tomorrow with them.

Sighing with contentment, she snuggled under the bedcovers, closed her eyes and fell asleep.

"Ali? Are you awake?"

"Hmm?"

Still more than half asleep, Alison pushed up on one elbow. She'd left the light on above the kitchen sink, and in the pale glow coming through her doorway she saw the twins standing by the side of her bed.

"Hey, guys, what are you doing up?" she asked as she glanced at the clock on her nightstand. It wasn't quite four-thirty in the morning.

"We don't feel so good," Jake said.

"No, we don't." Joey rubbed a hand over his forehead. "My head hurts."

"Mine, too. And my throat's really sore," Jake added.

"Yeah, mine too." Joey nodded in agreement.

Coming fully awake, Alison sat up and switched on the lamp on the nightstand. She should have known they were coming down with something, she thought, trying to beat back the wave of panic that threatened to wash over her. They'd been so lethargic and they hadn't had any appetite.

"Come on, you two. Why don't you climb up here?"

She patted the bed as she scooted over to make room for them. When they'd done as she asked, she looked from one to the other. Their little faces were pale, except for bright spots of red on their cheeks, and there were dark shadows under their eyes. Reaching out, she rested the back of her hand against first Jake's forehead, then Joey's. Both boys' skin felt unusually warm to her.

Obviously, they were coming down with something. But what? The combination of headache, sore throat and fever could be an indication of anything from flu to a strep infection. And, more important, what could she do to make them feel better at four-thirty in the morning?

"I think we need our dad," Jake said, a worried frown creasing his forehead.

"And our grandpa, too," Joey added.

Alison had to agree. But unfortunately, they weren't exactly within shouting distance. Of course, she could call Frank on the mobile phone. But there wasn't much he'd be able to do except offer advice. He wouldn't be able to ride back to the house until daybreak, and she couldn't see worrying him, perhaps needlessly, in the meantime.

For now, she might as well try to muddle along on her own and hope for the best. But how? Once again, panic almost got the better of her. If anything happened to the twins because she did something stupid—

"Your dad and your grandpa are up at the camp tonight," she reminded them gently. "But I'm here and I promise I'll take good care of you."

Nathan had run a fever a few times, and while he'd been several years younger than Jake and Joey, bringing down their fevers would more than likely involve similar methods. If she wasn't mistaken, she'd seen several books on child care on the shelves in Rebecca's office. Just to be on the safe side, she'd take a look at them. One of them should include detailed information on what to do when a five-year-old ran a fever and complained of a headache and sore throat.

"You guys stay here, okay?" she said, reaching for her robe.

"Where are you going?" Joey asked.

"To see if I can find something that'll help make you feel better."

"Tylenol?" Jake asked.

"You've taken that before?"

Both boys nodded, then Joey added, "The special kind for little kids. Our dad keeps it in his bathroom. Way up on the very top shelf of the medicine cabinet."

Nodding, Alison climbed out of bed and slipped into her robe, then hurried out of the bedroom. She stopped in the office first and found the information she wanted in one of the childcare books. Acetaminophen was the recommended analgesic for children with the twins' symptoms. And, as Jake had said, she found some of the chewable tablets in dosages suitable for younger children in Frank's medicine cabinet, along with a thermometer that she took back to her room, too.

Though the twins were running fevers, they weren't dangerously high. They chewed the little tablets she gave them, then gladly snuggled under the blankets on her bed. Within a reasonably short time, both boys were sound asleep again.

Alison dragged the easy chair close to the bed and curled up on it, her quilt wrapped around her, so she could keep an eye on them. She dozed a bit, but mostly she just sat and watched them sleep, rising occasionally to rest a hand against one boy's forehead, then the other's.

As the dawn light crept around the edges of the blinds on her windows, she took her clothes into the bathroom, washed and dressed. After checking on the boys again, she went into the kitchen, started a pot of coffee, then hurried out to the barn with Molly to check on the horses again as Frank had instructed.

As she'd expected, thick gray clouds filled the sky, and there was an unmistakable dampness in the icy air. There would be snow on the ground by evening, a lot of it. What she couldn't determine, however, was when it would start. She could only hope the forecast of late afternoon would prove to be true.

According to what she'd read in the childcare book, if the twins were still running fevers when they awakened again, she'd have to take them to the doctor. And that meant making a forty-mile round trip to Vernon.

She finally woke them herself around nine o'clock. They'd started to feel unusually warm to her again, and she wanted to give them another dose of Tylenol to make sure their fevers didn't soar. Nor did she want to delay their trip to Vernon any longer.

Somehow, she got them dressed and onto the back seat of Frank's truck, wondering all the time if she was making a mistake taking them out on such a cold, damp day. But if they had a bacterial infection, something like strep throat or tonsillitis, they could become seriously ill without the antibiotics only a doctor could prescribe for them.

The drive to Vernon went smoothly, and she found the clinic without any problem. But, much to her dismay, there were several people ahead of them, and they had to wait almost an hour before they got in to see the doctor. By the time the twins had been diagnosed with strep throat and she'd stopped at the pharmacy to pick up their prescriptions, huge flakes of snow had begun to swirl down.

Guiding the truck down Main Street, Alison shivered with apprehension as she recalled the last time she'd tried driving to the ranch in the middle of a snowstorm.

"You guys okay back there?" she asked, glancing in the rearview mirror.

"Yeah," they murmured in unison.

"Got your seat belts buckled?"

"Uh-huh."

At the pharmacist's suggestion, she'd given them each a dose of the antibiotic and some more Tylenol, and now the two of them, tucked under a blanket, looked ready to doze off again. Just as well, she thought, turning her attention back to the road. The doctor had said they should start feeling better by evening, but for now, she'd rather they stay quiet. She was going to need all her wits about her if she was going to keep the truck on the already snowy roads.

Of all the awful things she'd imagined happening while Frank and his father were gone, getting stuck in the snow with two sick little boys hadn't been one of them. If anything happened to them—

But no, she couldn't allow herself to think the worst. She had to concentrate on getting back to the ranch. Believing she not only could but *would* do it was half the battle, she reminded herself. All she had to do was take her time, and hang on to her newfound faith that everything would ultimately be all right.

She couldn't remember ever being more relieved than she was when she finally pulled to a stop by the front door of the house. She wasn't sure how, but she'd made it home, and for the time being nothing else mattered.

By late afternoon, almost half a foot of snow had fallen, and more continued to drift down. The twins were also noticeably better. They insisted on working on their gingerbread house, gladly ate last night's leftovers, and after all the sleeping they'd done earlier in the day, begged to stay up a little later than usual to watch television with her.

She finally got them to bed, then returned to the living room, feeling exhausted, yet oddly exhilarated. When she thought of all the things that could have gone wrong but hadn't, she couldn't help but smile.

She'd been lucky all around today. She'd gotten the twins to the doctor, she'd driven back to the ranch without running off the road, and within a few days, Jake and Joey would be well again. Now, if only Frank and his father would get home, maybe she'd finally start believing that she could safely share her life with someone she loved, after all.

Crossing to the window, she peered through the blinds. Though it was still snowing, the flakes drifted down in a desultory manner that impaired visibility very little. She doubted the men would have any trouble finding their way back to the house. Frank had told her the pasture was just a couple of miles to the south, and she'd turned on all the outside lights to guide them.

With a weary sigh, she closed the blinds and returned to the sofa. Maybe she'd wait up a little longer. It was after ten o'clock, and they could be coming in anytime now. And she really did love just sitting and looking at the Christmas tree and the stockings hanging by the fireplace.

She curled up in a corner of the sofa and snuggled under the quilt she'd tucked around the twins earlier. Gazing at the twinkling lights on the tree, she thought of all she'd gone through to get where she was. And, though she wished the route hadn't been quite so painful, she realized there was nowhere else she'd rather be right now than here with Frank and his family. Tonight, and tomorrow, and always...

Chapter Ten

"She's got the place lighted up like a Christmas tree," Bert chortled as he and Frank left the barn and headed wearily toward the house.

"Guess she wanted to be sure we could find our way home." Warmed by the thought that Alison had so obviously been concerned about them, Frank smiled as he dug in his pocket for his door key.

"Should have told her we could have done it with our eyes closed."

"I don't know about you, but I *did*," Frank muttered.

They'd ridden up the drive just after midnight, but they'd still had to bed down their horses and stow their gear before they could call it a night. Frank couldn't vouch for his father, but after the day they'd had, *he* was beat.

They'd managed to move the sheep to their winter pasture without any major problems, and they'd done so in record time. They'd gotten an early start that morning, and luckily the blizzard conditions the forecaster had predicted hadn't materialized. Though snow had fallen steadily since early afternoon, they'd been able to see where they were going and what they were doing with relative ease. And, of course, having his father along had been a big help.

"Thanks for giving us a hand, Dad," Frank said as he unlocked the back door, then stepped back to allow his father to enter.

"My pleasure." Bert offered him a tired smile as they stomped their boots on the doormat and slipped out of their jackets.

"You've got to be kidding."

"Hey, I like to know I can still be of some use around here." He hung his jacket on one of the pegs by the door, then turned his attention to Molly as the dog padded up to greet them. "Well, girlie, how did it go around here while we were gone? Our Ms. Kent keep those two young hooligans in line?" he asked, ruffling his fingers through her fur.

"I still don't think we should have left her here on her own," Frank grumbled, frowning as he rubbed a hand across the back of his neck.

Not that he'd had any doubt that she'd do just fine. He just hadn't wanted to take advantage of her. She hadn't come to the Double B to baby-sit his sons. But then, now that he thought about it, he'd lost track of her primary reason for being there quite a bit lately. Hadn't he? While he still wanted to see *Hunter's Edge* make the *New York Times*'s bestseller list, that was no longer the major reason why he wanted Alison to stay on at the ranch.

"She said she didn't mind."

"That was *before* she was stuck here with my sons for two days."

"Knowing Ali, she had a wonderful time with them."

"Yeah, you're probably right," he agreed, recalling all the times he'd seen her with them.

She'd been so kind to them, so patient and understanding, and so very, very loving. Anyone who saw her with them for the first time would more than likely think they were her children. She'd made a place for them in her heart, and that was only one of the many reasons he wanted her with him for the rest of their lives.

"Well, I don't know about you, but I'm going to bed," Bert said.

"Me, too." When he hesitated, his father glanced at him quizzically. "I...thought I'd just check on Ali first," he added, gesturing toward her bedroom. He'd noticed that her door was open, and thought he'd take a moment to look in on her just to assure himself that she was all right.

"You do that, son." Bert winked slyly, then disappeared down the hallway.

Shaking his head at his father's foolishness, Frank walked over to her bedroom doorway. He wasn't going to wake her. He just wanted to catch a glimpse of her before he went to bed. But when he glanced through the doorway, he saw that her bed was empty. He frowned for a moment, wondering where on earth she could be, then turned and headed for the hallway.

When they'd ridden up to the barn earlier, he'd seen the flicker of the colored lights on the Christmas tree through the blinds on the living room windows. And he knew how much she liked sitting in there in the evenings. She'd probably gone in there earlier, then fallen asleep on the sofa.

Just as he'd expected, he found her curled up under her quilt. He sat down next to her and smoothed a hand over her short, sleek, dark hair. She murmured something unintelligible and stirred slightly, but didn't open her eyes. She was probably as worn out as he was, he thought, barely resisting the urge to stretch out beside her and take her in his arms. And she looked so peaceful that he really hated to wake her. But if he didn't, she'd be stiff and sore all day to-morrow.

"Ali, wake up," he urged, rubbing her shoulder gently, not wanting to frighten her.

She murmured again, then opened her eyes.

"Frank?" She smiled with unabashed pleasure. "Oh, Frank, you're home." She sat up and slipped her arms around his waist, then rested her head on his chest. "I'm so glad...so glad," she sighed as she clung to him.

"Me, too." He shifted slightly and eased her onto his lap, cradling her in his arms. "Did you have any problems while we were gone?"

"Nothing major. Early yesterday morning, Jake and Joey woke up complaining that they had headaches and sore throats. Since they were also running fevers, I decided to take them to the clinic in Vernon. Turned out they had strep throat. The doctor put them on antibiotics and they were feeling a lot better by evening. They should be able to go to school Monday. And guess what?"

"What?" he asked, more than a little bemused.

"I drove home in the snow without running off the road," she stated proudly.

"And you call all that *nothing major?*" He hugged her close, marveling at how nonchalant she sounded.

When the twins had come down with ear infections right after Rebecca died, he'd panicked. If Bert hadn't been there to calm him down, he'd probably have lost it completely. Yet Alison had handled a similar situation on her own, both calmly and competently.

"It was just a minor crisis. We got through it none the worse for wear. The twins were almost back to normal by late afternoon. We worked on the gingerbread house for a while and they stayed up late to watch an old Disney movie with me."

"You must have been wiped out by the time they finally went to bed."

"I was. But I wanted to wait up for you. I guess I fell asleep," she admitted sheepishly.

"You should have gone to bed, too. But I'm glad you didn't." He bent and brushed his lips against her cheek, then took her mouth in a slow, sweet kiss when she tipped her face up invitingly.

He'd only been gone two days, but damn it, he'd missed her more than he'd imagined possible. He'd thought of her constantly, wanting nothing more than to be with her again. And now that he was...

"Come on, let me take you to your room." Still holding her in his arms, he stood and crossed the living room.

She clung to him wordlessly, feathering her lips along the line of his jaw, nearly destroying what little self-control he had left. Just inside the doorway of her room, he set her on her feet, holding her steady for a moment, then easing away from her. She gazed up at him with such longing, it was all he could do to stop himself from reaching for her again. If she hadn't been all but swaying with fatigue—

But he'd meant what he'd said about courting her. He wanted her, now more than ever, but he also wanted her to be sure that *she* wanted him. And for that, he was willing to wait until there was no doubt she had all her wits about her.

"When are the twins due another dose of their medicine?" he asked, brushing a wisp of hair away from her face with his fingertip.

"Around eight in the morning."

"I'll see that they get it. You sleep in, okay?"

"Oh, I don't mind—"

"But I do. You look like you're ready to drop. If you're not careful, you're going to end up getting sick, too. Then you won't be able to go to the twins' school program with us."

"Ah, I see. Misery wants company, huh?" she teased.

"Actually, what I was wanting, among other things, was to show you off to everybody." Seeing the surprised look on her face, he laughed softly, then bent and dropped a quick kiss on her cheek. "Get some rest, okay?"

"Okay," she murmured, smiling sleepily.

Maybe he could just lie down on the bed with her for a little while. Just hold her and—

Reluctantly, he turned and walked out of her room, closing the door behind him, then strode quickly across the kitchen.

He could tell himself that he'd stop with holding her and kissing her, but he knew better. When he took her to bed, he was going to make love to her—slow, sweet love. And he wanted her with him all the way. He wasn't going to settle for anything less. Not when he wanted her with him for always.

"Are they asleep yet?" Alison asked, glancing up as Frank returned to the living room.

From his place by the fire, Bert eyed his son quizzically, as well.

'Twas the night before Christmas, and all through the house, two little creatures had been stirring, nonstop, despite repeated attempts to get them to go to bed. They'd been so excited about Santa Claus, they'd literally been bouncing off the walls all evening, and that was after spending a couple of hours lining the drive with homemade *farolitos*. Alison had found herself wishing for just a tenth of their energy.

"Finally." Frank smiled wearily as he met first her gaze, then his father's. "So, I guess that makes it Santa time. You two ready?"

"Oh, yes." Alison returned his smile as she took his hand.

"The sooner, the better," Bert agreed. "It's already past *my* bedtime. And if I know my grandsons, they're going to be up at the crack of dawn."

"I'll get my stuff and be right back," Alison said as she and Frank and his father started toward the hallway.

"I hope you didn't overdo it," Frank growled, frowning down at her.

"I didn't," she assured him, then added as he eyed her skeptically, "well, not much."

"You're going to spoil them rotten, you know."

"Would that really be so bad?" she retorted mildly.

"No, not really," he admitted, smiling once again.

As she headed for her room, Alison had to admit that the past week had been her best yet on the Double B. But then, that was understandable since she no longer felt as if she were living under a black cloud of impending doom.

Not only had she taken care of the twins on her own without a major mishap, but Frank and his father had come home safe and sound, as well. When she thought of all that could have gone wrong, she considered the fact that nothing had a very good omen, indeed. And she'd finally opened herself up to all the possibilities that life on the Double B had to offer.

As she'd predicted, Jake and Joey had been well enough to go to school on Monday, and Tuesday night they'd participated in the school program. They'd looked just darling in their elf costumes, and they'd not only remembered their lines, but all the words to the songs she'd practiced with them. Had they been her children, she doubted she could have been any more proud of them.

Nor could she have been any more pleased to be with Frank than she had been. True to his word, he'd made a point of introducing her to everyone he possibly could, explaining that she'd come to the ranch to finish Rebecca's book. And, though he'd never come right out and said it, he'd also left the impression that she was now there to stay.

She'd gotten many curious glances, but everyone had been friendly despite her status as a stranger. That the Bradford family considered her one of them seemed to be enough to smooth her way.

The rest of the week had gone by in a whirlwind of activity. There had been a last-minute shopping trip to Vernon to buy the batteries both she and Frank realized they needed for the toys they'd bought for Jake and Joey. The twins hadn't had school Thursday or Friday, but Frank and his father had kept them busy so she could work on the manuscript.

Wanting to get as much of it done as she could before Christmas, she had written steadily both days. As a result, she had just one more chapter to write. With luck she'd have that finished just after the first of the year. And then ...

Then she'd have to see what happened next. She and Frank seemed to be moving toward happily ever after, but they hadn't made any specific plans for the future. She knew he didn't want to rush her into making any kind of a commitment. Becoming a permanent part of his family would require a major change in her life-style, and he obviously didn't want her to feel she'd made a mistake one day down the line.

As for her, now that she no longer felt like some sort of awful jinx, she was ready to move forward with their relationship. Yet she couldn't quite bring herself to ask him to make love to her, because she was still a little bit afraid that she might yet cause him to come to harm.

Wondering if she'd ever be completely free of that gnawing dread, Alison dug through her closet, retrieving the shopping bags full of brightly wrapped gifts she'd hidden there. Probably she was expecting too much of herself too soon. The promise of happiness after only four weeks sim-

ply wasn't enough to totally dispel three years of living with
the kind of deeply rooted fear and foreboding that she had.

At least with each day that passed she felt a little more
certain that her luck had changed for the better. Though she
hadn't said as much to him in so many words, she loved
Frank Bradford as well as his father and his two young sons.
She had almost from the first. And, so far, not a single ca-
tastrophe had occurred as a result. If that didn't give her
reason to believe she wouldn't lose them as she had everyone else, she doubted anything would. Except maybe cele-
brating Christmas right here with them twenty years from
now.

Telling herself that she *would,* she returned to the living
room, smiling once again.

Frank and his father were already there, setting packages
of all shapes and sizes under the tree.

"And you were worried about *me* spoiling Jake and
Joey," she teased, noting how many of their gifts were for
the boys as she added hers to the mounting piles.

"Guess we kinda got carried away," Bert said. "But then,
that's understandable. I think we all wanted Christmas to be
really special this year, didn't we?"

"Yeah, I think we did," Frank agreed as he met Alison's
gaze.

"Mmm, really special." Smiling, she set the box with the
belt she'd bought for him among the other gifts.

She'd wanted him to know how much she cared for him,
and aside from coming right out and telling him, she could
think of no better way to do it than giving him something
she'd chosen just for him.

After they finished putting all the larger gifts under the
tree, they tucked the smaller ones in the stockings hanging
by the fireplace until they were all stuffed. Even hers
brimmed with tiny surprises.

"Well, looks like we've got everything out, so I'm going to bed," Bert said as he gathered up the empty shopping bags and folded them together. "Good night to the both of you."

Standing together by the fireplace, Alison and Frank wished him good-night. Then, aware that they were alone together, Alison turned to Frank and smiled.

"I guess I should say good-night, too."

"Considering my father was right when he said the twins will be up at the crack of dawn, I guess we both should. But..." He caught her hand and drew her toward him.

"What?" she asked softly as she stepped willingly into his arms and tipped her face up.

She didn't have to ask, not really. Not when she saw the look in his eyes.

"You mean so much to me, Ali," he said, brushing his lips ever so gently against her cheek. "So much." He kissed her slowly, sensuously, leaving no doubt in her mind that he spoke the truth. "I want us to be together. But only if you're sure that's what you want, too."

"I'm sure," she murmured, and knew that she'd never meant anything more.

She'd found happiness here with Frank and his family. Even more important, she'd found love, the kind she knew could last a lifetime if only she was willing to take a chance. And as she pulled him close for another kiss, she realized that she was. More willing than she'd ever imagined she could be.

As if he needed no more encouragement than that, he scooped her into his arms, strode across the living room and turned down the hallway. He didn't stop until they'd reached her room, and then only to kick the door shut and slide the lock into place before going on to her bed.

He stood her on her feet beside it, then turned on the lamp on the nightstand.

"All right?" he asked, resting his hands on her shoulders.

"Oh, yes." She reached up and traced the line of his jaw with her fingertips.

"Good." He smiled as he fished a small box from his shirt pocket and set it beside the lamp.

"What—" she began, then realized with a rush of warmth just how thoughtful he was.

"I'll protect you, Ali. For as long as you want," he vowed gently.

"Have I ever told you that you're a kind and generous man, Mr. Bradford?"

"I think maybe once before," he replied. "But don't worry about repeating yourself. That's something I wouldn't mind hearing from you occasionally over the next fifty years or so."

"Then you will."

"I hope you mean that," he said, holding her gaze as he began to open the buttons on her blouse.

"With all my heart," she murmured, reaching for his belt buckle.

Within a matter of moments, they'd discarded their clothing. Then Frank lifted her onto the bed and sank down beside her, trailing his hands and mouth over her with an ardor that stole her breath away.

"You're so beautiful, Ali," he muttered, drawing her nipple into his mouth as he ran his hand down her body, then down again, stroking her with a subtlety that had her arching against him with a whispered plea.

"Not yet," he said, his lips feathering the side of her neck, his teeth tugging ever so gently at her earlobe, his tongue swirling against her sensitive skin as his thumb rubbed against her and his finger slipped inside her, teasing her with the promise of fulfillment beyond her wildest dreams.

She slid her hands over him with a sudden, unabashed urgency, her caresses growing bolder, then bolder still, as she fought fire with tender, yet provocative, fire.

Finally, he rolled away from her with a harsh groan, fumbled with one of the foil packets in the box, then turned back to her, settling himself between her legs. Smoothing her hair away from her face, he murmured her name, then took her mouth as he sheathed himself deep inside her.

He held her still for the space of a heartbeat or two, letting her savor the first glorious moments of their mating. Then, bracing himself on his forearms, he wove his fingers through hers, and began to move almost leisurely, his eyes holding hers.

Delighted by the tenderness of his claiming, Alison wrapped her legs around him, moving with him. As he increased the rhythm of his thrusts, she arched under him, and finally, inevitably, let him sweep her over the edge. As she cried out softly, he, too, found his release, shuddering as he called her name.

For a long while afterward, they lay still as their heartbeats slowed and their breathing steadied. Eventually, Frank reached up and switched off the lamp, pulled the bedcovers over them, then drew her into his arms again. Content to just hold each other, neither of them said a word.

Basking in the afterglow of their lovemaking, Alison found herself wishing the night would last forever. If only they could stay right where they were, cocooned in the warmth and security of their love, she'd never have to worry about Frank coming to any harm.

But, of course, that wasn't possible. The clock on the nightstand ticked off one minute after another, bringing them closer and closer to the moment when the real world would intrude once more.

"I should go," Frank muttered, as if reading her mind. "Jake and Joey are going to be up early and you need to get some rest."

"I wish you could stay," she said, nuzzling against his chest with her cheek. "Just a little longer..."

She knew he'd have to leave soon. The twins were under strict orders to wake him before they opened their gifts, and she was old-fashioned enough to believe it would be better if they found their father in his own bed. But she'd never thought she could allow herself to be this close to anyone again. Now that she had, she wanted to luxuriate in the wondrous sensation of once again loving as well as being loved.

"Mmm, you talked me into it," he growled, cupping her breast in his hand and teasing her nipple with his thumb. "But don't let me fall asleep."

"I wouldn't dream of it." Smiling, she nipped at his neck as she ran her hand down his chest and over his belly. "Although I doubt that's going to be a problem," she added, laughing softly as she encountered incontrovertible evidence of his renewed desire.

"Me, too," he agreed, rolling her onto her back and kissing his way down her body, turning her laughter into a moan of unwonted pleasure as he lured her toward another, even more intimate, kind of completion.

When they were both sated once again, she curled against him, tears welling in her eyes as she thought of how lucky she was to have found such a truly generous man.

"Are you all right?" he asked, sliding a fingertip under her chin and lifting her face so that she had no choice but to meet his gaze.

Though she couldn't see him that well in the darkness, she sensed his sudden concern.

"Never better," she hastened to assure him with a watery smile.

"I thought maybe you were . . . crying," he ventured, his voice husky.

"I do that sometimes when I'm really happy."

"You do, huh?"

"Yes."

"Well, since you're in such a good mood, I was wondering . . ." he began, then hesitated as if choosing his next words very carefully.

"What?" she prodded, snuggling against him.

"I know I'm asking a hell of a lot of you, but would you consider staying here with us? I love you, Ali, and I want you to be my wife. I want you to help me raise my sons and keep my old man in line. I want you to have my babies and grow old with me." He hesitated again, then continued quietly. "I wouldn't expect you to give up your work or anything. And you could do whatever you wanted to make the house *your* home."

"Oh, Frank . . ." she murmured, at a loss for words.

"You don't have to give me an answer right away. Just promise me you'll think about it over the next couple of weeks."

She gazed up at him, not knowing exactly what to say. Over the past two weeks, he'd made no secret of the fact that he had marriage in mind, but actually having him propose to her was more unsettling that she'd imagined it would be. With all her heart, she wanted to say yes. And yet . . .

Fear edged into the back of her mind, fear of loving and losing all over again.

If she went back to New York when she finished the manuscript, she'd have some wonderful memories to take with her, along with the knowledge that she'd left Frank and his family none the worse for her being a temporary part of their lives.

But how could she walk away from the possibility of a lifetime filled with love and happiness?

She simply couldn't imagine going back to her solitary life-style after being here with Frank and his family. Nor could she imagine leaving a man she loved so deeply for what could be nothing more than a foolish delusion.

Yet if she agreed to stay and marry Frank, and something happened to him or his father or the twins because of her—

"I . . . I promise I'll think about it," she said at last, hoping against hope that within the next week or so she'd somehow finally see her way clear to take another chance on life and love.

"Fair enough." He hugged her close. "Now I'd better get out of here so you can get some sleep."

He eased away from her with such obvious reluctance that Alison almost reached for him again. But the clock on her nightstand read four o'clock. And she knew as well as he did that if she coaxed him into staying any longer, there was a good chance the twins would find his bed empty when they went to wake him.

He slipped out of bed, pulled on his jeans and gathered up the rest of his clothes, then bent down to kiss her in the slow, easy way she'd come to love.

"Merry Christmas, Ali," he murmured.

"Merry Christmas." Smiling up at him, she stroked his face with her hand. "Sleep well."

"You, too."

He walked to the door and opened it, then glanced back at her. "I'll hold off the twins as long as I can before we wake you."

"That's okay. I'm anxious to see what Santa brought, too."

"I'll remind you of that about two hours from now."

"Surely they'll sleep later than *that*," she groaned.

"Don't count on it." Chuckling softly, he finally left her.

As her bedroom door clicked shut, Alison rolled onto her side and buried her face in her pillows, delighting in the way Frank's scent now mingled with hers on her bed linen. Then, with a soft sigh of utter contentment, she closed her eyes and drifted off to sleep.

"Wake up, Ali, *wake up,*" the twins pleaded in unison.

"Santa came last night and he left whole bunches of presents under the tree," Jake advised.

"For you, too. We saw your name on 'em," Joey added.

"And we know you're as anxious as we are to see what he brought," Frank teased, his deep voice much too cheery considering the late night they'd had.

"Oh, yes, really anxious," Alison muttered sleepily.

Glancing at the clock, she saw that it was just after seven o'clock. Grateful for the extra hour he'd somehow managed to give her, she started to sit up. But as the bedcovers slipped down around her shoulders, she suddenly realized she'd slept in the nude.

"Did you forget to put your nightie on last night?" Jake asked, eyeing her curiously.

"Umm, sort of," she admitted, not daring to meet Frank's gaze as she held the blankets up to her chin and lay back against her pillows.

"All right, you guys, let's give the lady a little privacy," he ordered.

As the boys scampered out of her room, she finally risked a glance at him. He'd obviously been awake for a while. His hair was still damp from the shower, he'd shaved, and he was dressed in a new pair of jeans and a green plaid flannel shirt. His eyes glinted with mischief and he had a downright wicked grin on his handsome face. Recalling how completely she'd given herself to him last night, she smiled, too. She really did love him, she thought, more than she'd ever imagined she could allow herself to love anyone again.

"I take it that means you don't have any regrets about last night," he said, his voice pitched for her ears only.

"No regrets at all," she assured him, wishing he weren't quite so far away, yet knowing it was probably better that he was. "What about you?"

"Not a one," he replied, gazing at her with such obvious desire that she had no doubt he spoke the truth.

"I'm glad."

"Me too." His eyes held hers a moment longer, then he gestured toward the doorway. "We'll be waiting for you in the living room."

"I'll only be a few minutes," she promised.

As good as her word, she walked into the living room not quite fifteen minutes later. She'd hopped in the shower, then dressed quickly in her new skirt, silk shirt and vest, her excitement mounting. The past three years she'd hardly been able to get out of bed at all on Christmas Day. But this year Frank and his family had given her reason to revel in the joys of the holiday season once again.

The boys stood by the tree, their eyes alight with anticipation, while Bert sat in his chair by the fire and Frank perched on one arm of the sofa.

"Can we start handing out the presents now?" Jake asked.

"Yeah, can we, Dad?" Joey echoed as Alison crossed to the sofa and sat down.

"All right," he agreed.

Moving to sit next to her, he put his arm around her and drew her close. Then, as the twins sorted the brightly wrapped packages and set them in front of the appropriate person, he nuzzled her neck and whispered softly, "You look beautiful this morning."

She smiled up at him, then blushed furiously as she realized Bert was watching them with an approving grin. At his thumbs-up signal, she sputtered with laughter.

"What?" Frank demanded.

"Your father." As she nodded toward the older man, he waggled his eyebrows. "I thought only St. Nick knew about us, but I have a feeling he does, too."

"Do you mind?"

"Not if you don't."

"Hey, I'm glad. The old reprobate has been bugging the heck out of me to woo you into staying since he first laid eyes on you. Decided you were the one for us, then made sure I knew that if I let you get away, he'd never forgive me. But don't let that influence your decision," he said.

"I'll try not to," she replied with a rueful laugh.

Sometime later, as they sat amid piles of torn wrapping paper, watching the twins try to decide which of their new toys they wanted to play with next, Alison once again felt the prickle of tears in her eyes. Sharing Christmas with the Bradford men was proving to be one of the most joyous occasions of her life. They'd been so good to her, welcoming her into their home and their hearts, and they'd given her so much besides the wealth of gifts spread out on the floor by her feet.

Frank and his father and the boys had gone overboard, she thought as she gazed at all the lovely things they'd bought for her. She especially loved the black cowboy hat banded with feathers, a more feminine version of the one Frank had worn when they'd gone to Santa Fe, and the pair of red leather cowboy boots. But what she treasured most was Frank's special gift to her.

Reaching up, she touched the silver feathers attached to the half-moon earrings she wore. Each time she put them on, she'd think of their day in Santa Fe, just as she hoped he would whenever he wore the belt she'd given him.

"You're not going to cry again, are you?" Frank asked softly.

"I'm seriously thinking about it," she admitted. "But not because I'm sad."

"That's good to know." He gave her a swift hug, then waved his hand at the paper littering the living room floor. "Should we clean up first or have breakfast?"

"Breakfast," Jake and Joey chorused. Then, eyeing Alison pleadingly, Joey added, "Pancakes would taste really good."

"Well, then, pancakes it is," she agreed. "But I'll need some help." She glanced at Frank with what she hoped was an inviting smile.

"My pleasure," he replied, a devilish gleam in his eyes as he stood and hauled her to her feet.

"Don't burn the bacon again," Jake admonished.

"We'll try not to," Frank replied, leading Alison across the living room as Bert snorted with laughter.

Somehow, despite a major lack of attention on Frank and Alison's part, breakfast turned out just fine. Afterward, they all lent a hand cleaning up the kitchen and living room, then Bert stuffed the turkey and put it in the oven to roast.

Around eleven o'clock, they all piled into Frank's truck and drove into Vernon for the noon service at the little non-denominational church there. After they returned home, they called Frank's sisters. Both Ellen and Elaine showed quite an interest in Alison and indicated they were looking forward to meeting her sometime soon.

The rest of the day flew by in a whirl of warmth and good cheer. All too soon, Alison and Frank found themselves tucking two very tired little boys into bed. Pleading weariness, Bert said good-night earlier than usual, as well. And then, as if by unspoken agreement, she and Frank wandered back to her room. Trembling with anticipation, they quietly closed the door. Then, gazes locked on each other, they slowly began to undress.

Chapter Eleven

"Sure you don't want to go with me, Ali?" Frank asked. Then he added coaxingly, "It's a nice day for a ride, and I promise we won't be gone too long."

From where she sat at the desk, Alison shook her head regretfully. "I'd love to, really. But I'm almost done with the manuscript, and I'd kind of like to start the new year with it out of the way."

A week had passed since the first night he'd made love to her, and though she hadn't accepted his proposal yet, at least not in so many words, Frank couldn't help but feel confident that very soon now Alison would agree to be his wife.

Truth be told, he already felt as if she were. She'd become such an important part of his life, and they seemed to get along so well together. And from the little things she'd said and done over the past few days, he'd begun to believe she felt the same way.

Still, he hadn't pushed her to make a firm commitment. He'd promised to give her time to think, and he had. But, oh, how he hoped that maybe tonight she'd say the words he so longed to hear.

He'd offered to take her out to celebrate the new year, but she'd told him she'd rather stay home. That, coupled with her sudden determination to finish Rebecca's manuscript, led him to believe that she wanted the first day of the new year to be the first day of her new life with him. Since he liked that idea, too, he nodded agreeably.

"I understand. But don't work too hard. Otherwise, you might end up falling asleep on me, and I want tonight to be really special."

"I beg your pardon, Mr. Bradford, but if I'm not mistaken, you're the one who zonked out on me last night," she reminded him, a teasing gleam in her dark eyes.

She was right, of course. After making mad, passionate love to her, he'd held her close and fallen sound asleep as if it were the most natural thing to do. Luckily, she'd had the presence of mind to set her alarm clock for four-thirty, so he'd had more than enough time to slip back to his room before the rest of the family began to stir. But he'd done so reluctantly. Even though the hour had been much too early for his liking, he'd loved waking up with her in his arms. And he didn't think he could wait much longer to make it a daily habit.

"That's only because you insisted on turning me every way but loose despite the fact that you knew I'd had a hard day," he protested.

"Me?"

She offered him such an innocent smile that he had no choice but to cross the office and haul her into his arms for a tantalizingly thorough kiss.

"Yes, you," he muttered, knowing that if he lived to be a hundred, he'd never tire of her. She truly had made his life complete.

"I'll try to be a little...gentler from now on," she vowed, lowering her gaze demurely.

"Don't you dare," he warned softly, then kissed her cheek and sat her back down in the desk chair.

"Where are you going?" She fiddled nervously with the papers on the desk as she eyed him questioningly.

"Just down to the south pasture. Since it snowed again last night, I thought I'd better check on the sheep and make sure Carlos and Benito have everything under control. I'll have the mobile phone with me in case you or Dad need to get in touch with me. I'm going to take Molly, too. And I should be back by late afternoon."

Although she'd never come right out and said anything, Frank knew that Alison worried about him whenever he had to ride out alone to take care of one thing or another somewhere on the ranch. As a result, he'd gotten in the habit of telling her exactly where he was going, what he planned to do, and about how long he intended to be gone.

He'd also taken her riding several times since they'd gone up to the camp. She could handle Shadow on her own now, and she also knew her way around a bit. She could already find her way on horseback to the Camdens' house or the south pasture.

He had not only tried to impress on her that he knew the ranch like the back of his hand, but that he was always careful, as well. Eventually, he hoped she'd realize that he wasn't in any danger on the Double B. Then maybe she wouldn't worry quite so much.

"I should have the last chapter ready for you to read by then," she said, her concern fading somewhat.

"How about if I look at it after dinner? Then, after everyone else goes to bed, we can celebrate the start of our new year ... together."

"Together," she agreed, her soft smile so full of promise it was all he could do to nod his head, turn and walk away.

It had been a long time since he'd wanted anything as much as he wanted Ali to be a permanent part of his life. And he had a feeling that after tonight, she finally would be. Tomorrow they could tell his father and the twins. Then all they'd have to do is set a date.

Feeling more lighthearted than he had in months, Frank headed toward the kitchen, suddenly eager for the day to be over so that the night could begin.

Standing by the office window, Alison watched as Frank rode down the drive, Molly racing along ahead of him, sending snow flying. She'd really wanted to go with him, but she'd wanted even more to finish polishing the last pages of the last chapter of Rebecca's manuscript.

As she'd told Frank, she wanted to be done with it, not only before the new year, but before she accepted his proposal.

Though it was probably selfish of her, she wanted them to start *their* life together with as much of the past behind them as possible. Most of hers would be left in New York City. And, of course, she gladly welcomed the twins and Frank's father as a part of their future as well as Frank's past. She also understood that to a certain extent *Hunter's Edge* would always be important to both her and Frank, but in a more distant way than it had been up until now. Rebecca's manuscript had brought them together, but Alison wanted nothing more than their love for each other to keep them together in the new year.

To that end, she'd worked hard all week, believing that only after the manuscript was complete could she accept

Frank's proposal. She knew she was probably being silly. But she hadn't been able to help how she felt, so she'd simply given in to the impulse.

"Whatcha doing, Ali?" Jake asked from somewhere close behind her.

Turning away from the window, she saw both boys standing just inside the doorway. Jake held their quilt and Joey the big box containing their pirate ship.

"Just daydreaming," she admitted. "How about you?"

"We want to work on our pirate ship," Joey said.

"But our dad told us not to bother you." Jake eyed her hopefully.

"One of these days we're going to have to find a way to convince him that you *never* bother me." Grinning, she gestured for them to come into the room.

"He said you were almost done with our mom's book."

"Almost."

"Are you going home after that?" Joey asked, gazing at her sadly. "We asked our dad but he said he didn't know."

"I'm not sure yet," she hedged.

Until she'd accepted Frank's proposal, she didn't want to make any promises.

"Will you be sure soon?" Jake asked.

"I think so. Now, why don't you get busy on that pirate ship and let me get back to work," she suggested as she returned to the desk chair and sat down.

The afternoon passed quietly with both Alison and the twins making headway on their projects. Around three o'clock the telephone rang, but Bert called out that he'd answer it in the kitchen. A few minutes later, Alison heard his footsteps in the hallway, then he spoke from the office doorway.

"That was Juan Ramirez. A couple of his kids got a little rambunctious and he needs some help replacing a broken window. I shouldn't be gone more than an hour or two at the most."

"Don't worry about us. We'll be fine," Alison assured him.

"Can we go, too, Grandpa? Can we, *please?*" Jake pleaded. "We haven't seen Georgie or Maria for almost two weeks."

The twins were good friends with the younger Ramirez children, and had been wanting to visit them since the Christmas holidays had begun.

"Well, I suppose so," Bert said, then turned his attention back to Alison. "Do you mind if they leave their pirate ship out?"

"Not at all."

"Go get your coats on, then."

As Jake and Joey ran down the hallway, whooping with excitement, Bert smiled and shook his head. "Wish I could bottle some of their energy."

"You're not the only one."

"Sure you don't mind staying here alone?"

"Of course not."

"I'll leave Frank's truck here. Keys are on the kitchen counter. And the numbers for the mobile phone and the Ramirez place are still posted on the refrigerator."

"That's great. See you later."

Vaguely, Alison heard Bert's old pickup sputter to life. Then the sound of the motor running drifted away as he drove off down the drive, leaving the house quiet once again. So engrossed in her work was she that Alison had no idea exactly when they left or how long they'd been gone when she heard Molly barking.

At first she assumed Frank was home. But then, she remembered the dog rarely barked just for the heck of it. Either she was warning that a stranger was on her property, or she was announcing that she wanted something. She was especially good at letting everyone knew when her food bowl was empty or when she wanted to be allowed inside the house.

More annoyed than anything by the racket Molly was making, Alison pushed away from the desk, stood and walked over to the window. She knew the dog wasn't barking a warning, but what could she want that Frank—

Gazing out the window, Alison saw that Molly stood a few feet from the back door. She was facing the house. And she was alone.

"What in the world..." Alison murmured as a tingle of fear trailed down her spine.

She'd seen the dog go off with Frank, but she'd apparently come home on her own. Why? To bark at the house? That wasn't like Molly at all. Nor did she normally sound quite as hysterical as she'd begun to sound in the few minutes Alison had been standing by the window. Something was wrong. Something was very, very wrong.

Her heart pounding, Alison raced down the hallway and across the kitchen, flung open the back door and stepped outside.

"Frank," she shouted as Molly ran over to her. *"Frank."*

There was no sign of him in the yard or down the drive, and the bar was across the front of the barn door, holding it closed from the outside.

Shaking with fear as well as the cold, she went back into the kitchen, lifted the telephone receiver and dialed the number of the mobile phone. After letting it ring a dozen times, she finally hung up. Something had happened to him. Otherwise, he'd have answered the phone.

For several moments, she stood, staring stupidly into space, wondering what to do next as Molly whined and pawed at her desperately.

"Okay, girl, okay," she said at last. "Just let me get my jacket and you can show me where he is."

Aware that her worst nightmare was coming true, Alison pulled on her jacket, grabbed her gloves and scarf and, with Molly at her heels, ran to the barn. She had to find him, and the best way to do so was on horseback, she decided, somehow managing to get a saddle and bridle on Shadow despite her trembling hands. He'd gone to the south pasture and she knew the way there. And with Molly along to help her find him—

"Oh, please, let him be all right," she sobbed, hauling herself into the saddle, then guiding Shadow out of the barn.

She should have known better than to think things would be different this time. Should have realized that her luck couldn't possibly change in a matter of weeks. As long as she'd held back, as long as she hadn't actually made a permanent commitment, nothing had happened. But once she'd decided to accept Frank's proposal—

"Just let him be all right and I'll go back to New York. I swear, I'll go back," she whispered as she urged Shadow into a slow canter.

She found him lying in the snow, Dusty standing patiently a few feet away, about two miles from the house. By the time she reined Shadow to a halt and slid out of the saddle, Frank was starting to stir. As she knelt beside him, he tried to sit up, then lay back again, groaning softly.

"Frank, I'm here," she murmured, then caught her breath as she saw the blood oozing out of the side of his head and staining the snow.

"Hey, Ali, don't look so scared." He squinted up at her, a wry smile tugging at the corners of his mouth. "I'm okay. Just fell off my horse and bumped my head." He closed his eyes for a moment, as if gathering his strength, then finally succeeded in sitting up.

"It's my fault," she cried. "I should have been with you. But I just *had* to stay at the house—"

Aware that she was babbling like an idiot, she gave herself a firm mental shake. She could chastise herself all she wanted later, and she would. But right now she had to get Frank back to the house so she could take him to the clinic. He'd done more than just "bump" his head, she determined, eyeing the nasty gash in his scalp that still seemed to be bleeding.

"I'm . . . I'm sorry," she murmured.

"Nothing for you to be sorry about. A rabbit shot out of those bushes over there and spooked old Dusty. I wasn't paying attention and ended up getting tossed." Closing his eyes again, he rubbed a hand over his forehead. "And, man, does my head hurt," he muttered. Then, gazing at her curiously, he added, "Not to sound ungrateful, but what are *you* doing here?"

"Molly came back to the house and kept barking and barking. When I realized you weren't with her, I tried getting in touch with you on the mobile phone. You didn't answer, so I came looking for you."

"Where was Bert?"

"He went to help Juan Ramirez fix a broken window and took the twins with him."

As a gust of icy air swept over them and Frank shivered, Alison eyed him with even more concern. She had to get him to the clinic, but first . . . "Do you think you can ride back to the house?"

"I've done it in worse shape than this," he admitted. "Just give me another minute or two, and you can help me up."

It took him a little longer than that, but eventually he managed to get back in the saddle. They rode slowly back to the house, and then, despite his protests, Alison insisted on taking him to Vernon. While he climbed into the passenger seat of the truck, she put the horses in the barn and scribbled a note to Bert so he wouldn't be worried.

To Alison's relief, Frank hadn't fractured his skull. However, he did have a mild concussion, and after stitching up the gash in his head, the doctor allowed him to go home only when Alison promised he'd go straight to bed and stay there no less than twenty-four hours. With the headache he'd indicated he had, she doubted she'd have trouble getting him to cooperate.

She called Bert from the clinic to let him know Frank was all right, but he and the boys still greeted them anxiously when they finally got back to the ranch. And though Frank grumbled about spending New Year's Eve in bed *alone,* he went willingly enough, and almost immediately fell asleep.

Somehow, Alison managed to get through the rest of the evening, pretending to be in good spirits for Jake's and Joey's sakes when all she really wanted to do was have a good cry. She was relieved when Bert and the boys decided to go to bed well before midnight.

Oddly enough, however, once she was alone, she didn't curl up in a ball and cry, after all. Instead, she calmly returned to Rebecca's office, picked up where she'd left off earlier, and finished *Hunter's Edge,* stopping occasionally to look in on Frank and wake him as the doctor had ordered.

Still suffering from a terrific headache, Frank spent New Year's Day in bed, as well. Though Alison wished he felt better, having him more or less indisposed was a little easier on her. Being with Bert and the boys and trying to remain cheerful was about all she could handle. Especially when she knew she'd be leaving the next day.

She'd done most of her packing after finishing the manuscript last night, then stashed her suitcases in her closet. Coward that she was, she planned to slip away before dawn the next day. She couldn't face saying goodbye to Jake and Joey or their grandfather any more than she could face saying goodbye to Frank. Nor did she want to give any of them a chance to tempt her into changing her mind.

For their good, she believed it was best that she get out of their lives once and for all. Actually, she'd known it all along, but she'd chosen to ignore her instincts. However, after what had happened yesterday, she couldn't allow herself to do that again. Frank's accident had been a warning, one she intended to heed no matter how much pain it caused her. She'd rather make a clean break and know that the four people she loved most in the world would be safe.

"What are you doing?"

Startled, Alison whirled away from the door that opened from her room to the side yard where she'd parked her rental car, almost dropping the suitcase she held in her hand. Standing across from her, just inside the doorway leading into the kitchen, Frank eyed her steadily. He was dressed in jeans and a T-shirt, but his feet were bare, his hair mussed and his jaw unshaven.

"You're supposed to be in bed," she said rather stupidly.

"I've been in bed almost two days. Couldn't stand it anymore. Thought I'd get up, put on a pot of coffee and take a shower. I heard you bumping around in here. Which brings me back to my question. What are you doing, Ali?"

"What does it look like I'm doing?" she retorted, tipping her chin up defensively.

He had no right to be up and about yet. It wasn't even five o'clock in the morning.

"From where I'm standing, it looks like you're leaving."

"Got it on one."

"Want to tell me why?" He took a step toward her, then raised his hands placatingly when she backed away from him.

"I left a note explaining." She nodded toward the white envelope on the dresser.

"You couldn't tell me in person?"

"I thought it would be easier this way."

"For which one of us?" he growled. "I asked you to marry me, Alison. You could have at least had the courtesy to refuse me in person instead of sneaking out like some kind of thief in the night."

"All right, then, I will. I've decided I can't marry you, Frank."

"Why not?" he pressed.

"I...I don't think living on a ranch is my style, after all," she said, not daring to meet his gaze, afraid that he'd see the lie in her eyes. "The past month was a nice little interlude. But when I gave it some thought, I realized I'd be happier somewhere less...provincial."

"Oh, really?" He stalked toward her angrily, pausing not more than two feet from her. "Look me in the eyes and tell me that."

"I'm sorry if you got the wrong idea—" She backed away from him, still refusing to meet his gaze.

He caught her by the shoulders and held her still. "Tell me what's wrong, Ali. Please, tell me so we can work it out," he coaxed, his voice suddenly gentle. "Something's scaring the living daylights out of you. I want to know what it is."

She almost gave in then. Almost set her suitcase down so she could put her arms around him and rest her head on his chest. Almost told him—

But how could she? She'd vowed that if he was all right, she'd get out of his life and stay out, and she didn't dare renege. She'd never been lucky in love, and she never would be. And she'd rather lose him by leaving him than by having him come to harm because of her.

"I think your imagination is working overtime, Frank. The only thing I'm afraid of missing is my flight back to New York," she advised him in a brittle tone of voice. "I'm sorry if you got the wrong idea about us. Obviously, I was just bored and restless. But I'll always remember you fondly."

"Oh, yeah? Well, here's one last little memory for you, darlin'."

Before she realized what he had in mind, he bent his head and kissed her, not with anger as she more than deserved, but with a gentleness that shattered her soul.

As he released her, she saw the anguish in his eyes and realized that she'd hurt him deeply. But that was for the best. He'd never forgive her now. Not even if she begged him on bended knee.

"Take care," he muttered, then turned on his heel and walked away without a backward glance, closing the door quietly on his way out.

"Oh, Frank, I'm so sorry," she sobbed.

Barely able to see through the blur of tears in her eyes, Alison opened the outside door, stumbled over to the rental car and loaded her suitcase into the trunk with the rest of her things. A few minutes later, after a last check of her room to be sure she hadn't left anything behind, she returned to the car and climbed into the driver's seat, started the engine and drove slowly, yet purposefully, down the drive.

"You going to keep stomping around here, snarling like a bear with a load of buckshot in his britches, or are you going to go after her?" Bert asked mildly as Frank slammed through the kitchen door and tossed his jacket on a chair.

Three days had passed since Alison had gone back to New York, three of the worst days in Frank's life. He wanted to believe that he *had* gotten the wrong idea about her, that he was better off without her, that he didn't need her or want her in his life. But he knew better. The way she'd kissed him back when he'd cornered her Monday morning had left no doubt in his mind that she loved him as much as he loved her. Yet she'd still run away, and he was damned if he knew why.

He hadn't thought she'd actually leave. Not after he kissed her. He'd been sure that she'd follow him out to the kitchen and tell him what was wrong. But then, he'd heard her car start, and he'd been too damn proud to run down the drive after her. Just as he was too damn proud to go traipsing off to New York City to try to win her back.

Or was he? After the past three days, pride had proven to be a rather cold companion.

"I'm not sure it would do any good," he answered his father at last, pouring himself a fresh cup of coffee, then sitting down across from him at the table. "Something I did sent her hightailing it out of here, and even if I could figure out what it was, I'm not certain I could convince her that I wouldn't do it again."

"You're right about that. You couldn't."

"What do you mean?" he asked with confusion.

"You fell off your horse and hit your head. Luckily, you've got a hard one. Otherwise, you could have ended up dead. Just like everybody else she's ever loved."

"*That* is what scared her?"

"Think about it, son. She spends the past three years living alone after her husband and son are killed. Then she comes here and we do our damnedest to lure her into becoming a part of the family. Once we do, she's reminded all over again how easy it could be to lose someone she loves. Rather than risk that happening again, she runs back to New York just as fast as she can."

"But death is a part of life. It's waiting for us all down the road. And I can't guarantee it won't catch up with me sooner rather than later any more than anyone else can."

"No, you can't. But you might be able to convince her that loving doesn't necessarily mean losing. You two have as much chance of growing old together as not."

"Not unless she's willing to risk it," Frank muttered.

"And I say there's only one way for you to find out."

"Can you handle things around here for a few days?" Frank asked.

"Of course. Take as much time as you need," Bert urged.

"What about Jake and Joey? I don't think it would be a good idea to get their hopes up."

While they hadn't been happy to hear that Alison had left, they'd seemed to be handling it well enough. Although they did keep asking when she was coming back.

"I'll tell them you've gone to see her, but I won't mention the possibility that you might be bringing her back. That way they can be surprised."

"They won't be the only ones," Frank said. "We could be wrong, you know. Maybe she really didn't want to live out in the middle of nowhere with a ready-made family."

"Didn't seem that way to me."

"Not to me, either," Frank admitted with a wry smile.

"Well, then, go pack a bag while I find out when the next flight leaves for New York."

Alison hadn't thought that once she got back to New York she'd feel quite so bad. Nor had she imagined she'd spend one day after another crying her eyes out as she slowly came to realize she'd made the worst mistake of her life. But she did because, without a doubt, she had. And, unfortunately, there was nothing she could do about it.

She'd burned her bridges where Frank Bradford was concerned. She turned her back on him and the love he'd offered her, belittling all that they'd shared, calling it nothing more than an interlude. He'd never forgive her for that, and she couldn't say she blamed him. Had he treated her as she'd treated him Monday morning, she'd never want anything to do with him ever again, either.

Blinking back yet another rush of tears, she traced a finger over the scene embroidered on the front of the Christmas stocking he'd given her. She should have left it at the Double B along with all her hopes and dreams, but she hadn't been able to part with it. Looking back, she wished she'd had a little less fear and a lot more courage. Maybe then she wouldn't have been so willing to believe that the odds were still against her. Now, however, it was much too late for—

The sudden buzz of her intercom startled her out of her reverie. Who on earth could it be? She certainly wasn't expecting anyone, not on a day like today. A mixture of freezing rain and snow had all but shut down the city since early afternoon.

Again the intercom buzzed, more insistently than the first time. Carlson knew she was home, but he rarely buzzed more than once unless she had a guest, which she'd already ruled out, or he had a package for her that required her signature. But it was Saturday, and the mail had already been delivered hours ago.

Setting the stocking on the coffee table, she crossed to the door and flipped the switch on the intercom.

"Yes, Carlson, what is it?"

"There's a gentleman here to see you, Ms. Kent. A Mr. Bradford. Shall I send him up?"

A Mr. Bradford...

Heart pounding, Alison rested her head against the doorframe and closed her eyes. Her first instinct was to send him away. But he'd come all the way from New Mexico and done heaven only knew what to get to her apartment from the airport. How could she refuse to see him? Especially when there was nothing more she wanted in the whole world.

"Yes, please. Send Mr. Bradford up."

As she waited by the door, Alison told herself not to get her hopes up. Perhaps he'd come about Rebecca's manuscript. Perhaps he hadn't been satisfied with the last chapter and wanted her to—

He rapped sharply on the door, and somehow, despite the way her hands shook, she managed to open the locks. He stood in the hallway, dressed as he'd been when they'd gone to Santa Fe, but looking half frozen, his eyes understandably wary.

"Frank..."

She wanted to hurl herself into his arms and beg him to forgive her, but she couldn't seem to move.

"Alison." He met her gaze silently for several moments, then continued quietly. "May I come in?"

"Of course."

She stepped back so that he could enter, then closed and locked the door as he walked into the living room. Turning to follow him, she caught a look at herself in the entryway mirror and cringed. She certainly wasn't any sight for sore eyes. She hadn't bothered to comb her hair in days; her face was pale, her eyes red-rimmed, and she was dressed in her rattiest sweats and a pair of old, floppy socks. Why he hadn't run the other way as soon as he'd had a glimpse of her, she didn't know.

Making himself oddly at home, he took off his hat and jacket, set them on a chair and surveyed his surroundings with obvious appreciation.

"Nice place," he said as she joined him. "I can see why you were so anxious to come back." He turned and met her gaze. "Although I can't say you look too happy to be here. Dare I hope that despite what you said Monday morning, you've missed us as much as we've missed you?"

"Oh, Frank..." His gentle, teasing tone was too much for her. Sobbing, she stepped into his outstretched arms and buried her face against his chest. "I'm so sorry. I never meant to hurt you, but I was so afraid. I thought my luck had changed. But then, just when I was going to accept your proposal, you got hurt, and I was so sure it was my fault, just like all the other times."

"Whoa, Ali, slow down," he soothed, stroking her back. "You were going to accept my proposal?"

"Until you got hurt. Then, I thought . . . I thought I was still bad luck to anyone I loved."

"How do you figure that?" he asked, taking a step back and tilting her chin up so that her eyes met his.

"My parents . . . If I hadn't insisted on going to Florida, they'd never have been on that plane when it crashed. And my brother . . . He wanted to leave the army after our parents died, but I talked him into staying, and eighteen months later he was killed. Even Len and Nathan . . . I should have insisted on taking the shuttle that day instead of letting them drive to the airport."

"Ali, you are *not* bad luck. One way or another, people die. And I'd like to believe that when it's your time, there isn't much anybody can do about it." He paused a moment, then added with heartfelt sincerity, "I'd also like to believe that we're a hell of a lot better off loving someone and losing them than not loving at all."

"But I'm so scared of losing you or your father or the twins," she admitted, tears welling in her eyes all over again.

"Don't you think I'm scared, too? I don't want to lose you the way I did Rebecca. But I'm not so scared that I'd rather spend the rest of my life without you. I'd rather have a couple of years, or a couple of months, even a couple of days, with you." Reaching out, he brushed the back of his hand against her cheek. "I wish I could promise you nothing is going to happen to any of us for the next fifty or sixty years, but I can't. All I can do is promise that, if you'll let me, I'll love you until the day I die." He took her hands in his and kissed her on the forehead. "Say you will, Ali. Say you'll come home to the Double B with me and be my wife. Say you'll help me raise my sons, have my babies and, God willing, grow old with me."

"What about keeping your old reprobate of a father in line? Is that still part of the deal?" she asked, smiling as she recalled the first time he'd proposed to her.

"Yeah, that, too."

Gazing up at him, she thought about all that he'd said. Looking back, she realized that she would have never traded the years she'd had with her parents and her brother or her husband and her son for the kind of sterile existence she'd had the past three years. And she'd rather have a few years, or a few months, or even a few days, with Frank than go on as she had been the past week.

"Have I ever told you how very much I love you?" she asked.

"Not in so many words."

"Well, I do love you, Frank Bradford. And, yes, I will marry you, help raise your sons, have your babies, keep your old man in line and, God willing, grow old with you."

"Want to seal that promise with a kiss?"

"A kiss would be nice . . . for starters."

Epilogue

"Okay, the stockings are up. I think that's everything," Frank said.

"Except for the star," Alison reminded him. Digging down to the bottom of the box on the floor by her feet, she lifted it from the folds of tissue paper she'd wrapped around it last year when they'd taken down the tree. "Who wants to do the honors?"

"How about you, Mom?" Scott suggested.

At eighteen, he was as tall as his father and, in his mother's eyes at least, almost as handsome.

"Yeah, Mom, you do it," Christy urged, her bright blue eyes dancing with mischief. "Dad will help you up onto the stool."

"Just wait, young lady. One of these days you won't be sixteen anymore," Alison admonished as she crossed the living room and, smiling up at her husband, took his hand.

"That's right. You'll be eighty-five," Bert chortled. "With a little luck."

Ah, yes, luck, Alison thought as she slipped the open end of the star over the tip of the top branch of the Christmas tree much as she'd done her first Christmas on the Double B. She could hardly believe that had been twenty years ago.

So much had happened since then. She and Frank had had their share of good times along with some bad. But they'd always had each other, and Bert and the twins, then Scott and Christy, too. And somewhere along the way, Alison had stopped expecting the worst. Oh, she'd never been able to take her good fortune for granted. But she'd counted her blessings and learned to enjoy the best life had to offer, one precious day at a time.

"I wish the twins were here," she said as she stepped down off the stool and put her arms around her husband. "But they would have to go and grow up on us, wouldn't they?"

As Scott and Christy eyed each other conspiratorially, Alison glanced up at Frank. "What?" she asked, sure that they were up to something.

"They will be."

"They will? When?" she demanded, barely able to contain her excitement.

"Christmas Eve. Jake managed to get leave and Joe sold another short story so he ended up with plane fare, after all."

"Might as well tell her the rest," Bert prodded.

"The rest?"

"Ellen and Elaine are coming, too, along with their families. Orson and Deborah, too," Frank said. "We thought about surprising you, but since you seemed kind of sad..."

"Oh, Frank, do you know how long it's been since we've all been together for Christmas?" she asked, tears in her eyes.

"Oh, no, Mom's gonna cry," Scott said. "Again."

"Because I'm so happy," she assured him. "So very, very happy."

* * * * *

Another wonderful year of romance
concludes with

Christmas Memories

Share in the magic and memories of romance
during the holiday season with this collection of two
full-length contemporary Christmas stories,
by two bestselling authors

Diana Palmer
Marilyn Pappano

Available in December at your favorite retail outlet.

Only from ▼ *Silhouette*®

where passion lives.

XMMEM

The Loop™

Is the future what it's cracked up to be?

This December, discover what commitment
is all about in

GETTING ATTACHED: CJ
by Wendy Corsi Staub

C. J. Clarke was tired of lugging her toothbrush
around town, and she sure didn't believe longtime
boyfriend David Griffin's constant whining about
"not being able to commit." He was with her every
day—and most nights—so what was his problem?
C.J. knew marriage wasn't always what it was cracked
up to be, but when you're in love you're supposed to
end up happily ever after…aren't you?

The ups and downs of life as you know it continue with

GETTING A LIFE: MARISSA
by Kathryn Jensen (January)

GETTING OUT: EMILY
by ArLynn Presser (February)

Get smart. Get into "The Loop"!

Only from 🔺 *Silhouette*®
™
where passion lives.

LOOP5

Stories that capture living and loving
beneath the Big Sky, where legends live
on...and mystery lingers.

This December, explore more MONTANA MAVERICKS with

THE RANCHER TAKES A WIFE
by Jackie Merritt

He'd made up his mind. He'd loved her almost a lifetime
and now he was going to have her, come hell or high
water.

And don't miss a minute of the loving as the passion continues with:

> **OUTLAW LOVERS**
> by Pat Warren (January)
>
> **WAY OF THE WOLF**
> by Rebecca Daniels (February)
>
> **THE LAW IS NO LADY**
> by Helen R. Myers (March)
> and many more!

Only from ▼*Silhouette*® where passion lives.

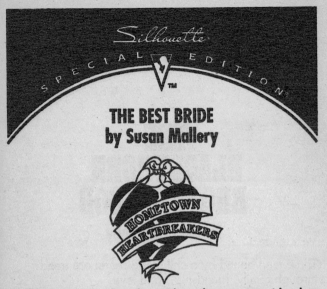

Silhouette

SPECIAL EDITION™

THE BEST BRIDE
by Susan Mallery

HOMETOWN HEARTBREAKERS

Hometown Heartbreakers: These heartstoppin' hunks
are rugged, ready and able to steal your heart....

Playing the field was what roguish Travis Haynes
did best—until he became a temporary family man.
Soon the unyielding lawman was weakened by a
little girl's touch—and completely undone by her
mother's kiss. But marriage-shy Elizabeth Abbott
wasn't about to become anyone's bride—
not even the oh-so-sexy Travis's!

Don't miss Susan Mallery's first book in her
Hometown Heartbreakers series, coming to you in
January...only from Silhouette Special Edition.

HH-1

Silhouette

SPECIAL EDITION ™

THE BLACKTHORN BROTHERHOOD

by Diana Whitney

Three men bound by a childhood secret are freed through family, friendship...and love.

Watch for the first book in Diana's Whitney's compelling new miniseries:

THE ADVENTURER
Special Edition #934, January 1995

Devon Monroe had finally come home, home to a haunting memory that made him want to keep running. Home to a woman who made him want to stand still and stare into her eyes. For there was something about Jessica Newcomb that made him forget about his own past and wonder long and hard about hers....

Look for THE AVENGER coming in the fall of 1995.

DWBB1

Silhouette

SPECIAL EDITION

™

The new year brings readers a
powerful new trilogy—

by Andrea Edwards

In January, don't miss A RING AND A PROMISE (SE #932).

Just one look at feisty Chicago caterer Kate Mallory made rancher
Jake MacNeill forget all about Montana. Could his lonesome-cowboy soul
rest as love overcomes unfulfilled promises of the past?

THIS TIME, FOREVER—sometimes a love is so strong, nothing can
stand in its way...not even time.

Look for the next installment, A ROSE AND A WEDDING VOW (SE #944),
in March 1995. Read along as two *old* friends learn that love is
worth taking a chance.

AEMINI-1

SILHOUETTE... Where Passion Lives

Don't miss these Silhouette favorites by some of our most distinguished authors! And now you can receive a discount by ordering two or more titles!

SD#05786	QUICKSAND by Jennifer Greene	$2.89	☐
SD#05795	DEREK by Leslie Guccione	$2.99	☐
SD#05818	NOT JUST ANOTHER PERFECT WIFE by Robin Elliott	$2.99	☐
IM#07505	HELL ON WHEELS by Naomi Horton	$3.50	☐
IM#07514	FIRE ON THE MOUNTAIN by Marion Smith Collins	$3.50	☐
IM#07559	KEEPER by Patricia Gardner Evans	$3.50	☐
SSE#09879	LOVING AND GIVING by Gina Ferris	$3.50	☐
SSE#09892	BABY IN THE MIDDLE	$3.50 U.S.	☐
	by Marie Ferrarella	$3.99 CAN.	☐
SSE#09902	SEDUCED BY INNOCENCE	$3.50 U.S.	☐
	by Lucy Gordon	$3.99 CAN.	☐
SR#08952	INSTANT FATHER by Lucy Gordon	$2.75	☐
SR#08984	AUNT CONNIE'S WEDDING		
	by Marie Ferrarella	$2.75	☐
SR#08990	JILTED by Joleen Daniels	$2.75	☐

(limited quantities available on certain titles)

AMOUNT	$_____
DEDUCT: 10% DISCOUNT FOR 2+ BOOKS	$_____
POSTAGE & HANDLING ($1.00 for one book, 50¢ for each additional)	$_____
APPLICABLE TAXES*	$_____
TOTAL PAYABLE (check or money order—please do not send cash)	$_____

To order, complete this form and send it, along with a check or money order for the total above, payable to Silhouette Books, to: **In the U.S.:** 3010 Walden Avenue, P.O. Box 9077, Buffalo, NY 14269-9077; **In Canada:** P.O. Box 636, Fort Erie, Ontario, L2A 5X3.

Name:_____

Address:_____City:_____

State/Prov.:_____ Zip/Postal Code:_____

*New York residents remit applicable sales taxes.
Canadian residents remit applicable GST and provincial taxes.   SBACK-DF

Silhouette®